BLOOD AND BRASS

Raven Taylor

PORTLAND PRESS NOVELS

Published 2025
First Edition
Portland Press Novels
a New Haven Publishing Ltd Imprint
www.newhavenpublishingltd.com
newhavenpublishing@gmail.com

Cover design©Pete Cunliffe

PORTLAND
PRESS

For my friends at Kirkby Stephen Silver Band —

Thank you for welcoming me so wholeheartedly into the world of banding. Your patience as I learn, your encouragement every step of the way, and your friendship mean more than I can say. You are, without doubt, the most community-minded, supportive, and welcoming band in the world. I'm so proud to play alongside you.

Prologue

The late spring afternoon was golden, with the low sun slanting across the field where the villagers gathered. The May Day celebrations were winding down, and the village band had just played their final piece. Beneath the shade of Lady Henshaw's oak, the men and women in their green blazers were packing away their instruments and folding up their music stands. The branches of the old oak were adorned with coloured ribbons, each one tied to represent its owner's wish, and they fluttered gaily in the breeze, full of promise.

Every year, on the first of May, the people of Bramwick gathered to pay tribute to the tree in a ceremony that not only celebrated the life of the late Lady Henshaw, for whom it had been planted, but also the workers 'rights movement her husband had been so passionate about. Borrowing from pagan tradition, the ribbons were fastened to the tree, and cider brewed from apples grown in the community orchard was raised in a toast to its health and poured in offering onto its roots. Then the brass band would gather below it and perform a concert which always ended with 'Slaidburn March'.

"I'm so proud of you, son." Pete Newell looked down at his boy, Nathan, and thought his heart might burst. "Your mum would be proud of you too."

Nathan stood before him in his green blazer, clutching his trombone and grinning broadly. He had been pleased as punch when he and his two best friends from Bramwick's youth band had been asked to join the adults this year in the performance at the May Day celebration. The band was an integral part of this folk tradition. It had been established by Lord Henshaw to give the local workers a respectable hobby that might focus their attention and keep them away from the pub. Nearly two hundred years later, it was still going.

"It's an honour to be chosen to be part of the May Day celebrations." Pete Newell smiled fondly at his son. "You know the story of the oak, don't you?"

"Lord Henshaw planted it to remember his wife when she died." Nathan had heard the story at school a thousand times.

"That's it. But it's not just for Lady Henshaw; that tree is for all the women of Bramwick."

5

"Even Mum?"

"Especially Mum." Pete wished she could have been there to see their son now.

The Henshaws' vast country estate had provided most of the men in the village with work during Victorian times, but over the years the land had been broken down into smaller parcels and sold off. Neglected, the once grand manor house fell into disrepair until it was eventually demolished in the 1960s.

Around the same time the tree was planted, the first Lord Henshaw put an agreement in place, assigning a portion of land to the people of Bramwick on a two-hundred-year lease. On this patch of land, he built a small building where the people could come together. He held a yearly Christmas dance there for his workers and many meetings, weddings and gatherings had been hosted there. The building also provided a home for his beloved Bramwick Brass Band. The land around it had a community garden where vegetables were grown, with a fruit orchard, and the surrounding field had seen many a summer fête and agricultural show.

Known simply as 'The Grange 'by the locals, it was a treasured community asset. In modern times, the hall was hired for birthday celebrations, played host to the mother and toddler group, the pensioners 'lunch club, the ladies 'yoga group, the men's domino meet, and the Women's Institute meetings to name but a few. It also still housed the brass band, who were valiantly fighting on despite their dwindling numbers. Their glory days were well behind them now, but they still turned out to mark all the major points in Bramwick's calendar from Remembrance Sunday to Good Friday, and, of course, the yearly celebration on May Day.

After the first Lord Henshaw's death, The Grange was maintained by a small group of trustees and volunteers from the community. They covered the nominal ground rent with money raised from local events. But the time on the lease granted to the village was almost up, and the current Lord Henshaw was greedily awaiting the day that the land would revert back to his ownership. The tiny bit of rent he received from the community group, and the lingering responsibility for maintenance on the building, irked him, and he knew he could get a nice sum when the land was eventually his to sell. However, with twenty years still left on the lease, the people of Bramwick gave little thought to a future without The Grange.

"Can I go and play with Simon and Rosie now?" Nathan asked his dad.

"Of course you can. Give me that."

6

Pete took the trombone case from his son and watched as he ran off across the field to where his best friend, Simon Hunter, was mucking around with that Rosie girl, the one who always looked like she'd been dragged through a hedge backwards. Pete smiled as Nathan caught up with them. All three had done themselves and their parents proud.

"Hey, Pete, lad." Fred Black, the kids 'music teacher and tenor horn player, stepped up beside him. "With youngsters like them, the band might actually have a future after all, eh?"

"Aye," Pete nodded in agreement.

It had been a wonderful May Day, one of those days when everything just goes right and everyone enjoys themselves, helped along by the glorious warm sunshine. The smell of summer blew from the fields and mingled with the scent of the barbecue that Sandy Brown was presiding over. That The Grange and the band might one day be gone was the furthest thought from anyone's mind as they soaked up the atmosphere, drank cider, and watched their children play. The oak tree looked on proudly over the scene, like an old sentinel keeping watch. Beneath its gnarled branches, the villagers laughed and drank, blissfully unaware that the land they stood on might not always be theirs. The ribbons in the branches fluttered on, whispering their wishes to the wind.

Chapter One

Nate

"Ey up lads, look who it is, if it isn't Nathan 'Nasher 'Newell," the man at the end of the bar sniggered and elbowed his drinking companion.

The Black Bull looked exactly as it had when I had left ten years ago. Same tired décor— hop garlands that hadn't been changed in years hanging faded and dust-laden above the bar, horse brasses that had long ago lost their shine adorning the stone walls, a moth-eaten fox's head staring with glassy eyes from above the fireplace— and the same tired old clientele propping up the bar.

"Oh aye," came another voice in reply. "What brings you back here? London kicked you out, did it?"

I glanced over my shoulder, irritated, to see two men in their sixties, both wearing tweed flat caps and green wellies, perched on stools at the end of the bar. One of them looked me up and down with a curious expression on his face. I appreciated that my studded biker jacket, with its safety pins and patches, and my red boots must look quite out of place somewhere like this. They evidently knew who I was, and although their faces were vaguely familiar, I couldn't quite place either of them. One of them, I thought, possibly used to drink with the Sunday afternoon crowd Dad had sat with when I was a kid. I used to get dragged along for an hour, given a glass of warm lemonade and a packet of salt and vinegar crisps, and told to sit and be quiet while the men put the world to rights.

I was about to throw a witty retort back at the men when Mrs Thornton bustled out from the kitchen and said sharply, "Leave off it, the pair of you. He's just lost his dad."

Mrs Thornton was the one thing that *had* changed. Her previously rich auburn hair was now streaked with grey, and she had grown considerably larger around the middle.

"Ah, of course, sorry," said the first man as he tipped his glass in my direction. "It's a terrible thing that. He was no age at all."

"He was a good man, was old Pete," said the second man. "When's the funeral? Thursday isn't it?"

"Yeah," I muttered, turning back to Mrs Thornton.

"Don't worry," she said to me, giving a kind smile. "Everything is all organised at this end. Your Aunt Ruth has been in touch and has taken care of pretty much everything, but I'm sure you know that already."

"She's been pretty helpful," I said, leaving out the fact that she had completely taken over all of the arrangements.

"Janice from the bakers is doing the catering. We'll have the back room all cleared out so there's plenty of space for everyone to gather. If you've any specific music you want playing, just let me know. We've got this newfangled sound system. Apparently, you can connect your phone to it and play anything you want, so that's not a problem."

Mrs Thornton smiled at me, and my stomach twisted uncomfortably. Janice from the bakery. The back room being cleared out. I was only eight when Mum passed away, but I remembered the gathering in that same back room afterwards. It was like déjà vu. No doubt all the same faces would be there this time around, only with more lines and more grey hair.

"Here we are then." She reached across the bar and handed me a key. "It's just at the top of the stairs, room three. Give me a shout if you need anything."

As I picked up my bag and slung my guitar case over my shoulder, one of the old men piped up, "Not staying at the old place then?"

I ignored him and headed for the stairs. I *had* actually planned to stay in the house I grew up in. I was broke and could have done without paying for accommodation, even at Mrs Thornton's modest rates, but after collecting the key from the solicitor, I had discovered that in the years I had been absent, Dad's hoarding had escalated. It had always been a problem, ever since Mum died, but now the cottage was crammed to the rafters with his accumulated possessions. I was tired, drained, and there wasn't even anywhere to lie down (it looked as if Dad had been sleeping in an armchair), and the kitchen and bathroom facilities looked barely usable, so I had made the decision to call into The Black Bull. God only knew how the old man had been living like that. I realised with a sinking feeling that as the sole executor of his estate, I was going to have to sort it all out before I could even think of putting it on the market. My dreams of a quick sale that would allow me to clear my debts and head back to civilisation had evaporated as soon as I stepped through the front door. I was going to have my work cut out, and the thought of having to spend an extended period of time in Bramwick caused a heavy sense of gloom to settle over me.

As I let myself into the dingy little room at the end of the corridor, the words of the man in the bar echoed in my ears:" He was a good man."

Was he, though?

As I closed the door behind me, sealing myself into the musty-smelling room, I felt my sense of despair deepen. I stared around miserably at my new surroundings. The ceiling was low with dark beams which were pockmarked with old woodworm trails, and I made a mental note to watch my head if I got up during the night. There was a tiny window in the far wall that let in very little light and opened onto a view of a typical grey Bramwick evening. There was a highly patterned carpet in a style that hadn't been fashionable since the seventies and a floral bedspread with frilly edges. On the small dresser was a tray with a tiny travel kettle and a selection of tea and coffee sachets. I dropped my belongings on the floor and sat down heavily on the edge of the bed.

When I had left Bramwick at the age of nineteen, I had sworn I would never come back, yet here I was. It wasn't just Dad's sudden death that had driven me back here, though, but a whole series of shitty events that included spiralling debts, the break-up of a six year relationship, and the apparent collapse of my music career. I wondered if it had not been for those other events if I would have even come back for the funeral. I might have just left it all to Aunt Ruth to sort out. I hadn't spoken to Dad in years.

My breakup with Freya, my now ex, had been sudden and unexpected. It was an event that would mark the start of everything else falling apart.

We had met backstage at one of my band's, Listed MIA's, gigs, back when we were nobodies— playing dive bars and barely scraping by. She was a tattoo artist working in a studio which didn't pay her enough for her talents. It had been a whirlwind— we moved in together too soon, I supported her when she opened her own studio, and we even made the ultimate sign of commitment and got a dog— a French bulldog named Milo. Sure, we had money worries. London's property prices, the band's income drying up, and too long living a lifestyle we couldn't afford all contributed to that. But we were happy. That was until Ritchie ruined everything.

She could have cheated with anyone— but it had to be the band's lead singer, Ritchie. The fallout had been painful. It had ended in a physical fight between myself and Ritchie. It wouldn't be the first time things had turned violent between us, and it could have been much worse if Maxwell, our bassist, hadn't been there to pull us apart.

Ritchie was one of my oldest mates. He was the cool older guy who'd quite literally saved my life when I ran away to London as a clueless teen. He was an arsehole and always had been. He was arrogant, selfish, and a master manipulator. But once he got up on stage he was unstoppable, casting his magic over everyone so we all forgave him for his shortcomings.

That was until he slept with Freya. That broke the spell for me.

11

After Maxwell pried us apart, I had walked out, and I hadn't been home or to the studio since. Mike, our drummer— the level-headed one in the band— kept calling. So did our agent. I ignored them all. For me, the band was over.

And then Aunt Ruth rang to say that Dad had died. She told me he'd had a heart attack and had sat undiscovered in his junk-filled house for over a week. Up until that phone call I had been sofa-surfing, with no idea what I was going to do next. Bramwick had seemed like a convenient place to regroup. Now that I was here, I wasn't so sure.

For a while, I just lay there on the floral bedspread, staring up at the tasselled lampshade as the murky daylight faded into darkness.

My relationship with Dad had always been... complicated. We'd been virtual strangers since I'd bolted to London. His death had shocked me, of course— but the guilt of not feeling more was somehow worse than the loss itself. I knew how I *should* feel, I just didn't feel it.

It wasn't that he'd been a bad father. In some ways, we'd been alright— just the two of us muddling through after Mum died. But that was back when I lived my life on his terms— mainly, playing trombone in the brass band.

Things shifted in my mid-teens though when I discovered punk rock and the guitar. Dad and I started to argue. The more I tried to build a life of my own, the more we clashed, until eventually I'd had enough and left.

From there, our stubbornness had kept us apart. Neither of us was willing to be the first to reach out. Months turned into years. I'd thought about him often enough, and I wondered if he followed my success from afar. I wondered if he was proud. He should have been, shouldn't he? I'd made it as a musician— wasn't that what he always wanted?

But, of course, it was the wrong kind of music.

When we landed our first record deal, I sent him a CD. It was a sort of an olive branch; I had hoped it might encourage him to get in touch, but I never heard a thing.

I sighed and turned over on the bed so I could gaze at the blackness pressing in on the window. I had grown so used to the bright lights of London that I had forgotten how dark it could get here. I supposed I could go down to the bar for a drink; that might be marginally less depressing, but when I sat up I was hit by a wave of reluctance that left me glued to the spot. All of those faces would be looking at me with a mixture of curiosity and pity. Bramwick's prodigal son returned to bury his father, sticking out like a sore thumb among the checked shirts and flat caps of the farming folk. I forced myself to stand up and cross the room, but when my hand touched the door handle, the knot in my stomach tightened.

It was ridiculous. Nasher Newell, who had once stood on stage and told a whole audience to go fuck themselves, who had held his own in many a pub brawl, who had left home at the age of nineteen without a penny to his name and forged a successful career for himself, was afraid of a bar full of farmers and women from the WI. But I felt as if I had left Nasher behind in London. That persona had evaporated as soon as I entered the Dales, and all that was left was plain old Nathan Newell who used to play trombone in Bramwick's youth band and who hung about with geeky Simon and hippy Rosie.

I tried my best to summon a bit of Nasher back as I shoved the door to my room open and stomped heavily down the creaky old stairs.

It was a Saturday night, and the bar was fairly busy. Mrs Thornton had turned the music on, and the air was full of lively chatter. This was a relief as it would be easier for me to go unnoticed. Mrs Thornton herself was nowhere to be seen, and there was now a girl serving behind the bar— she wouldn't recognise me, she was too young. I ordered a pint and took a seat in a quiet corner beneath a taxidermy deer head. I was about halfway through my drink when my hopes of remaining undisturbed were shattered.

"Look who's come slinking back! Thought you'd outgrown us country folk. Did London chew you up and spit you back out again, Newell?"

I looked up to see a man in decorator's overalls, spattered in paint, walking towards me. I groaned inwardly. Alan Fenn was the last person I wanted to see.

To say we didn't get on as kids would be an understatement. He was the school bully, him and his sidekick Tommy Deans, and we had been in many a playground scuffle together. Judging by his words and the sneer on his narrow face, he hadn't changed.

"Thought you were never coming back? You said only losers would hang around a place like this. Guess that makes you a loser now, then?"

The words stung more than I cared to admit. But Alan didn't need to know what a mess my life was now; as far as he was concerned I was only here for one thing.

"I won't be back for long. I just came to settle my dad's affairs."

I was aware that the room had fallen quiet around us as the patrons watched and waited to see how things might unfold. As I glanced around, I caught the eye of a woman who was sitting at the far end of the bar. On seeing me, she gave a mischievous smile, pushed out her chair, and stood up. I would recognise Rosie Bell anywhere, and my heart gave a small lurch.

She had been a part of my little group of friends when we were growing up. She was always tagging along with myself and Simon Hunter. She grew up on some kind of smallholding, and she was the girl who always had muddy knees and tangled hair. A bit of a free spirit, she wore garish, homemade clothes, usually patchwork dungarees, and she was forever fishing for minnows and catching toads in jars to bring to school. Come September, her arms would be covered in scratches from her blackberry picking adventures. She had always had a sort of wild charm, and I felt an almost imperceptible tug inside me as she crossed the room, carrying with her memories of hazy, sunny days, of the smell of hay in the fields, and of the swallows coming home to nest. A smile tugged at the corner of my lips as I observed her trademark patched-up dungarees and her explosion of red hair. She had been the subject of much ridicule at school because of her hippy parents but I had always thought she was pretty cool.

My smile soon died as she stopped just behind Alan and laid a hand on his broad shoulder. Surely to God, Rosie Bell, that sensitive child of the earth, that beautiful free spirit, was not with this brute.

"You alright, Mr Big City? Long time no see." She cocked her head quizzically as she smiled at me over Alan's shoulder. "I was so sorry to hear about your dad."

I gave her a brief nod. Didn't she remember what Alan used to call her when we were at school? Had she just forgotten what a bully he was?

Alan pulled out a chair and sat down opposite me.

"So how's things with the band and everything?" Alan asked, and I watched Rosie sit down next to him. The rest of the pub had, mercifully, gone back to their own business, and the idle chatter and clink of glasses rose again.

I took a swallow of my beer and said, "All good, thanks."

"Not what I've heard..." Alan said smugly.

"Yeah, well what would you know about it?"

I caught Rosie giving him a nervous glance before she settled a hand on his knee, and I clenched my teeth. There had been a time when I thought there might be something between myself and Rosie, but we had been kids then, and I had been so certain that she was going to end up with Simon anyway.

"I heard you broke up." Alan's tone was casual. "Wasn't there something on social media about a delay with the new album and a bunch of cancelled shows? It mentioned something about creative differences, that's a nice way of saying you broke up, isn't it?"

14

Bloody Maxwell and that damned Facebook page!

"We're just having a break, you know, while I deal with the death of my dad?"

"If you say so."

For a few moments, we were all silent, before Alan suddenly stood up and raised his glass and proclaimed, "I'd like to declare a toast!"

That brought everyone's attention back to us, and I sank back in my chair, head low. Rosie caught Alan's sleeve and mouthed 'don't 'while shaking her head at him. He shook her away and shot an irritated scowl at her.

"To Bramwick's own Jonny Rotten, back where he belongs! Welcome back, Nathan Newell!"

Not catching on to his sarcastic tone, the small gathering seemed to take his sentiments as genuine, and there was a staggered chorus of 'welcome home 'as some of the patrons raised their glasses while others just looked mildly confused. I downed what remained of my pint and made for the door.

Outside, the night was cool and still, and there was a mist hanging over the valley. Beyond the orange glow of the few street lamps, the black shape of the hills rose into the starry sky. There was a haunting beauty to the scene, and I felt a stab of resentment towards the nostalgia that threatened to creep over me. I lit a cigarette and stared gloomily out into the night.

The sound of feet crunching in gravel disturbed my thoughts, and I turned to see Rosie coming towards me, hands buried deep in the pockets of her wax jacket.

"Couldn't handle it in there, eh?" she asked, stopping by my side.

"I just came out for a smoke," I told her. "Want one?"

I offered Rosie the battered box, remembering all those stolen smokes we had shared in the hay barn in Wellman's field. The fire we nearly started. The fear that we would be caught.

"Nah, Alan hates the smell." Rosie waved the packet away.

"You two are together then?"

"Married for two years," she confirmed. "Together for, oh, going on ten now."

I hadn't noticed a ring when we were in the bar, and I bristled at the news. I tried to hold my tongue, but I couldn't help it; it was just too much of a shock that she would have ended up with Alan Fenn of all people.

"Ten years," I mused. She must have gotten with him not long after I left. "But when we were kids, he used to call you…"

15

"I know what he used to call me." She cut me off before I could finish. "We were kids then. People change; he's not the same person he was."

"Hmm." I dragged on my cigarette.

I found it hard to believe that people like Alan could change, and what I had seen in the pub didn't exactly back up her point. He had been one of those kids with a real temper, always kicking off about something and getting into trouble. I remember him once hurling his drumsticks at the teacher during a music lesson.

"So do you think you'll be around for long?" she asked. "It would be fun to catch up."

"I dunno," I said honestly. "My dad left a lot for me to sort out. You know the house was always bad, but Jesus Christ, it's got ten times worse since I left. So much stuff... unfortunately, it might keep me here for longer than I'd like."

"I always liked your dad," she said softly. "It was such a shame that he had to stop playing with the band."

"Yeah, because it meant I had to live his dreams for him," I said bitterly.

"I know you had a tough time towards the end..."

She trailed off. Tough was an understatement. My teenage years had seen us constantly arguing. He had this obsession with me going to study music at university, joining one of the bigger brass bands, one of the ones that entered competitions, winning awards, and becoming the superstar of brass that he always wanted to be. But I had other ideas. He was furious when I gave up playing the trombone in favour of the guitar. He said I could have gone places, but instead, I was wasting my time with all this punk music.

"Rosie, are you coming back inside?" a voice boomed, and Rosie jumped. We looked back to see Alan hulking in the doorway.

"Yeah, I'm coming." She gave him a wave and gave me an apologetic smile. "Ignore him, he's just jealous because he wishes he'd had the gumption to leave."

"Not you, though?"

"No, not me." She gave an affirming nod and wrapped her arms around herself, turning back towards the pub. "I'm right where I'm supposed to be. I wouldn't want to be anywhere else. See you around, Jonny Rotten."

I stubbed out my cigarette and watched her go back inside.

16

Chapter Two

Rosie

So Nathan Newell was back in Bramwick. That was not something I ever thought I'd see. When Alan had held his phone up to me, an immensely satisfied look on his face, to show me the post about Listed MIA suffering creative differences, I hadn't expected him to show up here. Even when the news got round the village about Pete Newell being discovered dead after having a heart attack, I still didn't really expect him to come. From what I had gathered, the two of them had parted on bad terms, and no one in Bramwick, including Pete, had heard much from Nate since.

It had been a shock all those years ago to find Nate was suddenly gone. He was always threatening to leave, and I didn't doubt he would one day, but I had assumed he would wait until he had some kind of plan. Everyone knew he had come to despise his life in Bramwick, but he was an intelligent guy, and we thought he'd enrol in college in Bradford, or even university in Lancaster. Instead he just took off out of the blue and from there had completely ghosted us all. His furious dad said he'd gone to London. The next we heard of him was a few years later when Listed MIA released their first proper album. Bramwick had been buzzing with the news that one of its own had made it big. Nathan Newell had proved them all wrong, and all his teenage bravado about how he was destined for bigger things had turned out to be true. There had been a lot of bitterness among our peers. I often heard old schoolmates slagging him off, saying his music was crap, that sort of thing, but I was secretly proud of him. Nate had known what he wanted, and he had grabbed it with both hands and found a way to make it work, unlike most of the people we went to school with.

I suppose I can look at it that way because I've never felt trapped here the way many of the younger generation do. I love Bramwick. I love how beautiful it is in the Dales, how nature is always on your doorstep, how the pace of life is slow and the sense of community strong. Bramwick people look after each other, and if you ever need anything, all you have to do is ask. You don't get that in London. Oh, and I enjoyed running my zero-waste food shop, and I *loved* my volunteer work at The Grange.

I think it was my upbringing that left me feeling rooted to the land here. I'm a farmer's daughter, of sorts, but ours wasn't your typical Yorkshire farm. In Grandad's day, it had been. He had many acres and kept sheep and cows and grew barley, wheat and corn, but over the years, it had been scaled down and had become something else, thanks to my mother's outside influence and her vision. We still had a modest herd of dairy cows, but they were almost like pets, and we knew them all by name. We had a flock of free-range chickens, a few sheep and goats, and we grew vegetables on a small scale. Much of the produce went into the little shop I ran on the main street. Before that, it had sustained our family. We were vegetarians, you see, which was also my mother's influence and a big part of why, when the farm passed to my parents, they stopped butchering animals for meat and took the business in a new direction. The main source of income for the farm was now the alpacas and the glamping pods. My parents had been offering alpaca trekking through the Dales since before it had become trendy. They had always been very bohemian and had been into reusing and recycling before *that* became a big thing too. It was just as well really, as their small farm enterprise didn't bring in a huge amount of income.

All of this was why Alan had taken to calling me 'Compost Queen' all through secondary school. He was mean to me back then, but isn't that often the way with adolescent love? The most popular boy in school can't possibly admit he's into the bohemian freak, with her homemade clothes and hippy parents, so he goes the other way and bullies her instead. I never would have imagined we'd end up married.

Alan had always had mood swings. I hadn't noticed it so much before we lived together but once we moved in it became more obvious. His bursts of anger could come suddenly and out of nowhere and could take you by surprise if you didn't know how to read the signs. I'd got pretty good over the years at predicting his emotions and I'd learned not to push him too far when he was going through one of his bad patches. Usually I could see a swing approaching and was able to navigate his feelings and calm him down before he really exploded. Experience had taught me that if I didn't mange to diffuse a situation before his temper got the better of him, it was best just to lay low, stay out of his way, and wait for him to calm down on his own.

His mood had already been low for quite some time when Nate appeared back in Bramwick. This bout of depression had started when he had been asked to take a step back from Bramwick Brass Band for a while. He, like myself, Simon and Nate, had been recruited into the band when we were in primary school. He took up the drums, which seemed to suit him as he enjoyed hitting things. Recently, he had turned up at a rehearsal drunk and mouthed off at Fred Black, our conductor, and the committee had taken the decision to suspend him, which had not gone down well at all. They were right to do what they did, of that I have no doubt, but in the face of Alan's ongoing fury, I was forced to stand down too in a show of solidarity, which really bloody annoyed me. Even worse, he had since been going around badmouthing the band, and it was looking increasingly likely his suspension would turn into an expulsion. I missed the weekly rehearsals and the camaraderie of my bandmates, and the resentment I felt around the situation had been putting extra pressure on my already strained relationship with Alan.

Following Nate's appearance in The Black Bull that night, his mood had worsened. He sat at breakfast that morning, scowling at his phone, scrolling obsessively through Listed MIA's Facebook page, and remarking viciously to me every two minutes about what a loser Nate was, to which I had to nod and pretend to agree lest his temper rise up again.

I looked across the table at Alan. He was holding his fork with one hand, digging through a pile of scrambled eggs, and gripping his phone with the other. He looked fixated on his screen, a sneer on his face, and I looked at him nervously.

He didn't look especially angry—I was certain he wasn't on the edge of blowing up, but there was definitely *something* up with him.

"Look at the state of him," he said at last, with a cruel laugh. He turned his phone around to show me a very unflattering picture of Nate slumped against a wall in what I assumed was the backstage area of some venue. "I cannot get my head around why you used to fancy *that*."

"How far back are you digging, Alan?" I questioned. The date on the post he showed me was three years ago.

"He'd never last a day at a real job," he said, ignoring my question and continuing to scroll. "He used to think he was so much better than us all; it's nice to see him finally taken down a peg or two."

I rolled my eyes and started clearing away the breakfast things. It was a bright morning and I was looking forward to a good day. I hoped Alan wasn't going to spoil it.

"I think you're getting a little bit too obsessed with him. Why are you letting this bother you? He'll be gone soon."

"Of course it bothers me that an old boyfriend of yours is back."

"We never even went out, you know that."

"That's right," he said with a sly smile. "He was into Hannah Ferguson wasn't he? Can't say I blame him really, she was hot, if you're into that whole emo girl thing. You weren't really his type, were you?"

He was being deliberately cruel to get a rise out of me. He was in the mood for a fight. I scraped the remains of the eggs into the bin. I wasn't going to let him get to me. But my heart rate had already increased and I felt a fluttering of nerves. The knife scraped across the plate and I looked out the window at the birds on the feeder.

"You were absolutely devastated when he left. Didn't you used to lie in bed at night and cry yourself to sleep because he wasn't interested in you?" He only knew this because he had found and read my old diaries. I'd never dared share my feelings about Nate with anyone other than those pages. "Pathetic, if you ask me."

I held onto the side on the counter as I felt the room growing smaller around me. Perhaps we *were* on the verge of an explosion. I decided I'd best tread carefully.

"Where is it you're working today?" I asked, changing the subject and trying to sound cheerful.

It was a Sunday, but it wasn't unusual for Alan to take jobs at the weekend if it meant extra cash and it suited his clients.

"I told you yesterday, over in Merrygill. That old woman with the big farmhouse has been moaning that the plastering in her kitchen isn't finished yet."

"The life of a self-employed tradesman," I sympathised. "No day of rest for you."

"Sadly not," he said, taking his jacket from the hook on the back of the kitchen door. "What are you up to today?"

"Oh, I don't know." The tension started to slip from my body as I felt the threat of an argument subside. "I've got a few bits to do over at The Grange. The apple trees need pruning. Might go and have a look at that."

"Right," he said, his jaw stiffening. The amount of time I spent at The Grange was a bone of contention between us. I shouldn't have mentioned it. "Well, have a good day anyway. I should be back around six. We can get a takeaway. I'll pick something up if you like."

It was ok, he wasn't going to have a go at me about how much of a waste of time my volunteer work was. "Pizza would be good," I said, and kissed him goodbye.

Chapter Three

Nate

I wondered if it might be worth just getting a house clearance firm to cart the whole lot off, but that would cost money, and I didn't have a lot of that to spare. Besides, there was always the slim chance there was something important or valuable among the junk: money in an old biscuit tin, bank books hidden in the back of a cupboard, that kind of thing. If I employed strangers to come in and blitz the place, these things could be missed. No, I was going to have to tackle it on my own. The thought was daunting. I was expecting Aunt Ruth to arrive in the village in the next couple of days, but she was old and a bit decrepit, and I doubted she'd be much help. I assumed she'd probably want to get back to Scotland as soon as the proceedings were over rather than hanging about to wade through her brother's hoard.

Aunt Ruth had already started to complain the last time I spoke to her about the fact that her brother had not included his niece in his will and had left everything to me. As a result, my cousin had decided that she wasn't coming to the funeral, using the lame excuse that there was no one to watch her dog. Other than Aunt Ruth and cousin Kelly, there wasn't really any family left, so I expected the funeral to be a small affair.

"Let's just get in there and get it done," I told myself as I hesitated at the garden gate. "The sooner it's dealt with, the sooner you can get it sold and get those debts cleared. Then it's clean slate time."

But how long would it take to sell? Property in Bramwick wasn't exactly in high demand. It struck me that I could be stuck here for months, and the thought was a depressing one. The reality was I was broke, and I needed to stop burning money at The Black Bull. I needed to at least get the place habitable as soon as possible, and standing at the bottom of the garden path, staring at the door and clutching a roll of heavy-duty bin bags, wasn't going to get me anywhere. I was grateful that I at least had the rusty old van that the band had used to lug our gear around. I wondered how many trips to the dump I would have to make in it.

I eyed the building suspiciously. It was a modest three-bedroom cottage, surely it wouldn't take me *that* long to clear...

I opened the gate, which squealed in protest, and made my way down the path, stepping over various discarded items— a bucket with a hole rusted through it, an old barbecue that had fallen on its side, a bald car tyre. I noted that there was a battered sofa around the side of the house, pushed against the stone wall and turning green as nature tried to reclaim it. I recognised it as the one we used to sit on when I lived there. At least he had got a new sofa since I left, that was something. I turned the key in the lock but had to shove the door with my shoulder to get it to open. It must have swollen with the damp weather. I stumbled over the threshold into the same musty staleness as yesterday. The air was probably teeming with mould spores and God knew what else. The first thing to do would be to open all the windows and get some air flowing through the place.

I made my way from room to room, flinging open the old single-glazed windows, navigating my father's encroaching hoard as I did so. Now that I had clean air drifting in, I considered how best to tackle this mammoth job. I didn't even know where to start, and the overwhelm that I felt threatened to stop me in my tracks before I even got going.

Get the essentials done first— make the kitchen and bathroom usable and then worry about the rest.

I tried to remind myself that I had stayed in some dire places as a youth when I first arrived in London, and this couldn't possibly be any worse, but somehow it was. I had grown used to my home comforts in recent years—Wi-Fi, Sky TV, hot water, heating…

In the kitchen, I turned on the hot tap and let it run, but after several minutes, it was still cold. I battled my way through piles of boxes in the utility room until I found the ancient boiler and managed to rekindle the pilot light. I wondered uneasily if the appliance was even safe. I could die in the night of carbon monoxide poisoning and sit here undiscovered for a week like Dad. I shuddered at the unwelcome image that crept unbidden into my brain of what state Dad must have been in when the police eventually forced their way in and found him in that armchair. I had noted on my first visit that there was a suspiciously empty space in the living room where I was assuming said chair had once sat.

Not wanting to suffer a similar fate, I made a note to pick up a carbon monoxide detector the next time I was in town. Hot water fixed, I returned to the crowded living room where Dad had died and hunted for the TV remote. I was pleasantly surprised to find that not only did it work, but Dad actually had a Netflix account set up on it. This meant he also had Wi-Fi. His viewing history showed that he was partway through a documentary about a cult in the US, a series he would never see the end of, and that he had recently watched his way through many old, classic films. The sight of his 'continue watching 'list that would never be returned to made a lump rise in my throat. I swallowed and tossed the remote back on the arm of the sofa.

22

Having established that I now had heat, electricity, and the bonus of Wi-Fi and Netflix, I resolved to get enough done by tomorrow so that I could check out of The Black Bull. I put in my ear pods, turned on my most energetic playlist, and soon the sounds of Rancid and The Dropkick Murphys were helping me power through the most mundane of tasks. Before long, I was sweating, as I filled bag after bag of stuff from the kitchen and hauled them out to the van. The farmhouse table was stacked high with neat piles of newspapers bound in twine, and I hauled these out as they were so I could take them to the recycling bins. By the door were several boxes of old shoes— boots, wellies, loafers— some relatively new and some encrusted with mud and worn to holes. There was even a pair of my old football boots left over from when I had given up the sport at thirteen. All of them went into bin bags.

The cupboards were stocked with enough cans of food that he could probably have survived an apocalypse. This was a good thing because it meant I could save money on meals. I kept anything that wasn't horribly out of date and that still left me with a *lot* of stuff. By mid-afternoon, the van was almost full, and the kitchen was just about usable. I was about to see if the kettle worked (there were plenty of teabags, but the milk had turned to cheese) when there was a knock at the door.

My first thought was that it was Aunt Ruth arrived early so she could pick through my father's belongings to see if she could find anything of value for my snubbed cousin, but when I pulled the stubborn door open, it was Rosie I found standing on the doorstep.

"Oh, it's you," I said, pulling the headphones out of my ears.

She folded her arms and looked at me reproachfully.

"Is that any way to greet an old friend?"

"Sorry, hi." I hadn't meant to sound so cold; she had just taken me by surprise. "What can I do for you?"

"What are you up to?"

"What do you think? Busy dealing with that lot." I jerked my head in the direction of the cluttered hall.

She leaned to her left and peered over my shoulder. Why was she here? Had she come back to gloat? To get a look at the place so she could report back to Alan about what a mess it was and they could have a good laugh together? But that didn't seem like something Rosie would do. Then again, marrying Alan Fenn didn't seem like something Rosie would do either.

"I figured you might need a hand."

I eyed her suspiciously. I couldn't quite work out why she was even still speaking to me after the way I had treated her and Simon.

"Wow," she said when I didn't answer. "If I'd known you were going to be so grateful, I'd have come over sooner."

She turned as if to leave.

I stared after her as she made her way down the path. I didn't need her help. Having her here would only complicate things.

"You know," she whirled back around, hair whipping over her shoulders, and glared at me angrily. "People in Bramwick help each other out; it's what we do, but I suppose you've forgotten that living in London?"

She turned away again.

"Wait," I called after her. "If you really don't have anything better to do, then I could use an extra pair of hands."

"Are you sure about that, Jonny Rotten?"

"Well, you're dressed for it." I nodded at her mucky overalls. Then I added, with a smirk," Compost Queen."

"Hey!" she exclaimed, but she was smiling now.

"Won't Alan mind you giving up your Sunday?"

"Nah, he's at work."

"What does he do?" This was exactly the kind of small talk I hated, but it seemed like the natural thing to say.

"Painting and decorating, building work, that sort of thing."

"Well, I might need some work doing round here to get it up to scratch." It was a peace offering, to show there were no hard feelings about how much Alan and I had disliked each other in school.

She nodded and said, "Hold on, I've got some boxes in the car."

I was back inside and had discovered that the kettle did indeed work when she appeared with an armful of flattened boxes. She dumped them on the now-clear kitchen table.

"Tea?" I asked, and when she nodded, I added, "There's no milk."

"You look like you've made a decent start already," she said, gazing around the kitchen. Then, with a wrinkle of her nose, she said, "It still needs a good clean, mind you."

She ran a finger along the dresser and looked at the dirt that came away.

"You don't look like you're any stranger to dirt," I said. I handed her a chipped mug with a picture of a Land Rover on it. I vaguely recalled buying that mug for Dad's birthday one year.

"I volunteer at The Grange," she told me. "I mainly work in the grounds. Remember the community garden and the orchard? But I'm also on the committee, which is actually a lot of work. Especially because Sandy Brown is also on it."

"God, Sandy Brown." I shook my head. "The biggest mouth in the village. So, is that what you do full time?"

"No." She shook her head. "I have the zero-waste shop on the main street, Nature's Bounty. It's a sort of joint venture between me and a friend, so I'm in there part-time too. I also help out Mum and Dad with the farm."

"That must keep you busy. I'm surprised you've got time to be hanging about with the likes of me." I smiled slightly. Gardening and running a zero-waste shop— there couldn't be a more Rosie way to spend time.

"For now," she said, blowing on her tea. "I might be about to get a little less busy."

"How come?"

"Well, you know the tenancy agreement granted to the village for the use of The Grange?"

I gave a nod. I remembered learning about the great Lord Henshaw, patron of the village, and his gift of the land at school.

"That agreement is almost up, and the current landowner, Danny Henshaw, doesn't look like he wants to extend the lease. Fed up of being responsible for it, I reckon, and he's looking to sell it off. There's a rumour he's got a developer all lined up and ready to go."

"That's a bit rubbish," I said, trying to sound sympathetic as I busied myself with attempting to open a drawer in the dresser that was wedged shut.

I cursed and swore as I rattled the drawer, and Rosie started to assemble the boxes.

"Yep," she continued. "But there's a tiny sliver of hope. Good old Lord Henshaw included a stipulation in the agreement that states if the time ever comes for the land to be sold, the people of the village should have the first option to purchase it, for whatever is a fair market value at the time."

"Oh yeah?" I tried to force a butter knife under the tiny gap I had created in the drawer to dislodge whatever was jamming it.

"We have until the first of May next year to raise the money," she confirmed. "We've been flat out fundraising, but it's not looking good. Five hundred thousand pounds is a lot of money, so it seems more than likely the land will go to the developer."

The drawer finally gave way and burst open under the force. Rosie giggled as I stumbled backwards.

"Sorry to hear that," and I genuinely was. I knew how special The Grange was to the village, and greedy developers buying up land didn't sit well with my punk ethics.

"Anyway," she said, changing the subject. "You really should have some kind of system here."

"You mean other than just chucking it all in bin bags ready for the dump like I've been doing?"

"Well, yeah, it's pretty wasteful just to send all this stuff to the landfill," she said scornfully.

"I could tell by looking at you you were still the Compost Queen," I said with a chuckle.

"A name I now proudly live up to. I also still answer to Patches, you know, though I don't wear clothes made by my mother anymore."

I laughed, remembering that nickname that I had bestowed on her.

"So they still have that farm with all the alpacas and stuff?"

"They do, though they're struggling a bit now they're getting older. Determined to keep going as long as they can though, and I do what I can to help. I've taken over most of the vegetable growing; it's where a lot of the produce in the shop comes from."

I lifted the contents of the now-freed drawer (it looked like a load of old bills) and dumped them into a bag.

"They should be recycled," she said. "So, back to this system. You should have boxes for stuff you want to keep, boxes for stuff that can be donated, boxes for recycling, and bags for rubbish."

"My way's much quicker," I insisted. "Plus I can tell you now I don't need boxes for stuff to keep; it's all going."

"You say that now, but you never know what you might come across. You might find some of this stuff actually means something to you."

"I'm not the sentimental type."

"No, you never were, were you?"

"What's that supposed to mean?"

"You must remember the last day of term when we were all given those school leavers hoodies? They had everyone's names printed on the back, and we all got our friends to sign them in Sharpie as a memento of our school days. You made a huge deal of chucking yours on that big bonfire we had at the graduation party. Didn't you make a big speech about how you didn't want anything ever to remind you of Bramwick Grammar or anyone in it?"

"Yeah, so what? I bet you still have yours, don't you?"

"I do actually."

"I just don't get emotionally attached to *things*," I told her. "My dad was sentimental about stuff, and look where it got him. I was never going to let this happen to me."

She looked around sadly. "It must have been really hard growing up like this. No wonder you never let any of us visit."

"Exactly."

"It doesn't change the fact that useful stuff shouldn't be going to the landfill," she said adamantly. "Can we at least agree on the donate boxes?"

"Fine!" I said, exasperated. I knew letting her help was going to make things take longer. "Why don't you go and start in the living room while I finish up here?"

At least if we were in separate rooms, I could put my headphones back in, and there'd be no more talk of graduation hoodies and The Grange.

"But how will I know if there's something you might want to keep?"

"I already told you there won't be."

"Ok," she said brightly. "If I find a big wad of cash, I'll just keep it."

"Obviously, if there's anything hugely valuable, then put it aside. Just use your common sense!"

"If you're sure…" She grabbed some boxes and disappeared into the living room.

An hour passed, and the kitchen was all but done. The last thing I had to do was box up the garish 1970s Denby tea set that had been displayed on the dresser since Mum's time and was now thick with dust.

"Nate," Rosie's voice drifted from the living room. "Come and see this."

"This had better be a stack of money or deeds to a mansion, Patches!"

When I put my head around the living room door, she was standing next to a neat stack of boxes holding a trombone. She put it to her lips and blew, pulling the slide in and out to make a comical noise.

"Why the bloody hell does he still have that?" I couldn't explain why the sight of the instrument irritated me so much. Perhaps because it represented everything my father had wanted me to be, all that I had rebelled against and struggled so hard to leave behind.

"You used to be really good at this," she said. "I was always well jealous of your talent when we were in the band. You were pretty into it all at one point."

"Yes, well, we all make mistakes. Thank God I saw the light."

"Remember that solo you played in assembly that time? It was really bloody good!"

I nodded. She was looking at the trombone with a nostalgic expression.

"God, you and me and Simon were so excited when we were asked to play at the May Day celebrations that year."

"Do you still play?"

27

"Not at this exact moment." She looked awkward, and I decided not to press her on what she meant by that. "But Simon does. He's first cornet now; he's pretty decent."

"Well, good for Simon." I took the trombone from her and laid it in one of the donation boxes. "I'm just glad I realised guitar is way cooler, or it'd still be 'Slaidburn' on a Sunday in a daft blazer with Simon Hunter instead of a sold-out London stage supporting The Radicals."

"Of course, because punk is so original and cutting-edge." She rolled her eyes at me.

"Well, at least it's not boring. It tackles real issues; we always have something to say. All brass bands do is play the same colonial shit they've been playing for decades."

"That's just not true!" she protested. "Look, I'm sorry; I can see I've touched a nerve. You wanted to get away and do your own thing, and that's okay, but it's also okay if your thing is staying put and playing in the brass band. The guys in the band are good people; they give a lot to the community, and that matters too."

"Yeah, I suppose you're right." I picked up the trombone again and turned it over in my hands. "Do you think they might have a use for this?"

"I'm certain they will," she beamed at me.

"As long as they don't mind this…" I tried to control the laughter that was bubbling up inside me and managed to keep a straight face as I held it out to her and pointed at the bell.

"What's that? Some kind of engraving?" She leaned in, squinting, before she staggered back, a fit of giggles erupting from her.

I let my own laughter surge from me, and for a few minutes, we were both completely incapacitated with the kind of laughter that consumes your whole body and makes your belly ache. I couldn't remember the last time I laughed so hard, and it felt good. When the laughter eventually subsided, Rosie wiped the tears from her eyes and shook her head.

"Band sucks?" She snorted as she tried to stifle another fit of giggles. "I don't remember this at all."

"I carved it when we were in third year, and Dad was insisting I keep going despite the fact I'd lost all interest."

"Well, you never know, there could be some kid in the youth band who might appreciate the sentiment."

"No doubt."

"They'll be practising tonight. Why don't you go and drop it in? I'm sure Simon would like to see you."

"Maybe I will. I guess you know the band is playing at Dad's funeral?"

She nodded. "The band was important to him, wasn't it? Why did he stop playing again?"

"Oh, he had some problem with his ears. He had to have this operation, and afterwards, he wasn't allowed to play anymore. Something to do with the pressure not being good for him."

"At least you were able to go on and have a career in music. That made him proud, didn't it?"

"If it did, it's news to me."

"He never told you?"

"We barely spoke after I left."

Admitting that out loud to Rosie made me feel ashamed. I know the lines go both ways, and he didn't make the effort either, but really, I could have done more to repair our relationship.

"Really? Well, he was obviously keeping tabs on what you were up to with your band as he was always talking about how well you were doing."

This surprised me, and I felt a pang of sadness.

"I should probably get going," Rosie said, glancing at her watch. "I could pop back for a bit tomorrow if you like? I'm only working in the morning, so I could bring you some lunch."

"Yeah, that'd be nice."

"Right, I'll see you then."

Chapter Four

Rosie

When Nate left, it had hurt. He had taken off without a word to either me or Simon. At first, I worried something awful had happened. But as time passed and he ignored our messages, it started to feel like we just weren't good enough for him anymore. In the year that led up to his departure, he had been working in the local petrol station, a job his dad made him take and which he constantly complained about. We always knew he was set on leaving Bramwick. His dream was to go somewhere bigger, meet like-minded musicians, and form a band of his own.

Simon and I knew how hard he worked at the guitar—he was as talented on that as he had been on the trombone. Music just seemed to come really naturally to Nate, and he had an incredible ability to come up with lyrics and melodies that were so catchy you'd find yourself singing them for days.

His dad had definitely made things difficult for him when he turned his back on brass in favour of punk rock. He had been a supportive and encouraging father when Nate was doing something he approved of, but he offered no encouragement when it came to him exploring his guitar playing and songwriting abilities. To begin with, it had upset Nate. He hated that he'd lost his father's approval. He wanted more than anything for him to share in his joy when he wrote a new song or mastered a complicated chord progression. But he told me and Simon on many occasions that his dad just wasn't interested. He called the type of music Nate was into 'nothing but noise'. He told his son he was embarrassed even to be seen with him when he started exploring his own fashion sense and began wearing ripped jeans and an old biker jacket on which he had painted various slogans in tip-ex. All of his father's criticism had definitely put a dent in Nate's confidence and had eventually led him to rebel so that the two of them were constantly falling out. More often than not in those days, Nate could be found sleeping on Simon's sofa bed.

So we understood when he left. We assumed he had had one last massive blow-out with his dad and had been pushed over the edge. What we didn't understand was why our attempts at communication went ignored. We had been there for him during those last few difficult years, always lending a friendly ear when he complained about how miserable and depressed he was. It felt like a slap in the face when he just cut us out of his life entirely.

A couple of years later someone shared a post on the Bramwick community Facebook page about his band and how they were set to support The Radicals on their next UK tour. I had no idea who The Radicals were but apparently it was quite a big deal. As his band's success grew, Fred Black, our old music teacher, had become quite evangelical about his former pupil's rise to fame. He may have gone on to choose guitar, but the foundations of his musical talent, Fred claimed, had been forged under him in the Bramwick youth band. For a time, he'd go to the local primary school and try to recruit new players with a presentation that leaned heavily on Nate's success. He wanted to show the pupils that the things you learned in the youth band could take you anywhere. It didn't quite work though, and all he achieved was to send a flurry of kids rushing to Mrs Simpson's lunchtime guitar club. In fact, so few kids had shown an interest in learning the cornet or trombone in the following years that the youth band had collapsed entirely. We all knew that with no new players coming through, it would only be a matter of time before the main band suffered the same fate. Not that we would even have anywhere to rehearse if Danny Henshaw got his way and The Grange was sold off to developers…

"Are you alright, love?" I hadn't realised I was staring off into space, lost in thought, until Mum's voice brought me round.

"Sorry." I gave myself a shake and picked up my tea.

"You looked miles away. I hope everything's okay?" It was a loaded question, and she didn't need to elaborate; we both knew what she was talking about.

"Oh no, don't worry, it's nothing like that," I assured her. She knew I had been having trouble with my marriage for a while now. "Alan and I are fine; it's getting better."

"Hmm." She looked at me over the rim of her mug with an expression that said she didn't believe me. "You'll be going to band tonight then?"

"Mum, you know I can't," I groaned.

"And why not? It wasn't you who got drunk and made a show of yourself."

I sighed. "Yes, but that was a one-off, and I need to show him a bit of solidarity, show him I agree that Fred's decision was a bit harsh."

"What was a bit harsh?" Dad came into the living room, overalls and checked shirt splattered in mud.

"Alan's suspension from the band," Mum filled him in. "Take those overalls off before you sit down, will you?"

"Serves him right if you ask me." My parents had never been huge fans of Alan. "I don't see why you should miss out because of his stupidity. You shouldn't be changing your life because of Alan's mistakes, love. That's not how I raised you." He waved the wrench he was holding at me to emphasise his point.

"It's not that simple, Dad." My mind wandered back to Nate and his old trombone. He might show up at practice tonight to hand it in. I could always make an excuse to pop along. I needn't stay for the whole rehearsal. I shut the thought down before it could go any further. "Anyway, did you get that toilet sorted?"

"Yes. Those stupid buggers in number three keep stuffing things down it that they shouldn't when it clearly states paper only."

There was a moment of silence.

"Guess who's back in the village?" I said, and when neither of them could guess, I told them.

"He'll be here for the funeral, I suppose," Mum said. "We thought we might go. What do you think?"

"I'm sure Nate would appreciate that."

"The band'll be playing, I assume?" Dad was still hovering in the doorway.

"They will be, yes."

"But not you?"

"Dad, will you leave it?"

"Ok, ok. I think you're being stupid, but I'll say no more."

"Anyway, I need to get going." I stood up and put on my jacket, bidding my parents farewell and stepping out into the mild evening.

As I walked across the lawn, I saw Flossy, one of the alpacas, staring at me over the fence from the neighbouring field. I went to say hello. She blinked her long lashes at me and gave a little snort. It was starting to get dark, and the view from the garden in the twilight was incredible. The farm was on the side of the hill, and you could see the village spread below, lights starting to twinkle, and the hills on the other side of the valley rising gently into the darkening sky. It certainly had been an idyllic place to grow up.

"How could anyone not love this?" I said to the alpaca.

I couldn't imagine why Nate harboured such a dislike for the place or why anyone would want to trade this for London, or any city. I considered myself very lucky to call a place like this home. I supposed we were just very different people, and that was why it could never have worked between us.

Chapter Five

Nate

I stood outside the hall and wondered what the hell I was thinking. In my hand I held my old trombone, my fingers gripping the handle of the case tightly. This was a stupid idea. I would drop it off another night. Better yet, I could give it to Rosie, and she could hand it in. I could hear the sound of brass instruments warming up drifting from inside the building as I stood there deliberating. A room full of people from Bramwick awaited me in there, filled with faces from the past, and the thought was far from appealing. I was just turning round to leave when a woman stopped me.

"Are you looking for the band?" she asked, looking at my trombone case.

"Oh yeah. Well, not really. I just have an instrument to donate. Could I give it to you?"

She gave me a surprised look. "No, no, you should come in. That's such a generous offer, and Fred will want to thank you."

I found myself being cajoled towards the door by this woman with her spiky blonde hair, and I seemed unable to resist as she swept me down a corridor and all but shoved me through a door marked 'Band Room'. For a few moments, I just stood there awkwardly. I could almost hear my fourteen-year-old self fumbling through warm up routines, feeling the sharp sting of Mr Black's corrections. I watched the bustle of the musicians unpacking their instruments and shuffling sheets of music, chatting amongst themselves and blowing their way through the odd scale. There were old, disused instruments hanging on the walls, and a black-and-white picture I recognised of a stern-looking Victorian gentleman— Lord Henshaw, the band's founder. I spotted my old friend Simon Hunter at the front of the cornet section, slotting his mouthpiece into his instrument. He had not changed at all. He still had the same haircut, the same glasses, the same faded blue jeans and jumper. Simon looked up, and when he caught my eye, a look of recognition went across his face, and I worried that he might not actually be pleased to see me, but then he broke into a smile.

"Nate Newell!" he exclaimed, his voice cutting through the hubbub, and everyone turned to look at me.

"Well, I never!" Another voice chimed in, and when I looked across the room, I was confronted with my old music teacher, Mr Black, still tall and wiry, only now his dark hair was snowy white.

"Mr Black," I said, suddenly feeling like I was fourteen years old again. "I didn't think you'd still be running things here..."

"And I didn't think I'd ever see you back in Bramwick, son, let alone with a trombone in your hand." His eyes glimmered with glee. "You've all heard me talk about him often enough, and now here he is. Everyone, this is Nathan Newell, my student who went on to become a famous rock musician."

They were all looking at me curiously.

"I just thought I'd drop this off," I started to explain. "It was among my dad's things, and I thought someone here might have a use for it. Sort of a thank you for agreeing to play at the old man's funeral."

"Let's have a look." Simon jumped up, and before I knew it, he had taken the trombone from me and was opening the case. "It's the same one, alright," he said with a snigger.

"I certainly don't remember seeing that when I was teaching you," Mr Black said indignantly as he caught sight of what had amused Simon. "I'd have given you what for if I'd noticed. Imagine scratching such a thing into a valuable piece of brass. 'Band sucks' indeed!"

There was an uproar of laughter from the others in the room.

"I know, very mature, eh?" I laughed. "I'm sure it'll buff out."

"I dare say it will." Mr Black nodded in approval as he took the instrument out of the case and put the two parts together. "Go on, let's see if you've still got it."

"I didn't keep it up," I said through gritted teeth, holding up my hands to ward off the instrument which Mr Black was brandishing at me. "I haven't played in years!"

"Nonsense!" my old teacher scoffed. "You might've traded harmony for anarchy, but I'll wager we can still get a scale out of you; it never leaves you."

"Really, I'm not here to play..."

"Come on, give it a go, for old times 'sake!" Simon piped up.

There was a chorus of 'Go on thens 'and 'Let's hear yous 'from the assembled players, and I realised I wasn't going to be allowed to leave until they'd seen me make an idiot of myself. With a groan, I took the trombone and adjusted the slide. My heart was actually thumping in my chest as the room fell silent and watched me as I settled the instrument on my shoulder. I hadn't played brass since I left Bramwick, and my mind was racing, trying to recall something, *anything,* that I had learned. Slide positions? Where the hell was C again? Mr Black had bet that I could still play a scale, but my mind drew a blank, and I was starting to sweat. I was a professional musician, in a room full of amateurs; this really shouldn't have been a big deal, so why did I feel so nervous? My mind was still desperately flailing about trying to retrieve lost knowledge as I raised the instrument to my lips. First position, slide all the way in! Of course it was! I took a deep breath, pursed my lips, and blew.

The noise that came out was shaky, but I was surprised how quickly it came back to me once I started; my hand seemed to have some kind of weird muscle memory that allowed it to find the correct positions without me even thinking about it, sending me wobbling my way up the scale of C and back down again. It was far from smooth; some of the notes cracked and wavered the higher I got, but I made it, and when I was done, there was a small round of applause.

"There, are you happy?" I thrust the instrument in Mr Black's direction, afraid that if I held onto it for too long, it would drag me back into the world of Bramwick Brass.

"I knew you could still do it," Mr Black said proudly. "When I teach someone, it stays with them for life."

When he didn't take the trombone from my outstretched hands, I put it back in its case with a look of mistrust, feeling like I was handling something dangerous.

"We're always looking for new players," Mr Black said. "We're here every Sunday and Thursday."

"Yeah, and we aren't picky either," Simon added. "We don't play in contests or anything like that anymore. It's all quite laid back, no pressure, just a bit of fun really."

"We're a friendly bunch, that's for sure," called the woman who had shown me in, peering over the top of her tenor horn.

"Thanks, but I don't plan on being here long. I'll stick to punk rock, I think."

Mr Black snapped the catches on the trombone case shut and handed it back to me. "I don't accept this," he said simply. "Keep it for as long as you're here at least."

I could see what he was trying to do, the sneaky old bastard. He was hoping sentimentality would get the better of me, that if I had to look at it every day, then I would pick it up and play it. I couldn't force him to take it, but I could put it back in the donate box. I said a brief goodbye and hurried off down the corridor, feeling a need to get out of there as fast as I could.

"It was good to see you, mate." Simon had followed me and stopped me at the main door. I continued to be surprised by the enthusiastic reaction to my return by my old friends after the way I had left things. I

35

was feeling guilty now about how badly I had handled my departure. "I know it's been what, ten years? But if you did fancy catching up while you're here…"

"That would be good," I said. The least I could do was not disappoint him now. "I'm staying at The Black Bull for now."

"Cool. I might drop in for a pint after work tomorrow then."

"Ok, see you then."

"Right, I'd better get back in there, or Fred, you know, Mr Black, won't be happy."

The band had broken into a merry march, and the tune drifted faintly down the corridor. That was the trouble with playing the trombone. I just wasn't interested in the types of music brass bands played. Simon had disappeared back to the band room, and for a moment I just stood there, feeling a bit shocked. How had this happened? I had vowed I would keep my head down when I was here and not get involved in anything or with anyone to do with Bramwick. Yet it was only my first day here, and already I had visited the brass band, reconnected with Rosie, agreed to have a drink with Simon, and I was stood here still holding the sodding trombone. All the ghosts from my past were already crowding in.

I started to walk. This wasn't the way it was supposed to happen. I wasn't meant to be playing trombones and having drinks with people from the past. I should have known that it wasn't possible to keep a low profile in Bramwick.

I had just crossed the bridge over the small beck at the back of the main street when I became aware of someone following me. I glanced back to see a dark figure stepping onto the bridge.

"What now?" I muttered. "I swear to God, if this is someone else from the past wanting to reconnect…"

"Oi, Sid Vicious!" These unimaginative names were already getting very tiresome.

I could make out the approaching figure now. It was Alan Fenn.

"Oh great, just what I need," I said quietly, before adding in a louder voice:" Alright, Alan?"

He had reached my side of the bridge now and was glaring at me menacingly. I could see he was holding a bottle of beer in his hand. I started to walk again.

"You think I don't know what's going on!" His words came out slurred. "Rosie spent half the day helping you clear your old man's stuff."

So she had told him. Then again, why shouldn't she? There was no harm in someone helping an old friend.

"Do you think I'm stupid?" Alan continued to advance.

"Look, calm down." I didn't feel in the least bit threatened. I'd dealt with worse than Alan Fenn in my time. "I didn't ask her for help. She just turned up because she's a good person. She likes to help people. It's who she is."

"Don't think you can tell me who my wife is. I know her better than you do."

"I'm sure you do."

"I don't like the idea of her spending time with you."

"Fine by me. I'd rather just get on with things myself anyway." That wasn't entirely true. Although I had been reluctant to accept her help at first, I had enjoyed her company and was quite looking forward to seeing her again tomorrow. But I wasn't going to tell Alan that, and it certainly wasn't worth getting dragged into whatever drama he had created in his head.

"She doesn't need to be wasting her time with the likes of you."

"Well, at least that's something we agree on. There's a first time for everything, I suppose." I started walking again.

"You always did think you were better than us, you arrogant bastard." Alan's uneven footsteps were following behind me.

"I'm not looking for trouble, Alan. I've got enough on my plate without this shit," I called over my shoulder.

"Running off to London, acting like this place is beneath you. You broke Rosie's heart."

I paused.

"Yeah, you didn't want her, and I was there to pick up the pieces." He took a lurching step forward. "Yet here you are trying to cosy up to her again, not because you actually like her, but because you can't stand the thought that she's with me."

"Oh come on, how old are we again?" This was starting to feel like one of the playground spats we used to have.

"Same with the band," Alan went on. He was grinning now, but his smile was full of malice. "You ditched that too, but I stuck with it, and now you're trying to get back in with them just to piss me off."

The guy's sense of self-importance was unbelievable. I was harbouring no grudges against him and had even been planning on sending some work his way, but if he wanted to act like we were still teenagers, then I could quite happily play along. I knew who would come out on top if this descended into physical violence, and I wasn't worried.

"You're more than welcome to my leavings, Alan— you can keep Rosie and the band."

A look of fury darkened his face, and he lurched drunkenly towards me.

"You stay away from Rosie, do you hear?" He was so close now I could smell the stench of booze on him.

"I thought I'd already said I would. Like I said, you can keep your compost queen; why would I be interested in her when I can have my pick back in London?"

I knew I should have just left it, but he had really wound me up now. I should have just walked away. My temper had got the better of me far too many times when I was younger. Once I had punched the frontman of another band after a show because I overheard him calling us a 'bunch of posers, 'and the scene had descended into chaos, with blows and insults being hurled in both directions. In the end, both bands had been banned from that particular venue. Then there was the bust-up with Ritchie after I had found out what happened with Freya. Nasher Newell would absolutely have punched him before now, though, so I was doing quite well at keeping things in check.

"Just go home, Alan; you're drunk." I applauded myself on my restraint.

"You're the one who should go home," he spat. "Coming here to my village and trying to get in with my wife and my band."

"Except they aren't your band anymore, are they? Didn't they kick you out for being a drunken mess? I can see why. Look at the state of you; it's pathetic."

"Say that again!" Alan had settled himself into a weak-looking stance, fists raised, beer bottle still clenched in one of them.

I wanted nothing more than to land one on him, to knock him onto his stupid, drunken behind, but instead, I turned away and said, "I'm not doing this."

"Coward!" The bottle Alan had been drinking from shattered at my feet, making me jump.

I dropped the trombone case on the ground and turned on him. "I guess we *are* doing this. Come on then."

He pitched forward towards me, landing a clumsy blow on my left cheek. The two of us clashed, exchanging angry punches and shoves. To give him credit, he did manage to land a few good shots on me despite his inebriated condition, but I soon got the better of him, sending him flying backwards and crashing into the railings of the bridge where he crumpled in a heap on the ground. Alan clutched his face and looked dazed, all the fight seeming to drain out of him. I wiped the back of my hand across my bloody nose.

"Have you had enough?" I asked, standing over him and breathing heavily.

Alan slurred something unintelligible between his fingers and struggled to his feet, clutching the railing for support. I retrieved the trombone and made my way back to the pub, leaving him where he was. I immediately regretted what had happened. There were sure to be consequences in a place as small as Bramwick.

Chapter Six

Rosie

On Monday morning, it was my turn to open the shop. I was not in the best mood to begin with when I left the house, and it soon became evident it was going to be one of those days. The previous night, Alan had gone out to the pub after coming home with a pizza, as promised, and things had gone downhill from there. When he got home, his shirt was bloodstained, and a black eye was forming. He wasn't making much sense, but I managed to piece together that he'd had a run-in with Nate. If Alan's jumbled version of events was to be believed it was Nate who had started the fight. I wasn't entirely sure I believed his story but I l didn't push him further. Instead I helped him to bed so he could sleep it off. In the morning, he had refused to talk about what had happened but had told me he didn't think I should see Nate anymore, and I abandoned my plan to go and help him again after my shift at the shop.

My walk to the shop on the main street took me past The Grange, and I was enjoying the rare sunshine, taking the walk as a chance to decompress from my troubles at home, when I noticed Danny Henshaw in the middle of the field near the oak tree with two men in suits, one of whom had a clipboard. Danny Henshaw was rarely actually seen in Bramwick, and I had a suspicious feeling that whatever he was up to, it wasn't good. As I was already in a bad mood, I decided to adjust my course and cut through The Grange so I could try and see what was going on.

Danny was casting his arms around in a sweeping gesture, evidently showing off the land. His receding hair was slicked back, and he was wearing a garish purple Ralph Lauren jumper that I thought clashed with his perpetual tan. He really was an odious character. When he saw me approaching, his lips parted in a wide smile that showed his glaringly white teeth. I did not smile back at him, but I noted with interest the logo on the clipboard one of the suited men was scribbling on. It said 'Mitchell Homes'. So it was true. This was the developer he had lined up for when we failed to raise the funds we needed to buy The Grange.

"A bit premature, all this, isn't it, Danny?" I said, coming to a stop and looking at him reproachfully.

His fake smile widened, and he turned to the men and said, "May I introduce Rosie Fenn? She's one of the committee members and volunteers that currently looks after The Grange."

One of the men extended a hand, and I ignored him.

"We have until May to raise the funds, Danny," I reminded him.

"Yes, and how's that going?" He looked down his long nose at me, somehow managing to look disdainful while never losing the smile.

"Very well, thanks. We're well on our way." We weren't, but I wasn't going to admit that in front of these people.

"Jolly good," he said. "You just let me know when you're ready to start talking officially."

He turned back to the developers and looked over the notes the man with the clipboard had been writing. I started to walk away, anger seething in me that he was so confident that we wouldn't be able to raise the funds. No doubt he would be getting way more than 'fair market value 'if he sold it to these people.

"Oh, don't worry about that," I heard him say to one of the men in a casual tone. "It's never going to happen, but we have to follow the procedure. Let them think that they had their chance. By May, this will all be over."

As I walked, I grew angrier and angrier. The community would sorely miss The Grange if it fell into the hands of those people. If it were gone, there would be nowhere for the local people to meet and connect other than the pub. The Grange was a true hub in the community, and I could not believe that people like Danny Henshaw thought money was more important.

I kicked a stone angrily and pretended it was Danny Henshaw's face. Clearly, he hadn't inherited his ancestors 'philanthropic nature. It broke my heart to think of the garden and the orchard that we worked so hard on flattened to make way for luxury houses. Houses that no one local could ever afford to live in.

"Luxury bloody houses," I muttered angrily as I pushed my way through the gates and back out onto the street.

They would most likely be snapped up by the hordes of people exiting London now that work from home was such a big thing. They had started to appear after lockdown, and while Bramwick was usually welcoming of what the locals referred to as 'blow-ins', this particular brand of new arrival had done nothing to integrate themselves into the local community, showed no concern for local issues, and pretty much kept to themselves at all costs. The only time you heard from them was when they appeared on the village Facebook group to moan about how far it was to the nearest Asda or about how they couldn't get a Just Eat delivery or an Uber, or about the smell coming from the fields when the farmers were spreading silage. It was beyond me how all of these things could come as a surprise. Did people not do any research before moving to a place?

As if the day hadn't started off badly enough, my first customer in the shop was Sandy Brown, also known behind her back as Sandy the Mouth. I groaned inwardly when I saw her come through the door, tugging her small grandchild along behind her. I knew she wasn't here to buy anything; she only ever appeared when there was urgent gossip she needed to spread. I said a cheery good morning, and she spent a few minutes making a show of browsing through the cabbages before she sidled empty-handed up to the counter.

"I heard there was a bit of trouble last night." She eyed me pointedly and pushed her glasses back up her nose as they began to slide.

I sighed. I knew Alan's fight would come up at some point today, and here was Sandy the Mouth, first on it.

"What do you mean, Sandy?" I asked innocently.

"Your Alan, getting into a fight," she pressed.

"Oh, that," I shrugged, trying to downplay the whole thing. "It was nothing, really. He's fine if that's what you're asking."

She shook her head, her pink candy floss hair bouncing, and sucked her teeth. "He's a thug that Nathan Newell. Have you heard the type of music he plays with that band of his? And the way he dresses, and all those tattoos."

Sandy waited for me to share in her outrage, and the small boy started tugging on her hand, restless and eager to get going.

"What happened? Why did he pick on Alan like that anyway?"

The way Alan had told it was that he had gone to the rehearsal room planning to have a civilised chat with Fred and had been faced with Nate 'lording it up on a bloody trombone in front of them all, showing off like he always did, 'and so he had decided not to go in. I could appreciate why this might have hurt him. His suspension from the band had hit him hard, and to have been faced with his old school rival in with the band while he was stuck on the outside must have been hard. I refrained from telling him that it had actually been me who suggested Nate go along and drop off the old trombone. I should have realised that suggesting Nate visit the band was a bad idea.

Thankfully, Alan had not disrupted the rehearsal and had left before anyone saw him. Unfortunately, later, while taking the scenic route home, he had run into Nate again, still with the trombone. He told me he had tried to avoid him, but Nate had spotted him and had apparently been intent on settling old scores and had decided to pick a fight.

"Jealous, I reckon," Alan had said. "Can't stand the fact that you and I ended up together."

I found myself wondering if Nate was ok. I hoped Alan's vicious temper hadn't got too out of hand.

"Oh, I don't really know," I said to Sandy, who was still staring at me. "Just a stupid drunken disagreement, I think."

Sandy huffed. "There's no need to downplay it, love. This kind of thing never happens in Bramwick. Then he comes back, and all hell breaks loose."

I had to suppress a laugh. Sandy the Mouth, dramatic as ever. It was only ten in the morning, and I suspected that by the time she had done her rounds for the day, the story would have grown even wilder, and she would have the whole place thinking innocent Alan had been violently set upon by a wild and crazed Nate.

"Thanks for your concern, Sandy," I smiled in what I hoped was a grateful way as I turned back to the laptop on the counter. "I'll be sure to tell Alan you were asking after him."

"He should press charges," she said, but her grandson had started to wail, and she had hurried him out of the door.

"Press charges," I muttered, shaking my head.

Sally arrived at one o'clock to take over the shop for the afternoon. She was wearing a black T-shirt that had the slogan 'I incite this meeting to rebellion 'printed on it in angry-looking text. Sally was a 'blow-in', but one of the ones who had got involved with village life, bringing her tenor horn to the band and eventually joining the Grange committee. She was older than me by twenty years, but when she had appeared at the band five years ago, I had liked her immediately. She was my kind of person, and we had become firm friends and had taken the plunge and opened the shop together two years ago.

She had, of course, heard about the fight, but she didn't press me for details, and I filled her in on what I had witnessed at The Grange that morning.

"Bloody Danny Henshaw," she cursed. "He doesn't even need that money; he's absolutely rolling in it, but it's never enough for his sort, is it? Greedy corporate bloody scum bag."

"That's him," I agreed as I went into the back to get my coat. "Sandy's already been in too, so you're probably safe for the afternoon. She's off doing the rounds now, telling everyone what a dangerous thug Nate Newell is."

"I quite liked him when he came to practice last night," Sally said.

"How was he? Alan said he was 'lording it up 'in front of everyone."

"I wouldn't exactly say that; he seemed sort of nervous if anything."

"Hmm." That didn't sound like the Nate I knew.

"I wish you'd come back to band; we miss you."

43

"I'm working on it," I told her. "Anyway, I best be off; I've a bit of work to do on the campaign. I'll catch you later."

Chapter Seven

Nate

The morning after my run-in with Alan, my ribs ached. He must have caught me pretty hard after all. Mrs Thornton had looked at me quizzically when I had tried to slink back to my room unnoticed. The bar had been relatively quiet, but she had spotted me, and despite my efforts to fob her off, by the morning, she appeared to know everything that had happened, as did the whole village, so it seemed. I wanted to tell her that it hadn't really been my fault, but it was useless as I knew that Bramwick people always defended their own, and I was no longer one of them. I decided there and then that I wouldn't be spending another night at the pub— it was Dad's place from then on, no matter what. So after breakfast, I gathered my meagre belongings and checked out.

The morning passed swiftly, and I made three trips to the dump, where I had an argument with the attendant who told me I couldn't come in with a van without a permit. The jobsworth finally relented and said he would make an exception after I explained about the death of my father, but he was adamant I would have to go online and purchase a permit if I wanted to come back another day. More expenses I could do without.

As it drew nearer to lunchtime, I found I was actually looking forward to Rosie's promised visit, but when two o'clock rolled around and she hadn't appeared, I figured she wasn't coming. I should have known really. Why would she come and waste her time here after what had happened last night? I tried to just forget about her and the incident with Alan because what did it matter when I was trying not to get involved with Bramwick business, but it annoyed me that he had probably gone home and made up some story about me starting the whole thing, and I kind of wanted to give her my version of events. She had mentioned a wholefoods shop on the main street, so mid-afternoon, I took a walk to see if I could find it.

It was a tiny little place, with colourful baskets of flowers sitting outside and a sign above the door which read 'Nature's Bounty'. Inside I found baskets of fresh vegetables, tubs of things like cereal that you could buy by the gram, and a fridge stocked with vegetarian sausages and the like. There were also shelves for locally made crafts— pottery, felted animals, goat's milk soap— and a small rack of brightly coloured hemp clothes. It was all very Rosie, and that made me smile. But I didn't find Rosie behind the counter— instead I saw the woman with the short, spiky hair who I had met at the rehearsal the previous night— the tenor horn player.

"Hello again," she said, looking at me with a curious smile.

"Hi, I was looking for Rosie, but I guess she's not here, so..."

"Hold on a minute," she stopped me. "I'm not sure you're her favourite person right now."

"God, is there anyone who doesn't know about what happened?" I grumbled. "Typical Bramwick rumour mill, no doubt churning out a completely inaccurate version of what actually went down."

She leaned on the counter and studied me. "I don't listen to gossip."

"Well, good for you, because I didn't start that fight, and if you're going to tell me about how Alan is some kind of saint and I should leave him alone, don't bother."

She laughed. "I know Alan isn't a saint, believe me. I'm Sally, by the way."

"Nice to meet you, Sally, but I'd better be off."

"Rosie's at The Grange," she called after me as I opened the door. "She probably won't listen to you, God knows she'll never give up defending Alan, but good luck getting your side of things across anyway."

I turned back and gave her grateful smile. Her accent didn't fit these parts, and I wondered if I might just have found an ally in this blow-in.

"Thanks."

I found Rosie in the vegetable garden pulling up weeds. When she saw me, she stood up and glared at me, arms folded, a trowel in her hand.

"You alright?" I asked her.

"What do you think?"

I leaned against the fence and pulled out a cigarette. "I didn't start it, though I'm sure that's what he's told you. He provoked me."

"Well, you shouldn't let him. He's not in a great place just now. Next time, just walk away."

"Fine. I'll keep away from him if I can help it. From you too, just like he asked."

"He asked you to stay away from me?"

"He did."

I don't know if it was my imagination, but I thought I saw her bristle slightly before she said, "Yet here you are."

"Here I am."

"Can I have one of those?" She pointed at the cigarettes.

"I thought Alan didn't like the smell." I offered her the pack anyway.

"Yeah, well..." She helped herself to one.

I flicked the lighter, and she leaned into the little blue flame, then leant on the fence next to me. For a few moments, neither of us spoke. It was just like those old days when we were kids sneaking fags.

"It's been worse since he was suspended from the band," she said.

"Yeah?"

"It really pissed him off when he saw you there last night."

"He saw me?"

"He did. He said you were showing off with that old trombone, trying to get in with them. To be fair, I can appreciate why that upset him."

"You can tell him the band is safe. I won't be going back. I was literally just there to hand in the trombone like *you* suggested."

"And yet he saw you putting on quite a show with it."

"Look, I wasn't putting on a show. Mr Black practically forced me at gunpoint to play a scale for him, and that's all it was. Then he refused to take the trombone because he has some mad idea that I might take it up again while I'm here, which I have absolutely no intention of doing. Ask that friend of yours from the shop. What's her name again? Sally."

"You met Sally?"

"Yes, and she'll tell you there was no showing off."

"Ok," she said, finishing her cigarette and straightening up. "I believe you, but stay out of Alan's way, yeah? For my sake as much as his."

"What's that supposed to mean?" But she had turned her back on me and resumed rooting about in the potato bed.

"I'm busy, and I know you've got things to be getting on with too."

Back at the house, I had now cleared enough space in the living room to sit down and move about freely, emptied my old bedroom, and washed the sheets so I would have somewhere to sleep that night. In doing so, I had unearthed the Wi-Fi router and was able to get the password so I could get online. The phone signal in Bramwick was so abysmal that I hadn't really been able to get online, and the first thing I did when I was reconnected was to go onto Facebook so I could look at Freya's profile. Judging by the pictures from the weekend of her out enjoying herself with her (our) friends, she wasn't taking the breakup too badly, which bothered me more than I cared to admit. My former bandmates, Maxwell and Ritchie, were even in a few of the pictures, and that bothered me a lot. Why was she still hanging about with Ritchie when she had claimed to be so remorseful over what had happened? It seemed as if life in London was rolling along as it always had without me while I was stuck here in this forsaken place. I hadn't had a single message from my so-called friends since I had arrived. No one had been in touch to ask how I was doing, if the funeral arrangements were going okay, nothing, it was radio silence. I tossed my phone angrily onto the sofa and then, suddenly remembering something, picked it up again. I had told Simon to come to The Black Bull for a drink, but I wasn't staying there anymore, and we hadn't agreed on a time to meet.

"Shit." I really didn't fancy hanging about the place waiting for him with everyone gossiping.

I went back on Facebook and searched 'Simon Hunter 'but there were, of course, hundreds of them. I searched instead for 'Bramwick Brass 'and quickly found their page. I scrolled back through their recent posts— a heartfelt share of the fundraising page for The Grange petitioning for donations was followed by videos of a performance at the summer fête and pictures of the band practising. Finally, I came across one announcing that 'cornet player Simon Hunter will be running a sponsored 10k in aid of our beloved Grange 'in which Simon himself had been tagged. I clicked on Simon's profile and sent him a quick message saying I would meet him around seven if he still fancied a pint. Simon answered quickly saying he would see me then.

I was dragging the last of that day's boxes out to the van when I heard a voice say my name.

"Oh no," I said quietly, straightening up. I had forgotten that she was due to arrive today. "Hello, Aunt Ruth."

I shoved the box I had been moving into the back of the van and turned to see a stout woman with a shock of ginger hair and a tweed suit looking at me critically.

"You look dreadful," she told me curtly.

"Um…thanks…"

"What happened to your face?"

I raised a self-conscious hand to my bruised cheek. "Nothing, it's fine. Did you just get here?"

"Yes, I've just driven from Glasgow. I didn't fancy staying at the pub, so I've booked a cottage through that thing everyone uses now—Airbnb. Do you know you don't actually get breakfast? Why do they call it Airbnb? It's false advertising."

I shook my head and fought back the urge to scream. Aunt Ruth had always been one of the most infuriating people I knew. She had been around a lot when Mum first passed away, helping Dad to adjust, but she and her daughter had soon drifted away, and once I was in secondary school, we didn't seem to see as much of them.

"Anyway, how are you holding up?" she asked, after I had shown her into the house.

"Yeah, I'm alright."

"Your father just died, you don't seem that bothered," she said accusingly.

48

"I'm just dealing with things in my own way. Sorry that you haven't found me wallowing and incapacitated with grief."

She looked at me suspiciously. "Terrible that he died before the two of you could sort out your differences."

"Neither of us were great at communication, I suppose."

"He was never much of a housekeeper either, was he?" she said, casting her eye around the living room. "That's why I stopped visiting. I couldn't bear to be in this place with all the mess."

"Some of us didn't have a choice," I reminded her.

I made her a cup of tea and prayed she wouldn't stay long. I was beginning to regret the relative tidiness of the living room. Perhaps if it had still been bursting with clutter, she might not have stayed at all. As it was, she sat down on the sofa and proceeded to complain about my tattoos, criticise my music for having too much bad language, told me I was too thin, and asked if I was eating enough. She inquired as to whether I had a girlfriend in London and quizzed me on what I was planning to do with the proceeds of Dad's estate. I sat and took it all in and waited for her to finally get round to what she had really come to talk about— the funeral arrangements. Apparently, I had been useless in that department too, and there being no one else, she had been left with no choice but to 'step in and take care of things'. I refrained from pointing out that she hadn't given me a chance. She had come steamrolling in, making calls and decisions before I could do anything at all. I nodded as she went over what time the church was booked for, what hymns she had picked, and the music that the brass band would be performing, and how many she had catered for with the buffet— too many in my opinion, not enough in hers.

"I can't believe we've found ourselves in this position again," she said sadly. "It takes me right back to when your mother died." Her eyes began to look moist as if she was about to cry, but she recovered herself and said, "Anyway, I should really go and get myself checked into this cottage. I've been given a code to collect a key from a safe or some such nonsense. What's wrong with people these days that you refuse to just meet you in person? How hard would that be?"

I stood up and followed her to the front door.

"I'm really sorry I can't stay to help." She cast her eyes over the boxes in the hall.

"It's no problem, really. I've had some help from a friend." It was only half a lie.

"Oh really? Who?"

"Just someone I used to go to school with."

"That boy with the glasses that you used to knock about with?"

"Simon? No, you probably wouldn't know her. Her name's Rosie."

"Oh, well, that's good."

"You're welcome to have a look and see if there's anything you want to keep," I offered. "But you'll need to be quick. It's disappearing fast."

"I might do that."

I tugged the door open, and she paused and put her hands on my shoulders.

"If you need anything, just give me a call," she said. "And try not to get into any more trouble. I'll drop back in tomorrow and see how you're getting on."

I waved her off and closed the door, glad to be on my own again. I still had an hour before I was due to meet Simon, and I didn't feel like doing any more clearing, so I went back to the living room, where I mindlessly flicked through the channels on the telly. When I found there was nothing worth watching, I decided I would get my guitar out for a bit, but what I actually found myself doing was opening the trombone case. The instrument shone in the light from the lamp as I ran a finger across it. There had been a time when I had really loved that thing, and I felt a tug of sadness for the boy I had been before I turned into a moody teenager who decided brass bands weren't cool. I put the trombone together and sat down on the sagging sofa. Blazers and 'Land of Hope and Glory' might not be my style anymore, but plenty of ska bands had brass sections. I raised the instrument to my lips and blew a long note, letting the pipes warm up. I moved the slider in and out and worked my way up and down a scale, just as Mr Black had had me do the other night. I really started to get a feel for it again, and it was much easier without a room full of people staring at me. There was something pleasing about the sound as it bounced around the small room, and it felt like I was reconnecting with an old friend who was pleased to see me.

I picked up my phone and Googled 'Ska music for trombone beginners 'and was faced with a number of results from Mighty Mighty Boss Tones to Madness. In the end, I opted for 'A Message to You Rudi ' by the Specials as it seemed to have a fairly straightforward little trombone solo. It took me the best part of an hour to master a passable version, but when I did, I found myself playing along with the song on Spotify, and I was really quite pleased with myself. And what was even better was the feeling that I was making music just for my own amusement— there were no thoughts of how it could make money— and music simply for pleasure had been absent from my life for quite a while.

"You must be delighted with this, I suppose." I glanced across at my parents 'wedding picture on the mantelpiece, and they looked at me approvingly. Perhaps I would hang onto that if nothing else.

50

Then a noise startled me. Someone was tapping on the living room window. I set the trombone down with a start and saw Simon peering through the grimy glass. He gave me a big grin and thumbs up and pointed at the trombone.

Shit, how long had he been standing there?

I glanced at my watch and saw that it was nearly seven. I had completely lost track of time. It always happened; often I would just get lost in the music, and the rest of the world would cease to exist.

"Alright?" I said casually as I stepped outside and pulled the door shut behind me.

"Sorry, I have to pass right by here to get to the pub, and I heard you playing."

I made a face. "I was just messing about."

"It was sounding good. I bet you'll be amazed at how quickly it comes back once you start."

As we walked, it started to drizzle, and Simon pulled up the hood on his duffle coat. I knew it couldn't be that same one he used to wear at school, but it certainly looked like it.

"Did Alan do that to you?" Simon asked, looking at my face.

"So you heard?"

"This is Bramwick, mate. Everyone's heard."

"Great."

"You're not the most popular person in the village right now," he told me. "Alan has been going around telling everyone you tried it on with Rosie, then attacked him."

"For fuck's sake!" It was one thing to have the whole village believe I had started the fight, but for them also to think I had 'tried it on 'with Rosie—that was a troubling accusation, and I sincerely hoped Rosie would have the decency to at least shut down that rumour. "And the whole place is on his side, I suppose?"

"Not me. He's still as much of a tosser as he was at school."

"And like I told him, I have absolutely no interest in Rosie."

"You used to take the piss out of her when she hung about with us, remember? Because her mum used to make her wear those awful homemade clothes. Remember that one dress that looked like a set of curtains?"

"I think it *was* a set of curtains once."

"She was never bothered, though, was she? She always just owned it and made it all part of her personality, and somehow it just worked the way it wouldn't on anyone else."

Once in the bar, I was relieved to see there was no sign of Alan and that the place was very quiet, with just two customers who paid us no

51

attention sat at the bar. The young girl was serving again, so thankfully I didn't have to deal with Mrs Thornton. It was warm and cosy inside with the fire crackling merrily, and there was a border collie stretched out in front of it, soaking up the heat. The smell of the wood burning mixed with the sweet scent of the beer was somehow comforting, and as we took our seats with our pints, I felt myself start to relax for the first time since being back. I had to admit that there was something uniquely welcoming about a Yorkshire country pub.

"No Alan," Simon said happily, echoing my own thoughts. "That might have been a bit awkward for both of us."

"Rosie said he had been chucked out of the band."

"Suspended, yeah, but he's doing his best to ruin his chances of ever getting back in, going around the village telling everyone who'll listen that we're all incompetent, unfriendly, horrible people, basically. He's launched an online hate campaign as well— he did it all through anonymous profiles, but it's obvious it's him. Ridiculous behaviour for a grown man, really."

I shook my head. "He'll get bored soon."

"I'm sure you're right."

We sipped our pints, and a slightly awkward silence descended before Simon broke it by saying, "Do you remember that time when Fred tried to make us learn 'The Floral Dance' for that competition? It was around about the time that you'd started to think you were too cool for the whole thing?"

I chuckled. I remembered it well, and I knew exactly what was coming.

"You weren't paying attention and were just generally acting up, and he made you go to the front of the class and told you no one was going home until you'd played your part for everyone. You agreed, became really serious, and then broke into the Imperial March, and everyone ended up in fits of laughter."

"Yeah, and I did a good job of it, and that's not an easy piece, but there was no way Mr Black was going to acknowledge that."

Soon we were caught up in our reminiscing, laughing, and joking about the things we used to get up to. It was quite grounding, talking with him about our shared past— he was just a normal, down-to-earth guy with none of the ego that my bandmates in London had.

We had just been recalling one World Book Day when I had come to school dressed as a punk, claiming I was inspired by the Sex Pistols' biography, when Simon said, "That was the year Rosie came in that patchwork dress."

"Yeah, what the hell was she supposed to be?"

52

"No idea. She just kept saying she was a 'free spirit'. Clearly, she completely missed the point of what World Book Day was supposed to be. I think she just thought it was fancy dress or something."

"I think that was when I started calling her Patches..." I had completely forgotten about the origins of that nickname until that moment. I smiled at the memory. Despite having no relevance to the day, her outfit had been endearing, and it had shone with her creative spirit.

Simon stood up. "I'll get another round in, eh?"

The night wore on, and the beer and conversation kept flowing as we reminisced about the treehouse we had built with Rosie and Andy Clark and how Mr Harris, one of the stuffy old custodians of The Grange, had made us take it down as he said it was an eyesore, and about the time Simon had dared me to drink five cartons of the class milk, and I had been sick all over Mr King's shoes.

"We were close back then, the three of us," Simon mused. "What happened?"

I shrugged and gazed into my pint, the laughter subsiding. "I dunno, I guess I was just desperate to leave, and you two were quite happy where you were. I needed to escape from the village, from Dad's hoarding, from that job I had at the service station that was slowly killing me, from everything. I just couldn't take it anymore, so I left."

"You could have stayed in touch, though. You never answered our emails or texts; it's like you just disappeared one day."

I gave a shaky laugh as I recalled the times I had seen my friends ' names appear in my inbox and how I had deleted the messages without even reading them. At the time, the sight of them had induced in me a visceral reaction that was hard to explain, and I couldn't bring myself to open them. But now I felt awful.

"I know, I was young and daft. I hadn't figured myself out yet. Still not sure I have to be honest."

There was a short, reflective silence, but then Simon brightened and clinked his glass against mine. "It doesn't matter. That was a long time ago, and it's good to see you."

Chapter Eight

Rosie

When we were in secondary school, Simon, Nate and I took music as an A-level. We were the only three in our already small school who had chosen to take our musical studies further, and as a result, our class was combined with three students who were taking intermediate music as a way to fill in holes in their timetable. Because Mr Black was not on permanent staff at the school, he often wasn't available to teach the class. So, knowing that we were more than capable, as he taught us in the youth band, and understanding that the intermediate students were mainly just there to mess about and waste time, the class often ended up unsupervised, and we were frequently left to our own devices. We had a double period of music on Friday afternoons. Mr Black always had to leave after the first period, and the second half of the lesson often descended into chaos. It fast became my favourite part of school, and I looked forward to that last period on a Friday afternoon all week. Nate had chosen guitar as his instrument, of course, and he usually used this unsupervised time to abandon the work Mr Black had set us in favour of showing us the latest song he had written. Even then, he knew how to pick out a good melody and how to string chords together in ways that just worked, and often we would all go into the weekend with his songs stuck in our heads.

He was always careful not to exclude anyone, which I really admired. He gave us all parts to play in these creations of his, even if it was just a few notes on the glockenspiel for Anne-Marie, who really didn't have a musical bone in her body. I absolutely loved the way he included everyone, and the patience and encouragement he showed to those who weren't as gifted as he was as he guided Julian to play a simple rhythm on the drum kit to keep us all in time, and demonstrated to Vicky how to play the three simple guitar chords that he said were all she really needed to be able to join in with anything we played. Usually he'd start by showing us what he had written that week, and to me it always sounded amazing with just his voice and the guitar. When he added the rest of us in it was always an absolute riot—we did not sound like a band of any kind—but he was never critical, and there was always lots of laughter and carrying on, which we all enjoyed. I always thought he could have been a good teacher, but when he returned I got the feeling London had changed him, hardened him up, and that success had left him with an ego that he didn't use to have.

It was during that year that I fell secretly in love with Nate. I wrote about him almost constantly in my cringe-worthy teenage journals, but I never told him how I felt because I was utterly convinced that he could never be interested in me in that way. I was awkward, I didn't consider myself attractive, and I certainly wasn't cool in my homemade clothes. When he briefly went on to date Hannah Ferguson that year I was absolutely devastated, and poured out that special brand of angst that is exclusive to love-struck adolescent girls into the pages of my diary without ever telling a soul how I felt.

That was also the year that the bullying really ramped up. I know I was different and perhaps a little odd, but I was generally well liked among my classmates. Other than some petty name-calling that honestly didn't bother me that much, I had never really been bullied before. It started with Alan, egged on by his mate Tommy Deans, sticking Post-it notes to my back when they passed me in the corridor with things like 'kick me, I'm a hippy 'written on them. They'd taken to running into me, with quite some force, whenever they saw me and then claiming it was an accident and calling 'sorry, compost queen 'over their shoulders as they sniggered and elbowed each other. One time Alan pulled out a clump of my hair when he was sitting behind me in maths and then began to exclaim loudly how revolted he was as I probably had nits. I had sat there, my face turning red and my scalp stinging, as most of the class laughed. One day in computing class, I returned to my desk to find the desktop picture on the monitor had been changed to that of a dead and decomposing barn owl because they knew owls were my favourite animal. I had been so shocked and upset that I had run from the classroom in tears.

At this point, I tried to speak to the head teacher, a ghastly woman called Mrs Keyes, who wasn't the most sympathetic. She suggested maybe I needed to try and fit in more and that I wasn't doing myself any favours by dressing the way I did (sixth form pupils were exempt from uniform). So I gave up trying to get the school to intervene. It escalated steadily over a period of six months, and it was getting less and less easy to brush it off. I was reaching breaking point, and it was making my school life miserable. I didn't let on to Mum and Dad what was happening, or perhaps they would have helped, but they were going through a rough patch with the business, we were having a bit of a tough time as a family, and I had the misguided notion that I shouldn't add to their worries. In the end, it was Simon and Nate who came to my rescue.

At the peak of it all, Alan and Tommy had taken to waiting for me outside of the music room on Fridays, because they knew the class was often unsupervised and there would be no teachers there to see them shoving me and shouting insults as I tried to leave. There came a particular afternoon when I had just had enough. It had been an especially stressful week and with music class nearing its end I saw them waiting for me, glowering through the glass in the door, and I burst into tears.

"This has really got to stop," Nate said. "It's getting ridiculous."

I watched as he strode to the door, taking the heavy electric guitar with him and wielding it like an axe above his head. He threw the door open and threatened to use the instrument to knock Alan out.

Alan and Tommy had then barged into the classroom, and although no one was actually hit with the guitar, a fight did break out. Even geeky Simon, bless him, waded in and ended up getting knocked into the drum kit, which caused a bit of damage. All four of them were in a huge amount of bother when Mr Jones from the classroom next door thundered in and broke them up. After that, the music class was not trusted to be on its own again and was supervised by English teacher Miss Jean from then on. As you can imagine, this heroic act only cemented my painful secret love for Nate.

So how did I end up married to Alan? I've asked myself that many times, believe me. It seems ridiculous now, but I can't downplay how much of an impact it had on me when Nate left. I was in a vulnerable state; a huge hole had just been ripped in my world, and I was left reeling. The one person who I cared about most in it was gone and had taken with him all my young hope. It shattered my confidence when my messages to him went unread, and I began to realise that I had meant absolutely nothing to him. Those months following his departure were extremely difficult for me. My confidence all but disappeared overnight. I was even more harsh on myself than I had been when he had started seeing Hannah Ferguson. I began to tell myself that I wasn't good enough— that my hair was too wild and red, that I wasn't thin enough, and if only I didn't have so many freckles or crooked bottom teeth, he might have liked me. Then Simon suggested we go to the young farmers 'dance together, just as friends. He was worried about me and how badly I was coping with Nate's disappearance. He said I needed to stop moping and get out and have a laugh. So I went. I was nervous and reluctant, and when we arrived, I almost turned around and left when I saw Alan was there. As soon as I laid eyes on him, I started to feel self-conscious and ugly.

I hadn't seen him since we had left school, and I had heard he was working an apprenticeship with his uncle. I told Simon I wasn't staying to be ridiculed by Alan, but Simon promised he would look after me. It didn't go that way, of course. Young farmers 'dances are notoriously rowdy and drink-fuelled affairs. The young folk of Bramwick usually only have one thing in mind when they go: sex. It didn't take long for Simon to end up pairing up with some girl, and I found myself left on my own and a little too worse for wear from the cider I had consumed. When I saw Alan making his way towards me, my heart lurched sickeningly. I immediately turned to retreat, but when he called my name, he didn't use his usual mocking tone. He was a bit drunk, and so was I, but his apology seemed genuine. He told me he was sorry for how he had treated me when we were at school, and his remorse seemed real. He explained how awful he felt, how he had just been a stupid boy, and promised me he had grown up. He said he was glad he had caught me as he had wanted to tell me this for a long time. We ended up snogging, much to Simon's bafflement, and things just sort of went on from there. For a while, it really did seem like he was a different person. He was kind, romantic, and incredibly handsome. Being asked out by the most eligible boy in Bramwick had been just what I needed to repair my shattered self-belief. Suddenly, I was the one strolling through The Grange with him while girls who had been popular at school shot me daggers. I stopped thinking about Nate and got lost in my exciting relationship with this new version of Alan.

Yet, as I watched him ranting and raving that evening, banging his fist on the kitchen table to punctuate his shout of "No, Rosie!" all I could see was the old Alan, the one who had shoved me and pulled out a chunk of my hair.

"You're not going, and that's that," he seethed. "I can't understand why you would even suggest it after what they've done to me. You promised to stand by me, remember?"

We were standing on opposite sides of the kitchen table, glaring at each other.

"Yes," I said carefully, trying to keep my voice calm and measured. "But that was when it was just a suspension."

Alan had had word that day that the committee had called a meeting and voted to make his suspension from the band permanent.

"And now that it's an outright bloody ban, there's all the more reason to support me!"

But I agree with them; you brought this on yourself when you decided to go around the place bad-mouthing them.

"The band means a lot to me, Alan, you know that. I have friends there. You can't expect me to just give it up because you messed up. Why should I suffer for your mistakes?"

I watched as his face turned a deep shade of scarlet, and he balled his hands into fists.

"So you agree with them?"

"What did I say when they first suspended you?" I asked angrily. "I told you to keep your head down, and I'd have a word with Fred, and it would all blow over. I was fighting your corner, I really was, but I can't possibly defend that ridiculous smear campaign you tried to start. You must see that!"

"I know what this is really about," he said, his eyes narrowing menacingly. "It's about *him.*"

It took me a second to catch on.

"It's because he's in the band now, isn't it? You were quite happy to miss it before that little development!"

"What? Don't be so stupid. I don't even think he's in the band anyway. He'll be going back to London soon."

He made a huffing noise. I felt like I was standing on a frozen pond that was giving way beneath me, and even the words I spoke caused another crack and made my safety that bit more precarious.

"Cherry had to go back down south because her mum is unwell, so the band is without a second cornet for the funeral on Thursday…"

"Are you kidding me?" Alan exploded, and his fist collided with the table again, making the salt and pepper pots jump and rattle. I jumped with them.

"You know they really need the second part."

"So this *is* all about him!"

"No, Alan," I said firmly. "This is about Pete. This would have meant a lot to him."

"Pete's dead. What does he care?"

I shook my head in disbelief. Then an image came to my mind of Nate at the classroom door with the guitar raised above his head. I was through arguing with him. "I'm doing this, Alan. I'm going back to band, and I'm playing at Pete Newell's funeral."

I whirled around and stormed out of the room, feeling angrier than I'd felt in ages. I heard him yell after me, "Fuck off then, compost queen."

Chapter Nine

Nate

The day of the funeral dawned grey, with the sky hanging heavily over the Yorkshire hills, almost obscuring them from view. It felt like the village was blanketed in a soft, quiet calm as if the whole place had decided to mourn Pete Newell. I woke up feeling cold and uncomfortable, with my nose stuffy and my throat scratchy. I wondered if I was coming down with something.

Aunt Ruth appeared at the door early and tutted when she saw I wasn't dressed yet. She wouldn't listen when I told her I didn't want any breakfast and insisted she would make me something while I went upstairs to get into my suit. As I tied my black tie, I felt anxious about how the service might go. I was grateful that Dad had left detailed plans about his wishes, and to Aunt Ruth for organising everything, but I still expected it to be a challenging day. I hadn't cried when I had learned that Dad had passed away. I'd felt a little anger, but mostly I had just felt numb. Dealing with Freya and the band had not left me in a good state to process the news about Dad. Today was the day for doing just that— a day to reflect and properly absorb what had happened.

It was a neighbour who had first raised the alarm. He had grown concerned when he hadn't seen Dad for a few days. The fact that his car had not moved for a while and the curtains had remained drawn had only heightened his worry. When he had knocked on the door and received no reply, he had called the police, who forced their way in. By then he had been dead for almost a week.

Now, as I stood in front of the mirror in my old room, a voice in my head spoke up and suggested that I should have made more of an effort to stay in touch.

"Look, I'm sorry," I said, sitting down on the bed. "If I'd known you were going to suddenly die at the age of sixty-nine, I might have tried harder, but I didn't. I thought you'd be around forever, and let's be honest, you never made an effort either. You could have come to London to see me— that's what most parents would have done if their nineteen-year-old had run away."

"Nathan, who are you talking to?" The voice came from the other side of the door.

"Just to myself, Aunt Ruth."

"Well, hurry up and get downstairs. Breakfast is ready."

On the landing, the smell of frying food wafted up from the kitchen. She must have come prepared as she didn't find the bacon and eggs she was cooking in Dad's fridge. She was wearing an old apron of Mum's when I stepped into the kitchen and she was dishing out a selection of fried items onto a chipped plate. My stomach growled at the sight of the food. I guess I was hungry after all.

"Oh, for goodness 'sake, Nathan," she said as she bustled towards me, and I wondered what I had done wrong now. She reached out and proceeded to tug at my collar, to straighten my tie, and to brush imaginary specks of dirt off my shoulders.

"I wish there was something we could do about this," she sighed in annoyance as she pulled again at my shirt collar, trying and failing miserably to make it cover the tattoo on my neck. "So unsightly. And these things in your ears, absolutely ghastly, and that hair— really not appropriate for a funeral."

She threw her hands up in exasperation and looked at me critically. I said nothing, just sat down at the table, and she set a plate of food down in front of me. The plate was joined by tea in Dad's Land Rover mug.

"Too thin as well," she muttered as she watched me eat. "Probably never cook yourself a proper meal in London, do you?"

When we arrived at the church, I was surprised to see how many people had turned out— it was way more than I had been expecting.

"Isn't this lovely?" Aunt Ruth remarked. "Mrs Thornton did say he was well-liked in the community, and she was expecting a fair number of people. It's a good job I listened and went that bit higher for the buffet."

I surveyed the many faces, some of whom I recognised and some I didn't, and was irritated when I noticed Alan lurking near the back. Surely he had no reason to want to show his respects— what did he think he was doing? But it soon became clear when I spotted Rosie towards the front of the church among a cluster of people in green blazers. She gave a kind smile when I caught her eye. I was glad that she appeared to be back with the band.

As I took my seat in the front row with Aunt Ruth and listened to the muted chatter passing between the mourners, I had never felt so alone in all my life. A whole community had come out to pay their respects to Dad, and I felt like they were all connected to each other by invisible ties. I, in contrast, was like a ship adrift in a stormy sea with nothing to anchor me down.

The service was short and simple; the vicar said all the usual things you might expect to hear about how Dad had been a valued member of the community, Bramwick born and bred, about how he had been a generous supporter of the band. I had been asked if I would like to say something, but I had declined. What could I possibly say about a man who had become a stranger to me? These people all knew him better than I did. Then the band was introduced, and I watched as the men and women in their green blazers made their way to the front. Simon gave me a solemn nod as they took up their places. As they arranged themselves in a semicircle, Mr Black, or Fred as Simon had called him, addressed the congregation.

"Pete Newell was always a lover of brass. A player himself once, his career was sadly cut short by injury. Yet he did not allow himself to become bitter and remained a valued supporter and champion of the band. We consider it an honour that he wished for us to perform this piece at his funeral. This is 'Jerusalem'."

Fred turned to face the band and raised his arms. The players watched and waited until the baton fell and the music filled the church. The notes echoed hauntingly off the walls as the melody rose and swelled to the rafters. It grabbed my heart in a way I had not expected. It was moving, and for the first time, I felt a real, deep sorrow for the lonely old man who I had never really understood. The finality of it all hit home in those brief moments as the music embraced me— he was gone, and I would never see him again. All those wasted years that had passed when I told myself that I would get back in touch, one day. I had thought that I had all the time in the world to repair our relationship. This was the man who had raised me alone under incredibly difficult circumstances after Mum had died. His hoarding and his guarded emotions may have been a constant source of frustration for me when I was young, but they were symptoms of a man who had lost the love of his life and didn't know how else to cope. He had never shown any interest in meeting anyone new because she had been his whole world. What must that have been like for him? He had probably assumed they would watch me grow up together, that they would grow old together. When the unthinkable happened he was left with a future he hadn't planned for. Then he had lost me too.

As I pondered these truths, I felt the tide of the music wash over me, the melody wrapping itself around me. It felt like my father was embracing me in a way he never could when he was alive. I was finally able to shed tears for him. That's the power of music, I guess. It can capture our emotions and stir them into a storm, or soothe them into a restful trance, or even make us cry. Aunt Ruth took my hand and gave it a squeeze.

Once the coffin had been lowered into the ground, where Mum already lay, it was time to go back to The Black Bull. Mrs Thornton had laid out a spread of sandwiches and cold sausage rolls big enough to feed the whole village. As I hovered near the back of the room with a silent Aunt Ruth, I felt like a gatecrasher at my own dad's funeral. I watched as the vaguely familiar faces of Bramwick loaded their plates with food and chatted freely among themselves. I was beginning to regret the decision to allow Aunt Ruth to organise this gathering. It was done. He was buried. What was the use in hanging about now? It felt all wrong.

Gradually, people drifted over in slow succession to offer awkward condolences, but before long, I found myself standing alone. Even Aunt Ruth had found someone to talk to, and I wondered if I could just sneak away.

I checked my phone. Nothing. Freya knew the funeral was today, and although we weren't together anymore, it seemed heartless that she hadn't sent any kind of acknowledgment. Neither had my old bandmates. No one had. My London life had moved on and forgotten me, and this just added to my growing sense of isolation and gloom.

I noticed that Rosie and Alan were still here, which surprised me. Alan appeared to be drinking whisky despite it only being three o'clock in the afternoon. Rosie had taken off her band blazer and rolled up the sleeves of her white shirt. I noticed that she had tattoos— some kind of floral design that snaked up her forearms. Aunt Ruth wouldn't approve. She caught me looking at her, and I watched as she leaned in to say something to Alan. She put a hand on his shoulder and glanced again in my direction. I was sure they were talking about me. Alan shot me an unfriendly look and gave a firm shake of his head in response to whatever she had said. She looked at him appealingly and said something else. He set his mouth in a grim line and firmly took her hand, removing it from his arm. She looked back at me and tried to take a step in my direction, but Alan stayed her by taking her wrist, and bent his head to say something into her ear. She shrugged and turned back to him, with a nod and a tense smile.

I decided to go over. If I could be the bigger man and smooth things over, then I would. As I approached, Rosie smiled, but Alan's mouth remained set.

"We're so sorry, Nate," Rosie said. "It was a lovely service, though. Very fitting."

"Thank you. And thank you for the music. He would have been made up with that."

I noticed Alan was still gripping her wrist.

"Look, mate," I said to Alan. "I wanted to apologise for the other night. We should have left all that shit behind us in the school yard. I'm ashamed of the way I acted. I'm just having a bit of a rough time right now. Not that that's any excuse."

Rosie reached up and gave Alan's arm a pat. "Alan's been having a bit of a rough time too, haven't you love?"

He shook her arm away but kept his grip on her wrist. He didn't say anything.

"Well, like I say, no hard feelings, eh?"

I put my hand out, and Alan looked at it for a few seconds before he released Rosie's wrist and briefly shook it without saying a word.

"Anyway, Rosie tells me you're in the building trade now. I could definitely use your skills for some of the repairs needed around Dad's old place."

"I've got a lot on at the minute," Alan grunted.

"Yeah? Well, I'll give you a shout when I know what needs doing anyway. It'll take me forever to clear Dad's junk, so you might have freed up some time by then."

"Maybe."

"Hey guys!" It was Simon calling from across the room, where he was sitting with some of the lingering band members. He gestured for us to join him.

"You go," Rosie said. "I don't think Alan is quite ready to face everyone yet, are you?"

I nodded and went to sit with Simon.

"I didn't get to introduce you properly the other night," Simon said as I took a seat at the table. "This is Brendan, George, and Sally."

"Oh, we've already met," said Sally. "I am sorry about your dad. I didn't know him well, but he always seemed like such a nice man, always volunteering to help out at concerts, serving refreshments, and the like."

"I liked your dad too," the man who Simon had introduced as George said. "He was always talking about you and your music, about his famous son who lived in London."

"Really?" I was hearing this a lot since being back in Bramwick, about how proud he was of me. Seemed like he had been telling everyone this apart from me.

"Oh aye," Brendan confirmed with a nod. "He liked nothing better than to tell us what you were up to, and how you started your music playing under Fred. Fred talks about you a lot too, his star pupil."

"He talks about you to the kids at school to try and get them to come along to the youth band," Sally informed me.

"But I gave up brass," I said, bemused.

"He knows that, but he tells them joining a brass band is a cheaper way to learn music than private lessons and getting that foundation will set them in good stead for whatever musical aspirations they might have," explained Brendan.

"He's right too," Sally agreed. "We have had a few kids over the years sign up because they want to be you. You're like his poster boy. Honestly, he talks about you so much we all feel like we know you. We never thought we'd actually meet you though. He says your career keeps you so busy you never really have time to visit Bramwick."

Sally gave me a look that seemed to suggest she had the measure of me, that she knew time wasn't the reason I never came back.

"Yeah, something like that," I swallowed nervously.

"It's a real shame you won't come and play with us," George lamented. "The band's really struggling at the minute. We don't have enough players really, and we could be about to lose our rehearsal space if Danny Henshaw gets his way. I think you could give us a real boost."

George was laying on the guilt, chipping in with his views, but I had stopped listening. I had noticed that Alan and Rosie now appeared to be having a disagreement. They were keeping their voices low, but Alan had his hand on Rosie's arm, and there was a distinctly angry expression on his face as he appeared to hiss at her through gritted teeth while she looked to be protesting, raising an open palm in a defensive gesture as she responded, patting him on the shoulder to try and placate him. Alan batted her away, and she turned and made for the door while he stalked after her.

"Trouble in paradise, I reckon," George commented, following my gaze.

"They haven't been getting on," Sally confided. "That is if they ever did…"

"Shouldn't someone go and see if she's okay?" The look of concern on Simon's face bothered me.

"I'll go," Sally stood up. "Make sure things haven't escalated."

I felt like they all knew something I didn't, and I shot Simon a questioning glance, but he just shrugged and said, "I'm going to have one more pint before I go. Anyone else want anything?"

Sally soon returned and informed us that Alan and Rosie must have gone home because there was no sign of them. A few concerned glances were exchanged.

"I'll check in with her later," Sally assured us, and the conversation started up again as Simon returned with a tray of drinks.

As I shared a pint with this small group, I found myself warming to them. They seemed friendly and down-to-earth. They were uncomplicated, very different to the type of people I spent my time with in London. They had also known my dad. The stories they told about his antics while helping out at concerts allowed me to feel a connection with him. I was hearing about a whole side of him I had never known. To these people, he had been a joker, a jolly soul, always happy to help out, who laughed a lot and was proud of his son. All I ever saw was a man who was depressed, who hoarded, and who had never got over the death of his wife. It's funny the masks we can put on for the outside world to hide how much we are suffering inside. Was it really any different to the mask I had created when I had turned myself into Nasher Newell? The one that had been fast disintegrating since my arrival in Bramwick. As I listened to them, I began to feel sad again. It upset me that I had never got to see the side of him that they did. They had no idea that once he closed the door to that house, he was often overwhelmed by memories and grief. When Sally noticed that all of their reminiscing was making me emotional again, she didn't hesitate in pulling me into a hug and patting my head as if she were comforting a small child.

I wasn't used to such feelings of genuine warmth. These people really seemed to care about each other, and strangely, about me too. There were no egos here, no big personalities that demanded all the attention, and I started to wonder if maybe this was exactly what I needed right now. It was uncomfortable, and my first instinct was to try and fight what I was feeling, to flee from it and never look back, but I stayed there with them.

"Well," George said, once I had got a hold of myself again," I think it's time I was off. Nate lad, I'm sorry again about your dad. If we can do anything to help, all you have to do is ask."

"He means it." Brendan stood up and offered his hand for me to shake.

"Remember there's a rehearsal tomorrow," Sally said as she too got up to go. "Just in case you fancy it, even if it's just to have a listen, get you out of the house for a bit."

"I'll think about it," I said with a smile.

"I'm a bit worried about Rosie," Simon said to me in a low voice once the others had departed.

"Oh yeah?"

"Things weren't pretty last time they had a rough patch like this."

"What do you mean?"

"Nothing," Simon said hastily, looking tense. "Just do her a favour and don't do anything to rock the boat."

"I'm confused. What does any of this have to do with me?"

"Alan's always been pretty insecure, just don't give him a reason to get jealous is all I'm saying."

There were a few moments of awkward silence before Simon stood up and clapped me on the back. "I should be going. You get some rest, yeah? It's been a long day."

The room was now slowly emptying around me, and I needed some air. It had been a revealing hour. Had I really been so wrapped up in

65

myself and my own angst as a teenager that I failed to notice that Dad actually did care about me? And if had been so proud, like they all said, why did he never get in touch to tell me?

I took the scenic route back to the house, feeling deflated, walking past the churchyard where I could see the fresh mound of earth where the old man lay. I paused and leaned on the wall, staring across the churchyard at the grave.

"I'm sorry, Dad," I said in a low whisper, and in my head I heard 'Jerusalem' start up again, which triggered another unexpected swell of grief. The tune followed me all the way back to the house, haunting my every step.

In the living room, the trombone waited for me on the couch where I had left it. Using my phone, I looked up a simple solo version of 'Jerusalem'.

"I must be mad," I said to myself before I lifted the instrument to my lips.

As before, the notes wobbled and shook at first as I forced them out, but after a few attempts, things started to settle down. There was definitely still something there; I could feel it starting to come back.

"Is this what you want?" I turned to the picture on the mantelpiece. "Would this make you happy? I know this doesn't make up for me being such a rubbish son, but does it at least help? If I go and try to help the band, would you think about forgiving me?"

I waited as if expecting an answer.

"But it's just for the time I'm here," I warned him when none was forthcoming. "Just until this place sells, because I still have a life to get back to, alright?"

I knew it was just my imagination, but I felt sure I could feel his approval radiating from behind the glass.

Chapter Ten

Rosie

It had only happened once, but that was all it took for Alan to get the reputation among the others as an abusive husband. He wasn't. I know that's what they all say, but it really wasn't the case with him. The single incident of violence had been over two years ago, yet I still felt like everyone was always watching us, checking up on me, expecting it to happen again every time we had a cross word. Trying to persuade them that Alan wasn't like that was no good. The idea had been planted, and it wouldn't shift. I frequently got bruises and scratches during my volunteer work in the garden at The Grange, especially as I've always been a bit accident-prone. Since the day Alan shoved me, the slightest mark on my body would lead them to ask, "Are you okay, Rosie?" The question always felt loaded as it was often delivered with a raised eyebrow and a not-so-subtle glance at whatever minor injury they had noticed.

It was lovely that people cared so much, but I had convinced myself that I was fine. I told myself over and over that I wasn't the kind of person who would stay in a relationship if it really was abusive. I was of the opinion that it's okay to slip up just once, and if you love someone, they deserve a second chance. It was little more than an accident anyway. I don't think he meant to hurt me, and he was so remorseful afterwards.

I shouldn't have reacted as quickly as I did after it happened. I think I was just so shocked in the moment that I didn't stop to properly process what had occurred. When I picked myself up off the floor, I was in such a panic that I made the whole thing seem much worse than it really was. I rushed out of the door, not thinking straight, and ran to Sally. She took one look at my rapidly swelling eye, and the tears on my cheeks, and knew exactly what had happened. Later, I would regret having rushed off like that as I felt the embarrassment and the shame of everyone knowing creeping over me. If I had taken a minute to pause, no one would have had to know the details; there would have been a million ways I could have explained away a black eye the next day. I had been upset and full of adrenaline when I went to Sally, and I had blown everything out of proportion.

It had happened during a stupid argument about how he thought I spent too much time on my phone. If I'd just let him have the phone in the first place, it would never have happened.

"Why is it you have so much time to spend on that thing but never any time for me?" he asked angrily, his grip tightening on the glass of water he was holding. "Who the hell is it you're talking to all the time?"

"It's mainly this stuff with The Grange." I set the phone down on the table. "I told you I was trying to put together a campaign to raise some funds. It's hard work, lots of messages, and people to email. Stuff with the shop as well, I was chasing up a stock order just now. I feel like I never stop."

"Must be nice to have so much time to spend on all your little projects while I'm left worrying about the bills."

"Come on, Alan, I don't spend *that* much time on my phone. Certainly no more than you do anyway."

"Yeah, well I'm running a business."

"So am I!" I exclaimed.

Alan laughed coldly and gave me a cold glance. "Yeah, right."

"Anyway, I'm putting it down for the night. There." I crossed the room to the kitchen table and set my phone on it. "It's on do not disturb. Sally and the shop and The Grange can all wait until tomorrow. I'm yours for the rest of the night." I gave him a smile and went to try and give him a hug, but he shrugged me away.

"I don't believe you," he said.

"What don't you believe?"

"That The Grange and that ridiculous shop you opened can mean you need to be on your phone all the time."

"What are you on about, Alan? What do you think I'm doing?"

"You could be talking to anyone for all I know. Probably messaging Simon, you seem quite close to him these days. Let's have a look, shall we?"

There was nothing on my phone that I didn't want him to see, but the very fact that he didn't believe me made me furious. When he went to pick it up off the table, I tried to snatch it back, and we ended up grappling fiercely as I tried to pry it from his fingers. Then he tried to shove me away, but he did it a little harder than he had meant to and I went flying, hitting my face hard on the corner of the table.

This all occurred during our last bad patch. He had always been jealous, but it seemed to really come to the surface whenever life wasn't going great. Something in Alan's world hit a bump, and suddenly I must be interested in other men. At the time, Alan's business was not doing too well, and he had been forced to take a job on a building site to make ends meet. He hated everything about it— from the hour-long commute to the foreman who he claimed had it in for him. Then one day he was sacked, and that led to him spending a lot of time in the pub with Tommy

Deans, which in turn led him to get the ridiculous idea in his head that there was something going on between me and Simon because we were "always messing about on the back row" at band and I was "never off my phone."

As he watched me get up off the floor that night, he looked truly horrified. After that, he really reined in his drinking. Then he had been suspended from the band, and it had crept up again, and this time it was Nate I was supposedly messing about with. I was mortified to find he had been going around telling people he had had to sort Nate out because he had 'tried it on 'with me. I had tried to do some damage control and make it clear this was not the case, but it's hard to put a rumour like that back in its box.

"Are you going to band tonight?" Alan asked moodily as he pushed what was left of his dinner around his plate.

"No, not tonight, we have that meeting about The Grange, remember?" I reminded him. "I'm half expecting Danny Henshaw to make an appearance now that I know he's back in the country."

"No thanks." Alan put down his knife and fork. "I hate those kinds of things, listening to the likes of Sandra Brown shouting her mouth off. It's all just a big waste of time anyway. I'll drop you off though and pick you up."

"Alan," I laughed, "it's a ten-minute walk."

"Yeah, but it's meant to rain." Alan's left knee was bouncing up and down, a sure sign he was wound up.

I glanced out of the window. It didn't look like rain. I knew exactly why he was insisting on driving me— he knew the band would be at The Grange, and he was worried that Nate might be there.

"You've got that big box of paperwork to take over, haven't you?"

"I suppose I have, but I could always drive myself."

"I'm just trying to be nice. I guess you don't want me to take care of you anymore." He gave me a cold stare. "Maybe I should just stop trying."

"No, Alan," I said, sensing a storm brewing. "It's lovely of you to offer. A lift and a hand in with that box of stuff would be great."

69

Chapter Eleven

Nate

I was late. And I knew how much Mr Black hated tardiness. I was late because I had spent too much time deliberating on whether I was actually going to go at all. By the time I did finally drag myself out of the house and across the village to The Grange, I found myself lingering at the front door for an age, trying to convince myself to go inside. As I stood there listening to the cacophony of notes clashing together as the players warmed up, I tried to give myself a pep talk.

"Come on, what's the worst that can happen? It's just a stupid brass band, you don't need to impress them, you're a professional musician, they aren't, this is just a hobby for them."

I straightened my shoulders, held my head high, and swaggered down the corridor, trying my best to summon the rapidly fading personality of Nasher Newell. On the way in, I accidentally crashed my trombone case against the doorframe, making an almighty racket to herald my late arrival. The room fell quiet as everyone looked at me with curious and amused expressions.

"Ladies and gentlemen, Bramwick's prodigal son returns!" Sally hollered from the horn section. Today she was wearing a T-shirt which said 'Deeds not words'.

There was a ripple of chuckles from the other players.

"Any one of these will tell you I don't usually tolerate tardiness," Mr Black said sternly, peering over his glasses. "But I'll let it go this once. I assume you remember where the trombones sit?"

"At the back where no one can hear us when we screw up?" There was a roar of laughter, and Mr Black motioned for me to sit down and shook his head in exasperation.

I muttered a brief "alright" to George as I sat down next to him, and he smiled encouragingly. I cast my eyes over to the cornet section, but there was no sign of Rosie. She had been with them at the funeral, so I had assumed she was back.

"Here we go," said Mr Black, setting a folder down on my stand. "Everything you need should be in here."

I fumbled to put my instrument together and was surprised that my hands shook as I did so.

"Ok everyone." Mr Black tapped his baton on the lectern. "Warm up this week is hymn number 60 in the red book."

"Apologies in advance," I whispered to George as I looked through the folder for the 'red book'. "I haven't done this in a long time and I'm way out of my comfort zone."

I did my best to keep up but my sight reading was rusty to say the least— this wasn't how we did things in Listed MIA; there were no little black dots and staves to follow when I played my guitar or sang, it all just came from instinct, and I felt that somehow this piece of paper put a barrier between me and the music and stopped us from properly connecting. It all seemed a bit too scientific— counting beats and reading dots— and I felt strangely separated from the ebb and flow of the music as I stumbled my way through the piece feeling like a fish out of water. My notes came out in laboured honks which led Simon to observe, "It sounds like someone is murdering a goose over there," to which I retorted irritably, "Haven't you got your own notes to butcher over there without worrying about mine?"

As the practice progressed I found I was really struggling. All the ease and confidence with which I usually performed on stage had abandoned me. This small hall with its gathering of amateur musicians was more intimidating than any of the sold-out venues I had played to. I was starting to sweat, and the knowledge that I was the worst player in the room did not sit well with my ego. I began to feel very self-conscious. George was patient though and kept offering useful tips and words of encouragement until I eventually did begin to settle a little. I was just starting to relax when I somehow lost count and managed to come in a whole bar early, to which Sally jibed, "Nice solo, Nate!" Then I messed up a simple rhythm and ended up completely out of time so Mr Black waved his arms for silence and gave me a stern reprimand.

"You were playing *on* the beat there, trombone two. You have *off* beats. Come on, you know that."

"Haven't you ever heard of syncopation?" I countered, feeling more and more irritable.

"That was not syncopation, Nathan. That was just plain wrong."

"It's Nate," I muttered.

When they moved on to a more complicated piece, I made the decision just to sit and listen for a while. They were a bit out of time, I observed, but this was mainly down to Alan's replacement on the drums, who couldn't seem to keep a steady beat. Mike, Listed MIA's percussionist, could have shown him a thing or two. They weren't bad though. They just needed a little refining, and once I had tuned into the frequent wrong notes and the odd questionable sound, I began to feel a little less self-conscious.

Soon, Mr Black called for a tea break, and I decided I hadn't done too badly at all. It was evident that Bramwick Brass had a lot of new and inexperienced players. They were hardly championship level, and that made me feel a little better about the whole thing. A lot of what I had learned as a kid was still there, and the practice had appealed to the part of me that always yearned to be making music with others. Sitting at home on my own playing guitar was all well and good, but it never gave me the same feeling that going into a rehearsal room or the recording studio did.

"We're not going to let Sally make the tea *again,* are we?" I heard Mr Black say to the group as I excused myself and went to look for the bathroom. "Go on, Simon. You know how a kettle works, don't you?"

As I wandered off down the corridor, a voice I recognised caught my attention. It was coming from one of the side rooms whose door was slightly ajar. As I passed, I glanced through the crack and saw that it was Rosie speaking, as I had suspected. She was addressing a small group of around thirty people, including an elderly lady who was knitting furiously, a distracted-looking man who was trying to stop a toddler from wriggling off his knee, and a middle-aged woman with a dog who seemed to be one of the only people who was actually engaged in what was being said.

"We're running out of time to raise the funds we need," she was saying. "Mr Henshaw over there would see The Grange turned into luxury housing for second homeowners, and we can't have that happen. The Grange isn't just a building and a patch of land; it's where we come together, it's the heart of our community, and Mr Henshaw has shown that he has no heart. He's already in talks with a developer because he's that certain that we can't do this. He thinks he's already won."

"Oh, come now, Mrs Fenn." A middle-aged man stood up and joined her at the front of the room, looking completely out of place in his designer knitwear, his dark tan, and his sickening smile that showed rows of perfect white teeth. I took an instant dislike to him. "Look around you. I hardly see much support for what you're trying to do. It's evident from how few people came out tonight and how little support your fundraiser has had that the people of Bramwick just aren't that bothered. It's true, I *have* been in talks with developers, but this needn't be a bad thing for Bramwick. Expanding the village could actually help the community."

"How, exactly?" Rosie stared at him with a look of utter contempt, and I couldn't help but smile at her feistiness. "It's not affordable housing you'll be building, is it? I've looked into Mitchell Homes. They only build luxury houses that no one from Bramwick could afford."

"Well, for one thing, part of the agreement for the potential purchase is that Mitchell Homes have agreed they will fund the construction of a new doctors 'surgery for the village— an important community resource you currently lack. They are very charitable and community-minded as an organisation; they like to give something back whenever they start a new development. We have details of this and all the proposed works in the brochures I have here, which will be distributed around the residents so they can make an informed choice about whether to support your takeover of The Grange or to allow us to take the village to a better future."

"So it's bribery now, is it?" Rosie snapped angrily.

At that moment, she saw me eavesdropping, and I made a hasty retreat back down the corridor.

"You alright? Did you get lost?" Simon enquired when I arrived back at the practice room. "Here, have some tea. I made it myself."

"What's going on in that room down there?"

"What do you mean?"

"Rosie's having some kind of meeting about The Grange."

"Oh yeah," Simon said." She has those from time to time, but I think people are losing interest."

"There was a guy in there with a bad tan talking about building a doctors 'surgery if he gets the land. It looked like things were getting a bit heated."

"That'll be Danny Henshaw," Simon scowled.

"I reckon she's got no chance," Brendan scoffed as he stepped up beside us. "I mean, I admire her determination and all, but she's up against Danny Henshaw and his millions. Even if she does raise the funds, which, let's face it, it is highly unlikely, he'll find a way around it."

"Not what I'd expect to hear from someone from Bramwick," I remarked. "I thought you'd all be right behind the campaign to buy The Grange."

"Most of us are," Sally said as she joined us.

"Support and interest *have* sort of dwindled, though, haven't they?" Simon said with a glum note in his voice. "What'll happen to the band if we lose this place?"

"I reckon the bands are just about on their last legs anyway," Brendan said unhappily. "I mean, look at us. There's hardly any of us left. We're just a bunch of beginners and retired people with nothing else to do. I think come a generation or two, brass bands will be a thing of the past."

"That's a bit of a defeatist attitude." I don't know why I said it. I certainly didn't care if brass bands had had their time, but something

73

about the condescending way that Danny Henshaw had spoken in that meeting with his plummy, stuck-up accent had got under my skin. It didn't matter what the context was. I would always root for the little guy against people like him.

"Well, thank you, Nate!" Sally smiled approvingly.

"Ah, what does he know? He hasn't got a clue," Brendan said dismissively.

"I know that one of the things that appealed to me most about the punk scene is how it stands up for the rights of the normal, everyday people, a bit like what brass bands have done over the years, I suppose, and I don't like seeing rich, entitled arseholes trampling over us mere peasants."

"So you're saying brass bands and punk have something in common?" Simon asked.

"Yeah." It wasn't something I had ever thought I'd hear myself admitting. "We've both historically represented the working man. We both offer attainable, down-to-earth ways into playing music."

"You're talking my kind of language, Mr Newell," Sally smiled. "We could use you on the campaign."

"Yes, well, let's not get carried away. I'm not around for long, remember?"

"Right, you lot, enough gabbing," Mr Black shouted. "Let's get back to it."

I muddled my way through the rest of the practice with mixed results. I managed to keep up quite well with some of the simpler pieces but found myself getting lost in some of the more complicated ones, which was frustrating as I knew that my teenage self would have managed, no bother. It seemed I had forgotten how much skill was involved in reading a new piece of music when you had no idea what it was supposed to sound like.

"You did well, son," Mr Black told me as we packed up.

"Wow, if Mr Black is offering me praise, I must have been *amazing*."

"It was good to hear you play again," he said, ignoring my sarcasm. "I'd be happy to give you a few individual lessons if you fancied it? I could have you back up to scratch in no time, I reckon."

"Sorry, but I'm broke. I can't afford private lessons." I shrugged.

"I wouldn't be doing it for the money. We could use someone like you in our ranks."

"But I'm not sticking around," I reminded him.

"I know, I know, only until the house sells, but you could still make a difference while you are here, raise our profile a bit, help inspire some youngsters to get involved."

Part of me felt horrified at the thought of the world finding out that Nasher Newell was spending his time playing in a small village brass band in Yorkshire. My reputation would be ruined, it would be a PR disaster, but the smug face of Danny Henshaw as he put down Rosie and her ambitions came back to my mind, and it really riled me.

"We really need it. In reality, Brendan is right. It doesn't matter if The Grange is saved, the band still might not have a future. If we can't inspire the younger generation, two hundred years of history will be lost."

"Two hundred years is a good run…"

"Come on, you're from here. There must be at least a part of you that would like to help. I heard what you said just there, and you're right. Punk music and brass bands, we aren't that different."

"Yeah, except brass bands just aren't cool, especially to kids and teenagers. It's all just so old-fashioned. You don't play music that they can relate to."

"We did a whole concert of Disney songs last year!" Mr Black protested.

"That's exactly my point. That might be fine for families and little kids, but what are you doing to hold onto them when they get older? They don't want to spend their Saturdays dressed in blazers getting the piss taken out of them by their mates."

"Well, that's exactly why we need someone like you. You understand these things."

"Thanks for the vote of confidence, but I don't think I'm the one to help you."

"Not even just for one concert? There's a big fundraising event coming up for The Grange, and if you were to play at it…"

"I'm really sorry, it's just not for me."

Mr Black looked crestfallen. "Fair enough. Can't blame me for trying, though, can you?"

The rest of the band had gone now, and I made for the door, leaving Mr Black alone sorting through a pile of music, the guilt weighing on me just a little bit.

"I thought you'd have been finished ages ago." I heard Alan's annoyed voice as I passed the room the meeting had been in, and I paused in the corridor.

"Sorry, it went on a bit longer than I expected, and with Danny Henshaw being there, there was a lot to talk about. You know he's actually trying to get people to stop supporting the campaign and get onside with letting the developers move in by promising them a doctors' surgery!"

"So that's another one of your little projects down the drain then?"

"Alan!"

"Well, you can't stand in the way of progress, can you? Look, you tried, but you can't fix everything. Some things are just doomed from the start."

"You're talking like it's already over."

"You know it is. Nobody cares anymore."

"I care…" It sounded as if her voice was cracking. "I don't want to lose this place."

"It could be a chance for a fresh start for you," I heard Alan reply. "Losing The Grange might give you the push you need to go and get a proper job."

"I have the shop too." It sounded like she was close to tears now.

"Because that's been such a big success. No one round here wants goat's milk soap and vegetarian sausages."

"You're being unfair."

"All I'm saying is I've stood by you, supported you for two years with these little ventures of yours, but I think it might be time you started pulling your weight a bit more."

"Pulling my weight? Who washes your socks and cooks your dinner every day?"

"There's no need to get upset," he told her. "I'm only trying to make you see that it might be time to move on. The shop hasn't worked, and it's clear The Grange is going back to Danny Henshaw."

"I'm not ready to give up fighting yet. We still have eight months, that's a long time."

"It's too long, Rosie," Alan snapped. "I'm not prepared to be the only one paying bills for any longer. You know you don't stand a chance against Danny, so stop wasting time on these ridiculous projects."

"Sometimes you can be a real bastard, Alan, don't you know that?" Her voice had turned to a series of sobs, and the door to the room swung open.

Rosie rushed out, swiping at the tears in her eyes, and I'm not even sure she noticed me standing there as she hurried down the corridor and out the door.

"Rosie!" Alan yelled after her as he too emerged into the corridor. Then he shot me a scathing look and added:" What the fuck are you looking at?"

I stared after him as he ran after her before I turned around and marched back into the practice room. Maybe it was just because I hated guys like Henshaw, or maybe it was the way Alan had spoken to Rosie, but suddenly, I found myself giving a damn.

76

"I'll do it," I said. "I'll take some private lessons with you, and I'll play at the fundraiser concert if you think it'll help."

"You will?"

"Yes. But if I'm going to help out while I'm here, you have to listen to some of my ideas; it can't all just be hymns and marches and Disney songs."

Mr Black smiled and then raised an eyebrow. "You have a deal, Mr Newell."

Chapter Twelve

Rosie

I was helping Mum to muck out the alpaca stables. She didn't really need my help, both my parents were still very active and capable, but I had to clear my head. The small farm where I grew up always felt like an oasis of calm, sitting there on the hillside with no immediate neighbours, just happy memories and the animals and crops. What Alan had said the night before had *really* hurt and had led to yet another blazing row. It seemed he was adamant that I should start looking for a 'real' job. He went off on a rant about how I was living in a fantasy world with the shop and The Grange and I had to come back to reality sometime. It worried me that Nature's Bounty made so little money. Alan was right—it wasn't a serious business, just a passion project for Sally and me, barely scraping by. It shouldn't really have been a problem, as what Alan earned was more than enough to pay the bills with a little left over. What was a concern was my lack of financial independence. What would happen to me if we ever did break up?

"Maybe Alan's right," I sighed. "Maybe it is time to give up, I feel like I don't have any fight left in me anyway after that meeting last night. It was awful, Mum, Danny Henshaw is just such an arse, and I'm not sure we can win against him."

"I hate hearing you talk like that, it's a good fight you're fighting, you know that, and the world needs people like you."

"Honestly Mum, I came away from that meeting feeling completely emotionally drained and defeated. What I really needed right then was a hug, a friendly ear, and some kind words, which I should have been able to get from the man I married. Instead I got reminded of how little I contribute and how financially precarious my situation is."

"Come here." Mum put down her rake and spread her arms. I went to her and she pulled me into a big, comforting cuddle. "Your dad and me have been talking. I think we should go in and have a little chat, we might have some good news for you."

We didn't tell Dad about the huge argument I had had with Alan but Mum explained about the horrible meeting with Danny Henshaw and my concerns about how little money the shop was bringing in.

"I think it's time to have a serious chat about what we've been talking about," Mum said, and Dad nodded in agreement.

"What's going on?" I asked.

"Well," said Mum. She looked at Dad with a small smile and I wondered what was coming.

"Your mum and I aren't getting any younger so naturally we've started thinking about retiring."

"Yes, what we really want to do is get a bit of travelling in while we're still able to. We'd love to go back to India."

I had heard many tales of the times they had spent backpacking there together when they were young. It had always sounded so romantic. Alan and I had never travelled together. We did have one holiday which I dragged him on to Malta, a sort of honeymoon, but it was chore to get Alan to leave Bramwick, never mind the country, so it remained our only trip. I would have loved to have seen India, and Africa, and so many other places.

"We've been thinking for a while about downsizing, getting a little cottage. The farm and the business are getting too much for us."

"You're going to sell it?" I asked, dismayed.

"We thought you might like to take over running it," Mum said.

"Me?" I felt my heart skip a beat.

"Why not? You know it as well as us and you're young and full of fresh ideas, you could breathe new life into it."

"I don't know what to say." I started to laugh, I felt so joyful.

"Just have a think, there's no rush," Dad said.

"Go and talk to Alan, see what he thinks too."

By the time I left the farm, my mood had improved vastly. I almost skipped down the hill, I felt so excited. My mind was racing with ideas of what I could do with the place. We could open a small farm shop with a vegetarian cafe maybe. I could host retreats and getaways. Perhaps we could even turn the old barn into a wedding venue…the possibilities seemed endless. It was so long since I had had any good news and this was definitely good news. It was so unexpected too; Mum and Dad had never even hinted that they were thinking of retiring. I couldn't wait to tell Alan—this could be just what we needed—and as I hurried down the road towards The Grange I felt like I was going to explode with happiness. And that's when I ran into Nate. Literally. I rushed around the corner onto Bridge Street and collided right into him. He reached for my shoulders to steady me as I stumbled and looked at me with a serious expression on his face.

"Sorry," I said, but I couldn't stop grinning.

"That's ok." The serious expression had disappeared and he looked relieved as he observed, "You look happy."

"I am."

"Ok then."

"Where are you going?"

"Just off to The Grange to meet Mr Black."

"I wish you'd stop calling him that," I grimaced. "Anyway, that's where I'm going so I'll walk with you."

"Right, but I don't want to make you late."

"Late?" I was confused.

"You came round that corner at quite a speed, you must have somewhere you need to be."

"I suppose I did." I felt the grin rise on my face again as I fell into step with him. "I've had some good news."

"Oh yeah? Is it about The Grange? Did the meeting go well last night?"

"You know it didn't; I saw you loitering in the doorway. But I might have something very exciting on the horizon. Mum and Dad want to retire and they've asked me to take over the business."

Saying it out loud brought the excitement rushing back and I glanced at Nate to see his reaction. He was still facing forward and his expression was neutral.

"They want to downsize and go travelling; they want to give me the farm."

"That's good of them."

"It's more than good. It's a dream come true. We can move out of that shoe box we're living in, and there's so much potential to expand on what Mum and Dad do. I'm thinking of maybe turning the old barn into a wedding venue. Small, rustic ceremonies are all the rage now. Guests could stay in the pods and they could have pictures with the alpacas. Can't you just picture them with little white bows round their necks?"

We were at the gates to The Grange now and Nate stopped and looked at me. He was smiling now. I hadn't seen him smile since he came back. In fact, come to think of it, in every picture and video I'd seen of him online over the years on the band's Facebook and the likes he was always either looking moody or snarling menacingly. But as I looked at his smile I saw the old Nate, the one I remembered from all those years ago, the one who had called me Patches, shining through.

"I'm made up for you Rosie, I really am, that all sounds amazing." My heart did a stupid little flip at the sight of that lopsided grin. "That farm is the only place I could have ever pictured you ending up."

"Thanks, Nate," I beamed. "Have fun with *Mr Black*."

I swung through the gates and skipped down the path towards the orchard.

Chapter Thirteen

Nate

The estate agent tried to hide her grimace as she glanced around the house. I'd done my best to clear away as much clutter as possible, but it was still a long way from show-home perfect. At least now you could walk around without tripping over anything. Unfortunately, shifting years 'worth of accumulated junk had revealed hidden problems—cracks in the plaster, stains and threadbare patches in the carpet, possible damp in the kitchen, evidence of woodworm in the dining room. Spiders. Dust. Dirt.

I wondered if I should get a cleaner in. I could barely afford it, but…

"It's a bit of a fixer-upper, isn't it?" the agent said, before quickly adding, "but that's not always a bad thing." She glanced at me. "Did you say it was your father's house?"

"Yeah. He passed away. He was a bit of a hoarder, and I've been trying to clear it out. I'm hoping for a quick sale, so…"

"Hmm." She moved the net curtain with a tentative finger, revealing mildew on the windowsill, then peered into the garden—which I hadn't even touched. The grass was knee-high, full of weeds. One of the fence panels had blown over, and a stack of old tyres sat in one corner.

"Beautiful view, mind you," she said, clinging to the positives.

She wasn't wrong. The house sat on the edge of the village, backing onto a field of sheep, with the rolling Dales beyond. On a summer's day, it was spectacular.

"Plenty of scope to extend, too." She scribbled something in her notepad.

Upstairs, as she moved from room to room, I became horribly aware of the musty smell. I'd also forgotten to make the bed—not that it was a habit of mine. She peered into my old childhood room and made more notes. The posters were still on the walls—Green Day, Rancid, The Offspring.

The bathroom was a disaster. The avocado-green suite had been there since my parents bought the place, as far as I knew. Worse still was the carpeted floor, now spongy from decades of absorbing every liquid that had ever hit it.

"Well," the agent said brightly, back in the living room. "The good news is it has a lot of potential. Decent size, pleasant views, lots of original features—people love that. The beams, the fireplace, the flagstone floors."

She swept her hand around the room, and I nodded.

"There's no shortage of buyers looking for a project. We just have to price it accordingly."

"And what does that mean?"

"I'd say we put it up at a hundred thousand to start and go from there."

A hundred grand for a three-bedroom cottage. That wouldn't even get you a studio flat in most parts of London.

"I'm in a rush to sell. I don't want it dragging on."

"We'll see how much interest there is first. We can always drop the price if need be."

"Or I could just stick it in an auction and be done with it…" I mused.

"Oh no." She shook her head. "You'll get way less than it's worth."

I agreed to do some more tidying before she returned to take photos. As she left, I started to feel better. Things were finally moving in the right direction. Once this was all dealt with, I'd be debt-free and ready to move on.

Maybe I'd start a new band. I might even ask Maxwell to come with me—after all, it was Ritchie I had the problem with. Ritchie, who had always rubbed me the wrong way. Who I'd fought with even before the whole Freya thing.

And I had a sneaking suspicion that, despite Freya's initial tears and assurances that it had been a stupid, one-time mistake, something was still going on between them. They were appearing in an awful lot of photos together on Facebook these days.

Why do people always want to shag the singer?

As I headed to my first lesson with Fred Black, I wondered vaguely—does anyone ever want to shag the trombone player? The thought made me chuckle.

Rosie, maybe?

The idea hit me out of nowhere, and I tried to crush it before it could take root. But then I rounded a corner, and she ran straight into me. She was brimming with excitement about her parents offering her the chance to take over their farm and camping business.

I didn't want to feel what I was feeling. It was inconvenient. But watching her smile, hearing her enthusiasm, I couldn't deny it. I was harbouring feelings for her.

I really could have done without developing a rebound crush on some country girl I went to school with.

When we finally parted and I went into the band room, Fred Black was waiting, sifting through music as usual. I wondered if he ever

82

actually went home. Maybe he didn't even exist outside of this room, outside of this band.

"Hello, Nathan, lad," he greeted me.

"It's Nate."

"Oh, yes, sorry." He smiled. "Come and have a seat."

"Thanks, Mr Black."

"It's Fred. You're not thirteen anymore."

But I *felt* thirteen again when he handed me a photocopied booklet. The basics—different note values, their positions on the stave, trombone slide positions.

"We're going right back to the beginning," Fred said. "I know you know this, but it's been a long time, and there's no harm in revising scales to begin with."

I sighed and ran my eyes over a page explaining minims, crotchets, and quavers.

"Is this really necessary? I'm a professional musician. I think I can just about remember what notes are what."

"Then you'll have no problem giving me a C scale. Hold each note for four. I'll count you in."

I wobbled my way up the scale, the notes long and loud. Things were a bit smoother on the way back down.

"Bit rusty," Fred noted. "Again. Crotchets this time. Breathe from your abdomen, not your chest—keep it controlled, don't blast."

He made me repeat the drill over and over until the notes were clearer, steadier.

"Very good," he said at last. "I think you're ready to try a tune. Page ten."

I flicked through the pages.

'Twinkle Twinkle Little Star'.

"Oh, come on! I'm not playing that."

"Why not?"

"It's baby music. Imagine if anyone saw me—they'd think I'd gone soft."

"Yes, yes, we all know you have an image to protect," Fred said dryly. "But while you're in here, you're just Nathan Newell."

I sighed and raised the trombone.

"On the count of four, then."

I took a deep breath and played.

Fred smiled widely when I finished.

"Not bad at all."

"Told you I was beyond this kind of stuff." I smirked.

Fred grinned. "Let's try something else."

He rummaged through a filing cabinet. When he turned back, he had a mischievous look in his eye.

"Aha! Here we are." He placed a new sheet of music on my stand.

I groaned as I scanned the notes.

"Oh, anything but *this*… The bloody '*Floral Dance*'! Can we go back to 'Twinkle Twinkle'?"

Fred chuckled. "I remember giving this to you just before you quit. You hated it for some reason."

I had. I'd loathed it. At the time, I hadn't really known why. But now, a memory dislodged itself and hit me full force.

"They played this at my mum's funeral," I said quietly.

How had I forgotten?

Fred nodded. "*We* did. Bramwick Band. It was your mum's favourite. Did you know that when they got married, before your dad had to pack in playing, the band played this at their wedding too?"

"No," I admitted.

"As they were leaving the chapel, we lined up outside and played as the guests showered them with confetti. Old Harry was finding bits of it in his tuba for weeks after." Fred chuckled. "They even posed for a picture in their wedding gear with their instruments for the local paper. It was rare enough to have a woman in a band back then, so it made a nice little story."

I frowned. "I don't really remember Mum playing."

"Oh, she did," Fred said. "Not as much after you came along, though. You were a handful."

I shrugged. "Dad never really talked about Mum. It was like this big taboo subject. I was so young when she died, I barely remember anything about her."

Fred patted my knee. "See, brass is in your blood, lad. But we don't have to play this piece if it's too much. We can find something else."

"No." The urge to play it took hold of me. "I didn't know why this piece made me so angry that day—the day I went home and did this." I pointed at the engraving on my trombone and smiled. "It only just came back to me about the funeral. But I'm not a hormonal teenager anymore. I want to give it a go."

Fred straightened up and reached for his baton. "Well, it does feel a bit like unfinished business."

He counted me in, and I began, but everything was off. My pitching, my timing—it was a mess.

"Come on, I know you can do better than that."

"I can't quite remember how it's supposed to sound. If I could just hear it, if you could play it once, I'd get it, no problem."

"Just focus. You can do it."

"But I usually play by ear. I'm really good at it—I only need to hear a tune once and I can pick it out."

Fred sighed. "That may be the case, but you're not in a punk band anymore. In a large ensemble, you need to read the notes, not just feel them."

I muttered, "This isn't going to work."

"Of course it is. You just need to get used to playing in a different way. You know the notes, you know the rhythms. Just clear your mind and play what you see."

I took a few deep breaths and studied the sheet music, breaking down the note values in my head. What was it Fred always used to say? *Subdivide!* I counted myself in and fumbled through the piece. Amazingly, I made it to the end without too much drama.

Fred grinned. "I knew you could do it. That's it, I can end my career happy, knowing I finally got Nathan Newell to play 'The Floral Dance'!"

I laughed. And, to my surprise, I actually felt proud of myself.

The lesson continued, and by the end, I was comfortably playing through 'The Floral Dance' and a few other beginner pieces, with Fred accompanying me on cornet. His teaching methods hadn't changed. He never handed out praise easily, but he wasn't overly critical either. If you wanted praise from Fred Black, you had to earn it. And that made it all the more meaningful when you finally got it.

As I sat there, I realised how much I owed him—and my dad. They had pushed me into music in the first place. If not for them, would I have ever picked up a guitar? Would I have written 'The World's End'? Would I have known the power of rhythm, of melody, of the way music could stir emotions in an audience?

I thought back to my first concert at ten years old, the pride on my dad's face in the front row. The thrill of playing a solo at the village fair, the applause, the congratulations. The excitement when Simon, Rosie and I were asked to join the main band for the May Day celebrations. I hadn't realised it before, but those early days had sparked something in me. An addiction to performing. The craving for applause. The rush of knowing I could move a crowd with just a few notes.

I had seen it happen at Listed MIA gigs. The way a whole audience tensed in anticipation when they recognised the opening chords of a song. The frenzy when I launched into the riff. The way the front row, crushed by the surge behind them, reached out with desperate fingers as if I were some kind of god. There was no drug in the world like that feeling. And in their own way, Bramwick Brass did something similar. Their music had given me permission to finally grieve my dad.

Fred's voice pulled me back. "That really was a pleasure."

"Really? I feel like I've forgotten most of what you taught me."

"Nonsense," Fred scoffed. "Would I ask you to consider playing at our next concert if I thought you'd lost it?"

I blinked. "The fundraiser? You think I'm up for it?"

"I do."

"When is it?"

"Two weeks."

"Two weeks?" I stared at him. "You never mentioned it was that soon. That's not enough time."

"Have a look at these." He handed me a folder. "Go home, give them a try. It's only six songs, nothing too difficult."

I hesitated, but something in me wavered. Rosie might be impressed if I did it...

"Alright," I said, taking the folder. But I wasn't convinced I'd be ready in two weeks.

Back at the house, I needed a detox. Too much brass. Too much Bramwick. I went up to my room and grabbed my favourite acoustic guitar.

"Ah, a proper instrument," I muttered approvingly, strumming a chord.

Hours passed in a blur. I played some old Listed MIA songs, then, out of nowhere, a new song started forming. I scrambled for a pen. With no paper around, I grabbed the cardboard sleeve from my microwave lasagna and started scribbling.

The excitement surged through me. It was happening again—that rush, that certainty that I was onto something special. The same feeling I'd had when I wrote 'The World's End'.

I leaned back, shaking my head in disbelief. "For fuck's sake," I muttered. "It's really, really good."

I never imagined Bramwick Brass could inspire me like this. And I wasn't quite sure what to do with the idea forming in my mind.

Chapter Fourteen

Rosie

"But I thought, after what you said the other day, that—"

"A real job, Rosie. I said a real job."

Alan had not greeted my good news with the enthusiasm I'd hoped for, and just like that, the happy bubble I'd been floating in all afternoon burst.

"I don't understand," I said, my voice small. "This is a chance for me to make a real success of something—for us to move into a bigger place. There'd even be space for children…"

I could picture it so clearly—my own kids growing up there, just as I had. Teaching them to respect nature, to work with the land and animals. Giving another generation the idyllic childhood I'd been lucky enough to have. I had always wanted a family, but there wasn't room in our current place, and until Mum's offer, I hadn't seen a way for that to change. Alan had said he wanted children when we got together, but I was starting to think that had been a lie. Lately, it had become just another sore point we avoided.

"You mean it's a chance for you to piss about with plants and animals while I go out and do the real graft," he said. "When you wanted to start the shop with Sally, I thought it was a stupid idea, but I supported you anyway. And I was right—it's hardly been a success. You've already proved you're not capable of running a business. You're too lazy to put in the hours. What makes you think this would be any different?"

I pushed my food around my plate. I'd cooked a nice dinner for us—spaghetti and homemade meatballs (veggie option for me)—but now my appetite had vanished, replaced by a dull, sick feeling in my stomach. I had wanted tonight to be a celebration. We could eat our favourite meal together, and I could tell him all about the plans I'd spent the afternoon making. Ideas for a café, for a wedding barn, for moving the shop up there and getting Sally on board.

But the conversation hadn't even got that far before he shut me down.

"And you go on about kids?" He spoke through a mouthful of spaghetti. Clearly, he hadn't lost his appetite. "How do you think you'd have time to run a business like that and look after children? You need to get your head out of the clouds. It's just another one of your stupid schemes, and I'm not prepared to support you through yet another hobby you try and dress up as work."

"This is a dream for me, Alan. Can't we at least talk about it? I've got so many ideas I want to run by you."

"I can tell you what we should be talking about." He dabbed at the sauce on his plate with a piece of garlic bread. "There's a recruitment day next week at that big hotel spa thing over by Merrygill. That old cow whose bathroom I was doing mentioned it."

I knew the place he meant. The big old hotel had sat empty for years before being bought out and was set to reopen as a luxury spa in the spring.

"I think you should go," he continued. "At least find something part-time to fit around the shop. By the time it opens, this crap with The Grange will be wrapped up, so your afternoons will be free by summer anyway, won't they?"

I set my fork down, blinking back the tears that threatened to spill. I had hoped tonight would be a celebration, that he would see this for the incredible opportunity it was. Instead, he was telling me I should turn down my parents 'offer and take a job as a maid or waitress, running around after rich tourists in a soulless corporate hotel.

My gaze landed on the unopened bottle of red wine on the counter. The tears burned again.

I got up and started clearing the dishes. I couldn't cry. Alan hated it when I cried.

"You not eating that?" he asked, nodding at my half-finished plate.

"No, I'm not hungry."

He pulled it toward him and started tucking in, muttering something about the veggie meatballs but shovelling them into his mouth anyway.

"Look, love, I don't mean to sound harsh," he said when he'd finished my food. He got up and pulled me into an embrace from behind and kissed the top of my head. "I'm only looking out for you. You get a bit carried away sometimes and I don't want you to make another mistake. I want to see you with a secure career. It'll be good for you to feel financially independent rather than having to rely on me."

"I suppose you're right," I sighed. I couldn't face another argument. "Do you want to do anything tonight?"

"I'm going out tonight," he said.

"Oh. Where?"

"Tommy asked me round to watch the football."

A small relief. The thought of spending the evening pretending everything was fine was too much. I watched as he grabbed his jacket and took his keys from the bowl by the door.

"I won't be late," he said as he left.

I took a deep breath, blinking fast. Then I picked up my phone and typed out a message.

Half an hour later, a knock came at the door.

Sally.

"You okay, love?" she asked, stepping inside and pulling off her boots. "What's happened?"

Sally was older than me, but one of my best friends. A mentor in the band and a fierce source of support. She had blown into the village not long after Nate left, a riot of pink spiky hair and an endless collection of political T-shirts (today's read 'Will Trade Racists for Refugees'). Even in her early fifties then, I had thought she was impossibly cool, with her Doc Martens and nose ring.

She was an outspoken feminist with no filter, which had shocked some of the older male band members at first. But once she'd established herself as a mean horn player, she'd started shaking things up in subtle ways, dragging the band into the modern era.

It was because of her that the men now helped at tea break. That we no longer had to wear tight, impractical grey pencil skirts as part of our uniform—now we could wear trousers like the men. That battle had been one of her finest moments, and I had hung on every word as she recounted her conversation with the committee. I wished I could have seen Roger's and Victor's faces when she told them that tight fitting, light grey skirts weren't practical when you had your period. Or when she pointed out how hard heels were to march in.

"Has Alan been an arse again?"

I nodded, and she pulled me into a hug.

"What's he done this time? Come on, where's this wine you mentioned? Get it poured, and we'll have a proper bitching session—get everything off our chests."

We drank, and I told her everything—Mum and Dad's offer, Alan's cruel words, his dismissal of our business.

"How dare he?" Sally said, outraged. "We've only had that shop two years, and we've at least broken even both years. Do you know how many businesses manage that? And he has the nerve to call you lazy? Does he even realise how much you do? Between the shop, The Grange, the community, and running this place? He hasn't got a clue, has he?"

"All I want is someone who supports me. Who shares in my happiness instead of tearing me down."

"Have you ever thought about giving women a go?"

I laughed.

"No, but seriously, love—Alan is an arse. You know that. Most of the band can't stand him. I've never understood how someone as lovely as you ended up with such a brute."

I sighed. "When we were at school, he was in the popular crowd. He was handsome, and all the girls fancied him. When he picked me, I was flattered. I couldn't believe it. When you're me, you don't say no when the most popular boy in the village asks you out."

Sally made a noise like she was trying to snort wine through her nose.

"And I was still reeling from Nate leaving. I wanted us to be something more."

She raised an eyebrow. "So he was an arse too?"

I shook my head. "No. He acted like one, but he's got a good soul."

She studied me, then shook her head.

"Don't," she said seriously. "By all means, leave Alan—I'd be right behind you—but don't latch onto someone else when you're vulnerable. It won't end well. If you go, go for you."

I gazed into the fire.

She was right. And now Mum and Dad's offer had given me a way out. The question was, would I take it?

Chapter Fifteen

Nate

Over the next few days, I felt miserable and lonely. I was unbelievably bored, and Dad's old house was starting to feel claustrophobic. I wasn't used to having so much time on my hands with nothing to do. My life had always been hectic and noisy, filled with activity and people. This quiet, sluggish pace felt unnatural and uncomfortable. I was climbing the walls.

I even found myself pulling on an old pair of walking boots I'd discovered in the house and going for daily walks in the Dales—completely out of my comfort zone. But at least under the open skies, I didn't feel quite so hemmed in. To my surprise, I could still name a lot of the trees and birds I saw on my walks, knowledge I had picked up from Rosie. Funny how things you learned as a kid stuck with you, while I could barely remember things said to me the week before.

I also scrubbed the house from top to bottom—another task completely alien to me, but at least I saved money on a cleaner. The half-hour drive to the nearest supermarket for supplies ended up being the highlight of my week.

The estate agent came back to take pictures for the listing, so at least things were moving forward. I watched as she adjusted the furniture, commenting on how the light was good that day, staging the place to show it off as best she could. I wondered again if I should just put it up for auction and be done with it. The sooner I could move on, the better.

More pictures had appeared on Freya's Facebook page—her with Richie and Maxwell. Even Milo was in some of them. I realised I missed the damned dog. Why had she got to keep him anyway? Surely I was more in need of the company than she was. I really should have taken the dog.

As angry as I was, I desperately missed them. I would even have welcomed Richie if he'd turned up at the door with a pack of beer. I wanted my old life back so much.

The trombone sat in its case, untouched, as my motivation and mood crashed. Dad stared at me from the mantelpiece, his expression locked in eternal disapproval.

Pick it up. You've got a concert to prepare for, remember?

That was what he seemed to say from behind the glass, standing there frozen in time with Mum at his side. But I felt so low that the concert was the least of my concerns.

It wasn't until the day of the next rehearsal that I finally forced myself to pick up the instrument again. Guilt hit me immediately. Fred would know I hadn't been practising—he always did. And if Rosie was there, I'd missed my chance to show her I could still play. When I was young and losing interest, I always had excuses—too much homework, not feeling well. But now? I had no excuse. I'd spent the past week doing bugger all other than moping around, feeling sorry for myself.

I opened the folder of concert music Fred had given me after our lesson. He hadn't been lying when he said most of it was simple. There was an easy-looking march, a version of 'When the Saints Go Marching In', and a couple of numbers from classic musicals. At least I recognised them all, so I wouldn't be fumbling around in the dark. I gave them a go and was pleased to find I could blow through most of them without too much trouble.

By the time I left that evening, my mood had lifted considerably. I was actually looking forward to band.

The first half of that evening's practice went better than expected. Simon and George were delighted when they found out I had agreed to play at the fundraiser.

During the tea break, Fred pulled me aside. I braced myself for a lecture about my lack of practice, but that wasn't it.

"We need to get you a uniform, given you're joining us for the concert," he said. "Come with me."

"Oh, right." I hadn't thought about the uniform. I remembered it from my youth and could only pray it had been updated since then.

I followed Fred to the back room, where a clothes rail held a row of familiar bottle-green blazers. He looked me up and down, pursed his lips, then rifled through the jackets.

"Here, try that."

I shrugged off my own jacket and pulled on the one he handed me, feeling utterly ridiculous and grateful there was no mirror. Unfortunately, the uniforms had not changed. The same garish green, the same hideous yellow piping on the shoulders and sleeves. Judging by the musty smell, I wondered if these were actually the very same ones from my childhood.

Fred tugged at the jacket in various places, trying to make it sit right. It felt shapeless and deeply unflattering. I remembered the first time I had been given one of these—when I was twelve, when Rosie, Simon and I had been asked to join the main band for the May Day performance. Back then, I had felt so proud, like I was finally part of a secret club. The appeal had worn off quickly as I got older and realised how uncool it was.

"That'll do," Fred concluded. "You'll need this too." He rummaged in a drawer and pulled out a matching tie.

"Um, thanks." I took it reluctantly.

"And you'll need a white shirt, black trousers, and black shoes."

"Not grey anymore?" At least something had changed. That made life easier—I already had everything from the funeral.

"No, black these days. More practical, apparently."

Fred looked me over again. I became acutely aware of my ripped jeans, my ancient T-shirt. His gaze landed on my red Doc Martens with their yellow laces, then on my hair, making the corners of his mouth pull down in a grimace.

"And you'll have to do something about that."

"My hair?" I asked, surprised.

"Don't worry, I'm not expecting a full makeover—just maybe don't spike it up like that."

I bit back the curse that threatened to escape. "Right."

"Good lad." Fred wandered off to grab a cup of tea from George.

"Oh yes, a proper bandsman now, are you?"

The voice behind me startled me. I had been disappointed when I hadn't seen Rosie on the back row of cornets, but now here she was. My stomach tightened as I turned to face her, aware that I must look like a right prat in the green blazer. Hastily, I pulled it off.

"It's just for the one concert. For the fundraiser."

"So you say, but once you've pulled that jacket on, you're one of us. No getting away now."

"Yes, well, we'll see. Anyway, you excited about the farm?"

Her face darkened, and she bit her lip, brushing a strand of hair behind her ear. "Alan isn't keen," she shrugged. "He thinks it's too much of a risk. He's probably right."

The change in her was unsettling. She had seemed so happy.

"He's right about a lot of things, actually," she continued. "About The Grange, about the shop. It's exhausting, fighting all the time. I'm just about done with it. Maybe a complete change of scene is what I need. If we're ever going to start a family, I need to be bringing in some money."

"What are you talking about?"

"I'm looking for a new job. Actually, I'm going to a recruitment fair this week—for that new spa opening near Merrygill."

"What, so you're just going to sit at a reception desk answering phones or something?" That didn't sound right. Rosie was meant to be outdoors, with soil under her fingernails, not cooped up in some fancy hotel. She was exactly where she was supposed to be, and now she was ready to walk away from it all?

"Why not? I looked up the company. They have a great reputation, they pay well—"

"And you'd rather do that than run the farm and the shop?"

"Of course not, Nate," she snapped, frustration tightening her voice. "But sometimes people have to be practical. Some of us have bills to pay, responsibilities. Not everyone gets to make a living chasing their dreams."

"I just can't picture it. Won't it make you miserable?"

She looked like she was about to cry. Before I could say anything else, Sally appeared, her T-shirt for the day declaring: 'Today we smash the patriarchy'. A classic.

"Hey, you're not upsetting her, are you?" She shot me an accusing look, draping an arm around Rosie's shoulder.

"Me? No. She's upsetting herself with this ridiculous idea of working at a spa."

Rosie carefully shrugged off Sally's arm. "I'm just going to nip to the bathroom."

As soon as she was gone, Sally turned back to me, arms folded. "She's not having the best time right now. She doesn't need you making it worse."

"How am I making it worse?" I asked, baffled. "I just don't see how giving up the farm—something she's always dreamed of—to work in a hotel is a good idea. It's not her. I've known her my whole life. She'll be miserable."

"No, you *haven't* known her your whole life," Sally corrected sharply. "You knew her *as a kid*. You don't know her now. You left, remember? You don't get a say in what she does."

I exhaled, shaking my head. "I know that. But I also know enough to see this isn't *her* choice. Alan's behind this."

Sally sighed, her expression softening. "Yeah. And honestly? I agree with you. But what can we do? It's her relationship. Her life."

The second half of practice did not go well for me. I was distracted, aware of Rosie sitting across the room. Every note I blew seemed to come out wrong, much to Fred's annoyance.

"Are you even with us, Nate?" he snapped when I somehow started playing 'Wellerman' instead of 'Morning has Broken'.

Later, back at the house, I stood in front of the mirror, wearing the bottle-green blazer over my funeral suit. What the hell was I getting myself into?

Chapter Sixteen

Rosie

Hearing that Nate was planning to play at the fundraiser took me by surprise. He looked completely out of place, standing in the band room while Fred fussed over his jacket. I couldn't blame him—I wasn't exactly a fan of the uniform either, with its cheap, man-made polyester that seemed charged with enough static to light up the whole village. At least the grey pencil skirts were gone.

But what really stood out was the contrast between Nate's spiked hair, piercings, and the bottle-green blazer. It sparked an idea. Why were we hosting such a small, old-fashioned fundraiser? No one would take notice of it. Sure, we might raise a few pounds, but it wouldn't be enough. We needed something that would grab attention—like Nate's punk rock persona and edgy style. We needed a protest.

Who better to talk to than Sally, my right-hand woman? She was no stranger to marches, sit-ins, or demonstrations—she had been involved in a number of protests over the years. So, I invited her to the next community group meeting.

"I'm not sure the people of Bramwick are capable of getting that riled up," Alex said thoughtfully, considering my proposal. Alex and I were part of the five-person committee coordinating the efforts to buy The Grange, along with Helen, Gerald, and the town gossip, Sandy Brown. Truthfully, most of the work fell to me.

"You might have a point," I admitted, remembering how reluctant people had been to get involved with saving The Grange.

"Rubbish," Sally scoffed. "You can get people worked up if you really have to. But being in Bramwick might make it tricky to have an impact. We don't have any motorways to blockade or underground trains to glue ourselves to."

Sandy shot Sally a shocked look. "You've glued yourself to a train? Isn't that dangerous?"

"No, not me personally, but it's been done," Sally said with a chuckle. "I chained myself to a bank's doors once, though."

"I could chain myself to the doors of the One Stop Shop?" Alex said, and I wasn't sure if he was joking.

"And what good would that do?" Sally responded. "So a few people can't get in for bread and milk—it's hardly earth-shattering. Plus, you don't want to mess with Greg and his business."

"The gates of the park, then?" Gerald suggested, and Sally shot him an annoyed glare.

"No one's chaining themselves to anything—at least not yet. Once the bulldozers arrive, then it might be a different matter…"

"So, what can we do?" Sandy said impatiently, glancing at her watch. "I have somewhere to be. Can we wrap this up?"

"The most important thing right now is press coverage," Sally said. "You need to raise awareness. Get the story out there. Involve the local press— with cameras there, you can have people waving placards and chanting. It can still be a fundraiser, but with a bit of anger and protest mixed in."

"I've already written to the papers," I told her. "No one was interested."

"Of course they weren't—who cares about a small village fundraiser? But we've got something that might actually grab their attention now."

"What?" I asked, genuinely puzzled.

"Nate," Sally said.

"I'm not sure I understand."

"A quick word to the press, telling them England's favourite anarchist is playing with us in the brass band…"

I hesitated. "I'm not sure Nate would thank us for that kind of publicity. He's trying to keep a low profile."

"Oh, come on! This is too good an opportunity to miss!"

"I'm sorry, but I'm not following," Gerald said, clearly confused. "Who's Nate, and what's he got to do with anything?"

"Well," Sandy started, ready to share some gossip, "he was born in Bramwick but left to get famous with a punk band. I've read some dreadful stories about him—drunken brawls, drugs, vandalism. There was a riot at one of his shows once, and the place was trashed."

I rolled my eyes. I wondered where Sandy had been getting her information.

"I don't think we'd want our venture associated with someone like that, to be honest," Sandy concluded. Alex and Gerald exchanged surprised looks.

"Maybe it wouldn't be the best idea," Alex said uneasily.

"Placards and banners, yes. You know, like 'Hands off our park,' that sort of thing," Gerald added.

"And a catchy chant, like 'Mitchell Homes, go home! We don't want your new homes!'" Alex suggested.

Sally looked appalled. "Just as well there *won't* be any press there, if that's the best you can come up with…"

"I think banners and chanting are a good idea," Sandy chimed in. "It would give the protest a feel without too much disruption. It's still a family day, after all."

"And what's the point of banners and chanting if the only people who see it are people from Bramwick?" Sally said, sounding exasperated.

"I'm tending to agree with the others," I said reluctantly. "I know it would be great to use Nate as leverage, but he's doing us a favour by playing. He's going through a tough time—just lost his dad, his girlfriend, and his band. The last thing he'd want is to lose his reputation too by having the whole country hear about him playing in a brass band."

Sally let out a long sigh. "Fine, but can we at least come up with a better chant?"

That evening, I attended a recruitment event in Merrygill. I dressed in a smart black dress and jacket, smoothing my hair into a neat bun. I knew how Nate must have felt in that band blazer—like an imposter. I could fit in most situations, talking to recruiters and mingling with candidates, but all the while, I felt like I was pretending to be someone else.

The conference hall was filled with banners about career opportunities with the Greenhill Leisure Group. A brochure showed a perfect-looking group of young people, grinning and embracing each other in uniforms. I didn't want that—a new "family" of grinning drones in white shirts. I already had a family—by blood and in the band. Why would I need another?

The evening was as dull as I expected, and I had to force myself not to walk out when the CEO gave a cringe-worthy speech about customer service and finding the "right people." I was definitely not the "right person," but I worried my smiling and nodding would give them the wrong impression. At the end of the night, we were told any eligible candidates would be contacted for interviews by the end of the week. I just hoped I'd never hear from them again.

Alan, however, seemed in a better mood when I got home. He took a genuine interest in hearing about my evening.

"You look great," he said. "You should wear stuff like that more often. It really suits you."

I thanked him, but his comment made me uncomfortable. Was this really what he wanted? A wife who wore dress suits, too much makeup, and spent her days with corporate drones? It was a depressing thought, but at least he was being nice. Maybe it was time to embrace a new version of myself. Perhaps this was what my marriage needed—a shift away from failed ventures and towards something else.

Chapter Seventeen

Nate

Sunny days were rare in Bramwick, but the day of the fundraiser dawned crisp and bright. As the morning wore on, the air turned warm and pleasant. I had worked hard all week on the pieces, meeting up with Fred to tackle the tricky bits I'd been struggling with. It had been enjoyable too. I wasn't perfect, but I had started to regain some confidence, believing I might just pull it off. But as I got dressed, a knot of nervousness formed in my stomach. The green blazer and tie made me feel ridiculous, draining away the self-belief I'd built over the past week. I'd never realised how much my clothes affected my confidence. Stripped of my usual attire, I felt exposed and uncomfortable.

"I'm going to completely humiliate myself," I muttered as I packed my trombone into its case. "I can barely play, and I look like an idiot."

At least this was Bramwick, so there wouldn't be many people around to witness my disaster.

When I arrived at The Grange, I saw several marquees set up with stalls selling local crafts and food. A few unenthusiastic protestors waved placards reading things like 'No to Mitchell Homes' and 'Preserve our Heritage.' Sally, in her band blazer, was standing next to them, trying to stir them up.

"Honestly," she said as I approached, "there's more life in a funeral home. Have you ever seen a more pathetic protest?"

She was right. It was pretty dismal.

"Let's see if we can wake them up," she grinned, pulling a megaphone out of a Tesco carrier bag. "Come on, people! Let's hear you!" she urged, and at the sound of her amplified voice, an elderly man winced and covered his ears. Sally waved her arms as she began to shout, "No to Mitchell Homes! No to Mitchell Homes!"

I watched as the small group of protestors half-heartedly waved their placards and joined in with the chant. I looked around the grounds and realised there were far more people than I had expected. There were even a few unfamiliar faces, people who didn't look like typical Bramwick residents. In the distance, I spotted someone from the local paper, camera in hand.

I turned back to Sally, who was still trying to rally the protestors. Her shouting grew more urgent as the photographer headed her way.

"Give me that," I said, grabbing the megaphone from her. It was painful to watch. I raised it to my lips. "Come on, Bramwick! Danny Henshaw and his cronies are breathing down your neck, and this is the best you can do?"

A couple of protestors glanced around in confusion, but soon they started waving their placards with more enthusiasm. I continued, my voice rising:" Let's make so much noise that the fat cats at Mitchell Homes hear us all the way in their head office! After me: Parks for people, out with greed, hands off The Grange, it's what we need!"

To my surprise, they began to chant along with me, the crowd growing as the noise swelled. The sun beat down on us, and the voices filled the air. I spotted Alan standing in the distance, watching the scene with contempt, a bottle of beer in hand. I stopped chanting, but the crowd continued, raising their voices in full force.

"Here, they're all yours," I said, handing the megaphone back to Sally, who gave me a grateful smile.

I hurried toward the gazebo where the rest of the band was setting up, still puzzled by the unexpected numbers.

"Decent turnout, eh?" Fred remarked. "Word must be getting around."

"Yeah," I said, eyeing the crowd suspiciously. Some of the faces didn't look like they belonged in Bramwick. A few looked like they had come straight from a Listed MIA gig.

"Rosie," Fred called, "can you go get Sally? She's getting carried away, and we need to warm up."

"Where did all these people come from?" I asked George as I set up my music stand.

"No idea, mate. Maybe they saw our plight on Facebook and wanted to help."

It didn't seem likely. As George trailed off, I saw Rosie and Sally returning to the gazebo, both smiling widely. Then Simon approached, handing me his phone.

"You might want to brace yourself. Someone's been talking to the press."

I took the phone, and my eyes fell on the headline: "Punk Star Nate 'Nasher 'Newell Turns to Brass: Fundraiser to Rock Village Park." Below was a photo of me from a Listed MIA gig, holding my guitar and screaming into the mic. The caption read, "Can the rebellious rocker save Bramwick's beloved Grange—and its band?"

"Who did this?" I demanded, waving Simon's phone around.

"Who cares?" Simon grinned. "People actually showed up!"

"Yeah, to gawk at me like it's some kind of freak show."

"Well, if we've got a star in the band, we might as well make the most of it," Sally shrugged as she followed Rosie into the gazebo, clearly pleased with herself.

"You!" I growled at her, taking a step toward her. "I didn't sign up to be your poster boy."

"Ooh, you're so punk rock!" she teased.

"Hey, hey! Enough!" Fred shouted, and Sally retreated. I sat down next to George, seething.

I noticed a couple of teenagers awkwardly trying to get a selfie with me in the background. I pulled my blazer tighter around me, wishing I could disappear.

"This is going to be the end of my career—right here, in a field in Bramwick."

As I picked up my trombone and began warming up, I heard the chant again: "Parks for people, not for greed, hands off our Grange, it's what we need!"

Once the warm-up was over, Rosie came over to me. "I'm sorry about Sally. She meant well."

"Oh, well, as long as she meant well…" But I felt my anger subsiding a little in Rosie's presence.

"Anyway, I just wanted to wish you good luck for your first performance. Most of these people are here because of you." She gave my shoulder a squeeze, and I immediately felt better.

The performance began, and it seemed to be going well. My nerves settled as I realised I could keep pace with George. As I got lost in the music, the worries faded—about the photographer, the kids taking selfies, and even Alan, who was lurking at the back, getting progressively drunk. It was miraculous. But as we launched into the final piece of the set, the commotion began.

"Oi, Nasher! Look at the state of you, all done up like a tin soldier or something."

The band faltered, exchanging nervous glances, but Fred urged us on. Alan was pushing his way through the crowd, scowling.

"The band must have gone mad, kicking me out and letting in the likes of you. You're only here because you're a celebrity—you can't even play!"

The music died, and the crowd murmured. Some pulled out their phones.

"Alan!" Rosie shouted, standing up and pushing her way to the front. "Stop it. You're embarrassing yourself."

"Oh, I'm embarrassing myself? What about you, running after him like he's some kind of hero? He's not going to save your precious Grange."

I lowered my trombone, my jaw clenched. "That's enough, Alan."

"Oh yeah? And what are you going to do about it?"

Alan took a few steps toward me, and for a moment, I thought I was going to lose control and take a swing at him. But Rosie stepped between us.

"Alan, go home," she said firmly, pointing toward the gates.

He hesitated but eventually turned, muttering under his breath.

"Well, folks," Fred said nervously, addressing the crowd. "It wouldn't be a village festival without a bit of local drama, would it? Let's start this again."

He counted us in, and we launched into the final piece, but the mood had been dampened.

Afterwards, I retreated behind the gazebo and lit a cigarette. I looked up. I was standing under Lady Henshaw's oak tree. Sally tried to apologise for the press stunt, but I was too frustrated to listen. It had all been too much: the photographer, the curious Listed MIA fans, Alan. I decided I was leaving. I didn't care if I had nowhere to stay—I'd rather sleep in the van than spend another second in Bramwick. I had loosened my tie and discarded my blazer somewhere.

In the background, the protestors had taken up their chant again, their voices renewed.

"Nate, I'm so sorry. He just... I didn't think he'd..." Rosie's voice broke through.

"You don't need to apologise for him," I muttered.

"He doesn't mean it. When he's had a few drinks, he says things he wouldn't normally."

"And I suppose getting drunk in the afternoon is normal for him?"

"He's having a tough time, Nate. It's just his way of coping."

"That makes it okay then?"

"He's not always like this..."

"Why do you put up with it, Rosie?" I snapped. "You deserve so much better."

The words hung between us. She looked down at her feet, embarrassed.

"It's not that simple," she said quietly, a tremble in her voice.

"I didn't mean..." I realised I'd crossed a line. "I just think you deserve better."

101

"He's alright really." She seemed to be talking to herself rather than me. "Thank you for today," she said, looking up again. She'd fought off the tears. "You know, for playing. You were great."

"I don't know if I can keep doing this," I admitted. "I'm not... I'm not the person they think I am."

"You were fantastic," she insisted, stepping closer. She held my gaze.

"I was all right," I said, taking another drag from my cigarette.

"Well, I think you were brilliant."

I didn't answer.

"I know Sally told the newspapers you were here," she said. "I did ask her not to, but I'm actually glad she did. It could make all the difference. *You* could make all the difference, if you really wanted to."

"Well, I think my career and reputation are ruined now," I replied. "Just wait until those photos of me looking like this get out—there'll be no going back."

"There'll come a point when you realise that image and reputation aren't as important as you think." She stepped closer, and I noticed the freckles still dotting her nose, faded since childhood but still there. "Besides, I think it suits you."

She reached out, fastened my buttons, and straightened my tie. Then she put her hands on my shoulders, rose on her toes, and kissed my cheek.

"Sorry!" she gasped, springing back and covering her mouth. "I have no idea why I did that."

She spun on her heels and hurried away.

"Rosie, wait!" I called, startled. But she didn't turn around.

I was still staring after her, my heart pounding, when Fred appeared.

"Ah, there you are," he said briskly. "A few people are looking for you out there, wanting autographs and photos, apparently."

"Right," I muttered. "You stall them, and I'll make a quick dash over that hedge."

Fred raised an eyebrow. "That hedge is full of thorns. Come on, surely you're not shy. This must happen all the time."

That was true. I'd always been accommodating to fans after shows, but today felt different. I wasn't Nasher Newell, the persona I used as a shield against the world.

A small crowd had gathered, snapping selfies and asking about Listed MIA. I smiled, signed a few autographs, but my mind kept drifting to Rosie and the kiss. It probably meant nothing, I told myself—just a friendly gesture, like something you'd do with your mum.

"Hi, I'm Michael Jones from the *Yorkshire Post*," a voice cut through my thoughts. A man with a camera shook my hand. "Would you mind telling me what someone like you is doing playing at a small-time village fundraiser?"

"I was born here. It just happened to be in the area and I was asked to help out."

"Great community spirit," he said. "I understand you were a bit of a rock star once."

I bristled. "I still am. This isn't permanent. I'm just here to sort out some family business, but I'll be back to making real music soon."

"Could I get a few photos with the trombone?"

"I don't think so," I said, starting to walk away, but Fred stopped me.

"Come on, lad, it's just for a local paper. It could help. Here, put your jacket back on."

Reluctantly, I tugged on my blazer.

"Let's get the band in the background," Michael said. Fred rounded them up.

"I got some great shots of the locals with their placards," Michael said as he adjusted us. "I'll write a good piece, to help your cause."

He positioned me at the front, telling me to look "menacing" and "give it some attitude." By the time he finished, I felt like a complete idiot. Meanwhile, the brass band seemed to be enjoying the attention. I kept searching for Rosie, but she had disappeared.

"Right, I've got an idea!" Fred bellowed after the photos were done. "Let's round up those folks with the placards and march to the pub. Make it look like a real protest!"

"Oh, I love that!" Michael agreed enthusiastically.

"Trombones to the front!" Fred ordered as he lined us up.

"Are you kidding?" I muttered. But I was quickly cajoled into formation, given a piece of music I'd never seen before, and a lyre to hold the music while marching. Behind us, the protestors with their placards lined up. As we started, the village seemed to follow us.

The band played 'Slaidburn', but I faked it—I had no idea how it went. The protesters took up their chant again, matching the rhythm of the march. Michael jogged ahead of us, snapping pictures.

It must have been quite a spectacle.

When we finally reached the pub, I decided I was going to get very drunk.

Chapter Eighteen

Rosie

The second time Alan used physical violence against me was the day of the fundraiser, and I swore it would be the last.

As I left The Grange that day, my mind raced. The memory of the kiss I had planted on Nate lingered, twisting my insides with guilt. I had no idea why I did it. There had been a sudden spark when my lips touched his cheek, a rush of warmth for that kid I had once been so besotted with. I had promised myself I was done with Nate all those years ago when I chose Alan. I had buried my feelings deep down and hadn't thought of him in years. But now Nate was back, and he was in the band, and the kiss, no matter how brief and innocent, had brought up something I wasn't ready to confront. The shame I felt as I rushed off was overwhelming because I was still drawn to Nate, and that truth felt like betrayal to Alan and our marriage. I had to find him.

I tried The Black Bull first and was surprised to find he wasn't there. I had expected he'd have ended up there in search of a pint and perhaps Tommy Deans so he could have someone to rant to. I started to grow frantic as I hurried home, hoping he had made his way back there. What if he was staggering about the streets somewhere causing even more trouble?

When I arrived, the front door was sitting wide open, which meant he was home, which was good. However, the sense of relief did not last long. As soon as I walked through the front door, I heard a loud crash coming from the sitting room. My heart started to race as I rushed in the direction of the noise and was confronted by a chaotic scene. I covered my mouth with my hands and let out a gasp. The living room was in disarray, and I stupidly wondered for a moment if there had been an intruder. There hadn't, of course. The coffee table was overturned, nicknacks were smashed, our wedding photo lay on the floor with a vicious crack in the glass. Alan was standing in the middle of the carnage with his back to me like some kind of hulking monster, but when he heard me enter, he turned slowly, a menacing look in his eyes. I was still holding my cornet case, so I set it down and tried to stay calm.

"Alan, love," I said, hoping to sound calm and reassuring. "It's okay, let's sit down and have a talk about it, yeah?"

His eyes narrowed and he gave me a look of pure disgust. I took a tentative step forward, as if approaching a dangerous wild animal. I paused, and when he didn't move, I took another careful step forward. Then another. My shoe crunched on a bit of broken porcelain and I looked down to see the remains of an owl figurine crushed into the carpet. I bit my lip and felt a stab of sorrow. Sally had given me that. It was just a daft little thing, but Alan knew there was sentimental importance attached to it. I took another cautious step, holding his gaze with my own. His eyes were bloodshot. I could hear his breathing, heavy and menacing through flared nostrils. I was close to him now and I reached out, my hand trembling, and tried to lay a reassuring touch on his shoulder while forcing a little smile to my lips.

"It's okay." It was the same voice I had been known to use with the cows if one of them was distressed and I was trying not to startle it. "I'm sorry about what happened at the fundraiser. I think sometimes I forget how hard this whole thing is on you."

I could feel his heavy breathing as his shoulders rose and fell under my hand. He didn't say anything. He knocked my hand away.

"This has to stop, Rosie."

"I know," I said, barely disguising the tremble in my voice. "I'll stop going to band. You're right, it's not fair on you."

I hoped this might be enough to bring him back down. If I could show him I was on his side…

It didn't work. Alan lashed out at me and caught me in the face. The blow sent me sprawling back on the floor. I landed heavily and my left wrist twisted as I put my hands out to break my fall. For a moment I felt dazed. I just sat there. When I looked up at Alan I thought he looked as shocked as I felt. I felt pain shooting up my arm from my wrist and my face was burning where he had caught me. I started to cry.

For a heartbeat I thought Alan was going to crouch down and comfort me. Surely the shock on his face would lead to remorse. But then the look of disgust returned and I felt my breath catch in the back of my throat. I was starting to hyperventilate.

"Stop fucking crying," he said. I pushed myself backwards. My injured wrist screamed as I leant on it. My back hit the sofa and I cowered against it. "You're pathetic, you know that?"

"Alan, listen to me," I pleaded. "I said I'll quit the band. What else do you want me to do? Just tell me?"

I hated that I was grovelling like this but I was in survival mode. One wrong word could land me another blow.

"It's not just about the band," Alan seethed. "It's him. I saw the way he was looking at you."

"So let him look, I love *you*, you know that."

"And you," he continued. He was pacing back and forth now. "Just like when we were teenagers. Trailing after him like a misty eyed schoolgirl."

"I won't have to see him anymore if I don't go to band." I got to my feet, shaking and starting to feel dizzy. If I could only say the right thing he might calm down.

He looked at me. His breathing was slowing now and he had stopped pacing.

"It's going to be alright," I said.

He took a step towards me and raised his hand. I flinched as he reached out for me. His fingers brushed my cheek and his touch was gentle. But his eyes were like cold, hard flints.

"Rosie my love." His words were dripping with danger. Every muscle in my body was tense. "I'm going to make sure you don't go back to that band."

His hand fell to his side and for a moment I wondered what he meant to do. Did he mean to hurt me so badly I'd never play again, like old Pete Newell? But he turned and made for the door. When I saw what he was heading for, I dashed after him, grabbing his arm. I immediately cried out as pain seared in my wrist. He turned and struck me hard across the face again, sending me stumbling back. He grabbed my cornet bag from beside the door, snapping the catches open and taking the instrument roughly in his hands. I felt a trickle of blood run from my nose. The cornet was a flash of silver in his hand, light reflecting and casting patterns on the ceiling before he hurled it at the stone fireplace. It soared across the room and collided with the hard surface, sending a metallic ringing sound through the air. I lurched towards it, but he got there before me, and he brought his boot down heavily on it. Then he did it again. And again. My heart broke as I watched the metal crumple, folding in on itself and splitting at the newly formed corners. My beautiful cornet. My pride and joy; a gift from Mum and Dad on my twenty-first birthday. Now it lay among the stray ash and soot in the hearth, crumpled beyond repair. All the concerts we had played at together, the rehearsals we had shared. That instrument had seen me through some of the happiest times of my life, comforted me when I was down, lifted me to dizzying and joyful heights with its beautiful sound. I knew then that that was the end for me and Alan.

Chapter Nineteen

Nate

In the pub, the drink flowed as one pint turned into two, then three, until I eventually lost count. Many of the band members soon started to look quite tipsy. Sally had come over and apologised profusely for her stunt involving the press. She had taken off her shirt now to reveal that under it she was wearing a T-shirt with the slogan 'eat the rich 'emblazoned across it. Although she said she was sorry, her tone suggested she was anything but. However, I was feeling the effects of the drink and enjoying the camaraderie, so I was willing to forgive her.

One person was missing though, and that concerned me. She had taken off after kissing me, and I hadn't seen her since. When I asked Simon, he looked at me with a worried frown and said he hadn't seen her either.

"I suppose she must have gone to check on Alan," I mused. "That was some performance he put on back there, wasn't it?"

"It was." Simon's frown had deepened now, and he cast his eyes around the room, finally settling on Sally and calling her over.

"I think someone should go and check on Rosie," he said to her quietly. "No one's seen her since the concert finished, and, well, you saw how Alan was..."

"Shit." Sally put her gin and tonic down on the table, sloshing the contents over the sides. "Shit! What a crappy friend I am! Too caught up in marching and chanting and drinking."

I watched as she pulled her blazer on.

"I think I should go with you," Simon said, an anxious expression on his face.

"Can someone tell me what's going on?" I asked. "She's probably staying away because she's embarrassed."

And not just by Alan's behaviour...

"Why? She's got nothing to be embarrassed about."

I wanted to ease their minds and tell them she was probably just avoiding me. I was the reason she had left, not Alan.

"We should make sure." Simon was also putting his jacket on.

"Why do you both look so worried?" I was puzzled. A couple of the others hadn't joined us in the pub either but no one was sending out a search party for them.

Simon paused, looking conflicted. Sally had gone to retrieve her bag, and he glanced quickly from her to me before he leaned in and said quietly, "Sometimes he loses his temper; we just need to know she's ok."

"What, he hits her?" I exclaimed incredulously, and Simon tried to shush me, but it was too late. Sally was on her way over and had heard my loud outburst.

"Great, so now he knows. Nice work, Simon."

Simon went red.

"I'm coming too," I said.

"Are you crazy?" Sally looked at me like I had gone mad. "Can you imagine how much worse it would make things if you showed up?"

I considered this. I felt a sudden surge of protectiveness towards her, and I wanted to rush out with them and—if need be—batter Alan. But what if all of this was my fault? It made me feel sick to think Rosie might have been hurt because of me.

"Can you let me know if she's okay then?" I looked helplessly at Simon.

"Yeah, mate," he nodded. "Don't worry though, I'm sure she's fine. Just have another drink, enjoy the night. We'll be back soon, I'm sure."

But it was difficult to enjoy the night after that. The drink continued to flow, and I did my best to join in as the band members laughed and joked together, high on the energy of the day. But the more time that passed without the return of Simon and Sally, the more anxious I grew. I kept checking my phone to see if Simon had been in touch, but an hour passed, and there had been nothing. People kept handing me drinks, patting me on the back, and telling me what a great success the day had been.

Eventually, Simon reappeared, without Sally. I excused myself from Brendan and George, who had been telling me a story about the time the band had a drink fuelled outing to Saddleworth back in the days when they were still at full strength. I hurried over to Simon, trying to read his expression.

"Is everything okay?" I asked.

"Yeah, we found her. She's going to stay with Sally tonight. She didn't fancy coming to the pub, so they've gone home with a bottle of wine."

"She's alright though?"

"She will be," Simon said. "Don't worry, Sally'll look after her."

I tried to press Simon for more details, but he fobbed me off and assured me there was nothing I should be concerned about. He went to the bar and came back with shots for me, Brendan, and himself.

Soon, Simon appeared to be back in the swing of things, looking a lot happier and enjoying the atmosphere. This made me relax a little. They had just had an argument, that was all. If anything terrible had happened Simon wouldn't be here enjoying himself. As I began to let my guard down, I realised that I was starting to really like the members of Bramwick Brass. They were a good bunch.

"Now then." Fred, as sober as ever, tapped on his glass to get everyone's attention. The noise died down, and everyone turned to look at him. "I've finished tallying up the donations from today. Between the buckets and the QR codes for cashless donations our performance today raised an incredible two thousand pounds."

A cheer went up from the assembled band members.

"This is, of course, all going to be given to the campaign to save The Grange. I want to point out that this is just the money we as a band took in. I don't know yet how much the WI, the bake sale, and the other groups managed to raise. You can all be proud of yourselves though, because it's a lot more than we anticipated."

"Yeah, and I think we all know who we can thank for how well attended the day was!" Simon cut in, looking at me.

"Yeah: Sally!" I shouted back, and there was a rumble of laughter and cheers.

As I listened, the seeds of an idea that had been planted in my head the previous week were making their way back to the surface.

"I'm sure if the lovely Rosie were here, though, she'd tell us it's still not enough." Fred set his jaw and looked determined. "Despite all our efforts, we're still far from where we need to be, and time is running out. But Bramwick Brass is part of this village's history, and The Grange is part of our history, and we'll keep fighting until there's nothing left to fight for."

There was another round of hearty cheers and applause.

I thought of Rosie, back at Sally's. She should be here, celebrating the success, not drowning her sorrow with Sally.

"Oh look, the rock star has something to say," Brendan shouted as the attention shifted away from Fred and onto me.

I had stood up on a chair and was waving my hands for quiet. The Grange and this campaign were important to Rosie. If I had contributed in any way to her troubles then I wanted to make it up to her. I wanted to give her something to smile about when I next saw her—and I thought I knew how.

"Come on then, Jonny Rotten, let's hear you!" It wasn't said in a mocking way—it was just friendly banter.

Now that they were all looking at me, I felt stupid standing on the chair, so I stepped down before I spoke.

"Right, I'm not very good at making speeches," I began. "But I've got an idea. It might sound a bit mad at first, but hear me out. It's like Fred was saying: events like today are great, but even with me and our friends from the newspaper, they aren't going to be enough to save you or The Grange. You need something big, you need to think outside the box…"

They looked at me expectantly, and I continued.

"Last week, I wrote a new song. It was you lot who inspired me, so I've been thinking, well…you're going to release a single."

There was silence for a moment before someone at the back laughed, and a few murmurs started to rise as they shot confused glances at one another.

"Who's releasing a single now?" asked a bemused George.

"Just hear me out! With my contacts in the music industry I think I can help you do it."

Fred looked at me skeptically. "Five minutes back in the band, and you already think you can arrange brass music?"

"Ah, no, because this is going to be different. What I'm thinking about is a collaboration between you guys, me, and hopefully some of Listed MIA."

I tried to explain. In truth, I hadn't really thought it through properly, and I certainly hadn't spoken to Maxwell or the others. I pictured Rosie's face when she found out. This could be a way for them to make some serious money.

"If you're up for it, I think we have the potential to do something special, and raise the funds you need to save The Grange."

They were paying attention now. So was the rest of the pub.

"But for it to work you need to trust me and embrace the fusion between brass and punk."

For a moment, it looked as if they were struggling to process what I had said, and there was a short silence and a few raised eyebrows. Then Simon shouted from the back of the room, "I think it's a bloody brilliant idea!"

There was a chorus of agreement and the sound of many glasses being clicked together, and I grinned at them.

"Let's hear it then," George demanded. "This song that you say you wrote."

"What? Now?"

"Aye," Fred agreed. "Let's be having it."

"No, this really isn't the place, I don't have any of my gear…"

"Hang on!" Simon called over his shoulder as he dashed across the room and retrieved an old guitar that was hanging on the wall near the bar. By now, the whole place was looking at us, and half the village seemed to be in the pub that night.

"Here we go." Simon handed me the guitar.

I took the battered old instrument from him and tried my best to give it a brief tune. It was an old nylon-stringed number, hardly ideal for a punk song, but they were all egging me on now, and I was drunk. I strummed the guitar a few times and winced. It sounded tired and ready to pack in. I looked at them all, took a deep breath, and launched myself into it.

"We march in step, but we're out of line,
Might have our roots, but these are different times,
Tunings sharp, and our temper's hot,
Every note a war, and we've fired the first shot.

From the past, we're breaking free,
From the chains of our history,
Play it loud and make it last,
Our legacy in blood and brass.

This isn't just music but a call to arms,
If you're brave, stand up and address all the harms,
We're not just players in a dusty hall,
We're rebels who scream with a brassy call.

No more marches for kings and wars,
No more pride in colonial scores,
This is a sound for the people of today,
Using our horns in a different way.

Rip up the score and start something true,
Music should be for the many and not just for the few,
Re-write the march and break new ground,
Voices rising with a whole different sound."

I might have got a bit carried away; the performance was perhaps a little too enthusiastic for a village pub. Poor old Mrs Thornton's guitar had probably never been battered like that before. Soon almost everyone was caught up in it, and they were even singing along to the chorus by the end. When I finished, they gave me a huge round of applause and cheers, and I stood there grinning.

"Well," said Fred nervously, tugging at his collar. "We might need to change a few words…"

"No." I set the guitar down and shook my head firmly. "Nobody changes the words."

"But they basically just crap all over the whole tradition of brass bands," Brendan said, sounding a little annoyed.

"No, they don't." Simon pushed his way to the front and stood by my side. "He's saying it's all well and good having traditions and roots, but sometimes you have to try something new. If we stop being so stuck in our ways, we might actually do something that gets people's attention."

Fred looked doubtful, but now George was nodding in agreement. Brendan still looked a bit miffed.

"I suppose the traditional way to settle this would be with a vote," Fred said, looking around at them. "Hands up all those in favour of giving Nate's idea a go, questionable lyrics and all…"

I watched as hands began to shoot in the air, and Fred started to count them. "Fifteen if you count me too, hardly a landslide but a decent majority."

"Nice one, mate." Simon slapped me on the back before he started to sing the chorus in a drunken, off-key voice.

Simon and I were among the last to leave The Black Bull that night, and we walked down the dark road together, swaying slightly, laughing and carrying on like we were two fifteen-year-olds again.

"I wish Rosie and Sally could have been there to hear that song. They would have loved that, especially Sally."

That brought the tone back down to a more serious level, and we stopped laughing.

"Is she really okay?" I pressed.

"No, not especially." The drink seemed to have loosened Simon's tongue. "I hope she doesn't go back to him this time."

"He hurt her again, didn't he?"

"Yeah," Simon confirmed.

My guts lurched. My head was already spinning and I was hit by a wave of nausea.

"It took us ages to find her," Simon went on. I pursed my lips as I felt the bile rise. "She wasn't at the house when we got there. There was just an open front door, and Alan passed out in the living room. We couldn't get an awful lot of sense out of him."

"That bastard," I said through gritted teeth.

"The living room was a bit of a mess—smashed ornaments and stuff." Simon swayed slightly as he walked. "But when we saw her cornet lying on the floor…"

Simon shuddered visibly and he stopped walking and put a hand on a lamppost to steady himself. He looked sicker than I felt.

"God, I wish I hadn't had that last pint." He swallowed hard and hung his head.

"What about the cornet, Simon?" I was starting to sober up as a cold dread crept up my spine.

"It was like finding a body at a crime scene or something." Simon shook his head. "I couldn't stop staring at it, lying there all silent and twisted."

"How bad is it?" I could feel my heart starting to race. If he had done that to her cornet what had he done to her?

I couldn't believe I had let the pair of them go alone. I had been drinking myself stupid and getting carried away playing music when I should have been beating the living shit out of Alan.

"I mean, she's not great." Simon straightened up. He started walking again and I followed. "She's got a busted lip and a sprained wrist, but she didn't need a doctor or anything."

I was starting to shake now.

"We found her sitting under the oak tree." Simon slurred his words as he explained.

That had always been her special place. Where she used to go to think.

"I'm going to kill Alan," I raged. There was a bin out in the street and I kicked it violently, imagining it was Alan's head. It clattered to its side and spilled its contents onto the path. Somewhere in the distance a dog howled.

"Honestly, it would be better if you just stayed out of it," Simon urged. "Rosie's strong. I really think she'll do the right thing this time. She promised us that was the end of it."

"That's something, I suppose." But my anger was still bubbling. "Did you call the police?"

"She didn't want them involved."

"But why isn't she pressing charges?"

"It's not always that simple, mate."

We walked in a sombre silence for a time before Simon said, "You're doing this for her, aren't you?"

"What? No, it's for all of you."

"But mostly for her." It wasn't a question this time. "Bloody good tune though, mate."

I glanced at Simon, and he started whistling the chorus.

113

"Yeah." I couldn't help but smile. "It's going places that one. I have that feeling."

And suddenly it became even more important that I found a way to make it work.

Chapter Twenty

Rosie

I hurried down the garden path in a panic, blinded by tears. That was it. I couldn't stay after that. Nothing he could do or say would make up for the pain in my wrist, my swollen lip, and the ruined cornet. He had always been abusive. I had lied to myself for years. I had told myself things could be worse, that the good made up for the bad— but it didn't. His toxic moods had trapped me. I forgave him every time he turned on the charm and told me he was sorry. Well, not any more.

"Stupid, that's what I am, stupid!" I cursed myself as I yanked the garden gate open.

As I fled down the street, I could hear him calling after me, and I glanced back to see him stumble out of the front door.

"Rosie, come back, I didn't mean it! I'm sorry, Rosie!"

I paused and turned around, striding back towards the house. My tears were subsiding now and giving way to anger.

"Rosie," he tried to smile as I approached him. He looked utterly broken. "I'm sorry. It'll never happen again. Just come back inside, we can talk."

"No, Alan."

He threw himself to his knees and grabbed my leg, sobbing like a small child.

"Rosie, I love you, I can't live without you."

"It's over, Alan. I'm going, do you hear me?" I shook my leg hard, and he fell away. "I am never coming back."

"But I need you," he snivelled. Karen Granger from next door was at her window now. She twitched the curtain but quickly retreated when I gave her a look.

"I don't care, Alan," I said in a low voice as I stepped away from him. "You can't keep doing this to me."

"I can't live without you, Rosie," he snorted as I started to walk away again.

"You'll learn."

"I'll kill myself." His voice now sounded angry and desperate. When I glanced back, he was on his feet again. "I mean it, Rosie. I'll do it. Then what'll happen? Could you live with that on your conscience?"

I faltered. Was he serious? No, it was just another of his manipulation tactics. He'd made similar threats before. He drove off after one argument, telling me he was going to crash the car into a wall. I'd called Sally, and she'd driven me around looking for him. I'd been frantic with worry. We'd found him at Tommy Deans' house, playing computer games like nothing had happened.

"It's your choice. I can live with it." I started to walk again.

As I made my way down the street, I expected him to try and follow me, but he didn't. I could hear him still wailing about my conscience and how he really meant to do it. I didn't believe him.

When I got to The Grange, everyone had gone, and the marquees and stands had been packed away. It looked beautiful in the late sunshine, with the leaves on the trees beginning to turn a golden hue and the gorgeous backdrop of the Dales. It was quiet and peaceful as I made my way across the field, past the orchard and the vegetable garden, to Philomena Henshaw's oak. I sat down on the grass and rested against the tree's broad trunk. It had always been a place that felt safe. I'd often gone there to sit and eat my lunch when I was at school. When Alan and Tommy's bullying had been especially bad, this tree had been a sort of sanctuary. I would sit there under the protection of its welcoming arms and feel connected to the earth via its deep roots. I would think of Lady Henshaw, and of how much Lord Henshaw must have loved her, and hope that one day someone would love me that much. Sometimes I talked to her. At primary school, we had been taught all about Lord Henshaw's philanthropism, but in high school, a favourite history teacher of mine told us about his wife. She was often overlooked in the records, but she was a huge driving force behind educational reform for girls in Bramwick. After that, she became a figure I admired in an almost spiritual way.

Sometimes Nate and Simon would join me. The place was not spiritual for them— they liked to use the tree as a climbing frame. They would haul themselves up through the branches and sit like monkeys with their legs dangling. I was always happy to remain on the ground where I could feel the grass and my connection to nature.

And so it seemed the natural place to retreat to that day. There I was once again fleeing Alan's tyranny and seeking protection and guidance from my old friend with her wizened bark and whispering leaves. Some of last year's May Day ribbons still clung to the branches. People said that the wish would only come true once the fabric had rotted away. Nature's Bounty provided the ribbons; they were made from biodegradable materials so they wouldn't harm the environment. They were guaranteed to eventually disintegrate, ensuring all wishes would be granted. Some just took longer than others.

I don't know how long I sat there, alone with my thoughts, but my mind was much calmer by the time the light started to slip from the sky and the first stars appeared. I stood up and took the ribbon that was tied in my hair and fastened it to one of the low-hanging branches. Wishes weren't just for May Day.

"If you can hear me, Philomena," I addressed the late Lady Henshaw, as I always did, by her first name," help me stay strong, don't let me go back to Alan. Let me take on the farm, make a success of it, and save The Grange, all on my own, because I am enough just as I am."

"Look, told you she'd be here!" I turned to see the outlines of two people coming towards me. It was Simon and Sally. "She always comes to the tree when things get bad."

I waited awkwardly as they approached, my swollen face and wrist throbbing.

"Oh my God, Rosie!" Simon exclaimed when he saw me, and I reached up to touch my lip. "That absolute bastard! Wait until I see him!"

"Oh, love!" Sally put her arms around me.

"It's okay," I said as I pulled away from her, and I even managed a smile. "I'm alright."

"No, you're not!" Simon said indignantly. "Don't lie."

"No, maybe not, but I will be."

"This can't go on," Sally said kindly.

"I know." I took a deep breath. "Don't worry, it's over. I won't be going back. I won't be defending him anymore. You're right, he's a bastard, and he doesn't deserve me."

"You can say that again!" Simon looked absolutely furious.

"All the others are asking after you," Sally said. "They'll still be at the pub if you want a drink?"

I shook my head. "I don't think I want to face them just now."

"Nate wanted to come, but we had to stop him," Simon told me. "We didn't think it was a good idea."

I thought back to the kiss again and my cheeks coloured.

" He seemed genuinely concerned about you, though."

"Can I stay with you tonight, Sally?" I couldn't think about Nate. "I don't think I can face Mum and Dad quite yet either."

"You know you can," Sally said, and the three of us started walking.

"I can go and let myself in if you give me a key," I offered. "You get back to the celebrations."

"Not at all," said Sally. "I'm not leaving you. God, that's just made me even more bloody angry. You deserve to be there celebrating with us and he's ruined this day for you too."

"It's alright," I said. "Some other time."

Sally linked her arm with mine as we walked.

"That was quite something today though, wasn't it?" I said.

"You didn't even see the march, did you?" Simon exclaimed.

"What march?"

"Everyone sort of marched to the pub," Sally explained. "There were placards waving and chanting. That man from the paper was taking a lot of pictures, so I expect you'll see them tomorrow. It was pretty good for Bramwick!"

"Good work," I said with satisfaction. "And honestly, I'm glad you didn't listen to me. I'm glad you went to the press. Nate owes me and Simon, so he'll just have to suck it up, won't he?"

"You know, I think we might just be in with a fighting chance now, don't you?" Sally rubbed my arm and smiled.

"I think you're right. I just feel it. Something's shifted."

We had come to the main street now, and we paused. "Are you sure you don't want to go to the pub?"

"I'm sure."

"Alright then," said Simon. "I'm heading back in, so I'll leave you two to it. I promised Nate I'd let him know you were okay. Don't worry, I won't tell him what happened."

"It's fine, Simon," I was actually quite touched that Nate cared. "Everyone will know soon enough, so you might as well just be honest."

"If you're sure…"

"I am," I said with a firm nod. "I dunno, I know he's been gone for ages, but don't you think he still feels like an old friend? It's like no time at all has passed…"

"You know, I sort of know what you mean," Simon agreed. "It's a Bramwick thing; I think we share a connection that never really goes away."

It wasn't the kind of thing I'd expect Simon to say, and I suspected he had had a few before he and Sally came to look for me.

"Hey, where does that leave me?" Sally said indignantly.

"Oh, you're honorary Bramwick now, Sally," Simon told her. "You're not like those other blow-ins; you've made yourself one of us."

"Well, that's good to know. You enjoy the rest of the night, Simon," Sally said.

"It feels a bit wrong now, to be going back in and celebrating." Simon rubbed the back of his neck.

"Go," I said, patting his arm.

"If you're sure…"

"You heard her, leave us girls to have a good old chat."

118

"I'll see you both soon though, yeah? And if you need anything just give me a shout. I'm here for you Rosie, remember that."

I thought my heart might burst as I watched him go back into the pub.

"Come on," Sally said. "Let's get you up the road. A good night's rest at Sally's and you'll feel much better. It'll all work out."

I wished I could believe her. But my world had been turned upside down and things were never going to be the same again.

Chapter Twenty-One

Nate

When I woke the next morning, I had a hell of a hangover. My head was splitting, and my mouth was so dry I felt like I had just trekked across the desert. I peeled my cheek from the pillow and scrabbled around on the floor for my phone. I found it lying among my clumsily discarded band uniform, and it was almost out of battery. There were a number of notifications blinking at me, and I sat up, squinting at the screen.

First, there was a message from Maxwell, who had sent a link to an article with the headline 'Brass Punk Revolution 'with a very unflattering photo of me standing in front of the band holding the trombone, a scowl on my face. Maxwell's accompanying message read 'What the actual fuck, mate? I'm seriously worried about you.'

The next message was from Fred reminding me we had agreed to meet later to' have a look at this song of yours.'

There was also a message from Freya, and my heart lurched when I saw her name. My excitement died when I found that her message was even more unkind than Maxwell's. She called me an embarrassment. I hastily deleted it and hit the block button.

A few more people from London had decided it was a good idea to reach out to poke fun at me, and I had been tagged in what seemed like an endless stream of social media posts. It seemed that, thanks to Sally, the whole of the country had seen me looking like an idiot.

All of this was infuriating but it all paled in comparison when I recalled Simon's account of finding Rosie. I started to feel sick and cold again. I wanted to know how she was doing, wanted her to know I was thinking of her. I had started to type out a Facebook message to her telling her I was there if she needed to talk, but I swiftly deleted it. Simon had warned me not to get involved. She seemed to have a strong network of support in the band, she didn't need me.

I wanted to just stay in bed and rot, but unfortunately, there were a couple of house viewings booked in that morning. I stormed about, muttering to myself, trying to straighten the place up as best I could. I didn't hold out much hope for a sale from either of that morning's visitors. The middle-aged woman with her daughter poked about and complained about how much work needed doing as if she hadn't even read the listing. The couple with the toddler seemed too preoccupied with trying to wrangle their wayward child to actually pay any attention to what they were looking at.

I couldn't stop thinking of Rosie. Twice I found myself typing out messages to her and deleting them.

Eventually I left my phone at home and wandered around to the local shop where I had a glance through the *Yorkshire Post*. Sure enough, there was a full-page article about the previous day's events. Unlike some of the things that had been sent to me via social media, this article appeared to be fairly well written, and the lead picture was of the march down to the pub. Although you could see me in that picture, and others, and I was mentioned quite extensively in the text, the piece somehow seemed more measured. It did a good job at shining a light on the plight of The Grange rather than just trying to sensationalise the fact that there was a 'rock star 'there playing trombone. I was sure Rosie and the band would be happy with such a heartfelt article. I hadn't bought a newspaper in years, but I did that day.

Back at the house, I found myself clipping out the article, and I stuck it on the wall above the fireplace next to Mum and Dad's wedding picture.

"There we go," I said to my old man. "You've a real reason to be proud of me now. Look at your son using his fame to help the village; bet you'd be absolutely made up. Shame it took you dying for this to happen."

When it was time to meet Fred, I set off in the van feeling quite excited about the proposed project. Simon was waiting with Fred at the door when I arrived, and he helped me carry in the gear I had brought, which consisted of my electric guitar, a small amp and PA, and a microphone.

"I hope you don't mind," Simon said as we hauled the equipment into the band room. "I've been dying to have a proper listen to the song. I haven't been able to stop singing it."

I smiled.

"Plus, I thought you might need some moral support with old Mr Black. You know what he's like. He can be a bit stuck in his ways."

"Hey, I heard that!" Fred called from behind us.

"That really was some fantastic press for the village," Simon commented. "Have you seen it? It's everywhere."

"Tell me about it," I grumbled. "Hey, have you heard from Rosie?"

"Yeah, I went round to see her this morning. She seemed much better, looking forwards not back, I think."

"Typical Rosie."

"Told you she was strong."

In the rehearsal room, I set up my equipment, and as I plugged the guitar into the amp, it gave a satisfying buzz. "Back in the comfort zone," I said, smiling happily.

"Well, don't get *too* comfortable," Fred warned. "We may still need your other talents."

I pulled the guitar strap over my shoulder and adjusted the mic stand. Simon and Fred moved towards the back of the room and stood looking at me expectantly, arms folded. When I didn't do anything, Simon gave me the thumbs up.

"Alright, Nathan, let's hear it," Fred prompted.

"Ok, but you have to imagine how it'll sound with a full band. You won't get the full impact with just me and no bass or drums."

"I can give you a beat if you want?" Simon offered.

"Ok, just a simple four-four."

Simon positioned himself behind the drum kit, and I asked him to count me in. It felt strange performing a solo piece to my old music teacher and best friend from school, but I soon became so lost in the music that I forgot they were even there. I had been eager to get plugged in and hear how the song might sound at full volume, but I hadn't dared do it at the house for fear of disturbing the neighbours.

It did not disappoint. As I belted out the words and strummed the chords loud and fast, I again felt that tug in the pit of my stomach that told me I was onto something special. When I was done, Simon cupped his hands around his mouth and let out a loud whoop. Fred stood quite still, looking thoughtful, a small frown furrowing his brow.

"Brilliant, just brilliant," Simon said as he came towards me, clapping enthusiastically.

"What did you think?" I nodded at Fred.

"It's not what we're used to…but it has potential."

"Good old Mr Black, as enthusiastic as ever." Simon rolled his eyes.

"No, no, I think it can be done. I can hear something in that middle section just after the bridge in particular. We'll add some bits and pieces here and there, but I think that part is where the big brass number could come in. If I can get a recording of it, I can come home and work on something."

"That's not quite how it works," I said. "It needs to be more organic than that. Simon, have you got your cornet?"

"Of course I do." Simon darted enthusiastically across the room and grabbed his bag.

"Mr Black, err, Fred, sorry, you'll need an instrument too."

"Why? What are we going to do? We don't have any music yet."

"You won't need it. Why don't you grab something that can give us a bit of bass?"

"I don't understand."

"I think we're going to have a jam, Fred." Simon gave him a wink.

"See, he knows how it works."

"A jam?" Fred looked incredulous. I knew he'd probably never free-styled anything in his life. He would probably feel very uncomfortable without either his baton or a piece of music sitting in front of him. It felt quite good to have the shoe on the other foot.

"Go on, get an instrument."

Fred made his way to the back room, shaking his head in disbelief.

"Play that chorus again, mate," Simon urged as we waited for Fred to emerge. "Just the riff, no words."

I obliged. Simon bobbed his head along to the beat, his fingers hovering over the keys of his instrument.

"Keep it going," he encouraged, and I lopped the riff back around.

On the fourth time round, Simon felt confident enough that he had a feel for it and he lifted the cornet to his lips and blew a few tentative notes. As the tune repeated again and again, Simon added in more and more notes as he grew in confidence. Soon he hit a groove that saw the pair of us jamming along perfectly in sync with each other.

"That wasn't bad," I said when we let the notes die.

"You know what this reminds me of?" It made me happy to see the exhilarated grin on Simon's face. I knew what he was thinking.

"Last period on a Friday afternoon," I confirmed.

Fred was now hovering at the back of the room, clutching an enormous tuba. "I always thought the two of you as musicians had a sort of chemistry when you were kids. You haven't lost it."

"Care to join us?" Simon invited.

"Look at his face," I laughed. "Enjoy this moment, Simon, we finally get to be the ones who make Mr Black uncomfortable."

"That's enough of that, you two," Fred said in his best stern teacher's voice. He hoisted the tuba across the room and sat down with it. "I can jam with the best of them. Come on, let's see what you've got."

We spent a good couple of hours messing around with melodies and arrangements, making rough recordings on our phones. It felt good. By the time we agreed to call it a day, we were all pretty pleased with ourselves, and the atmosphere was not unlike it was after a good session in the studio with Listed MIA—only there had been less bitching and less hostility.

"I wonder if we could get you a trumpet instead, Simon," I mused. "A trumpet is way cooler, and you could fill in all those fiddly bits in the verses."

"Wait a minute, there are no trumpets in a brass band," Fred reminded us.

"Well, if you want to be a classicist about it." Simon looked at me questioningly.

"Yes, I do actually. We're still Bramwick Brass Band after all." Fred was adamant. "Right, well, I think we've made a good start. I'll have to write out some parts for the others before next practice, and we'll see how we go. I'll see you both on Monday."

By the time Monday's rehearsal came around, I found my mind wandering back to Rosie. Would she be there? She might not even know about our plans to record a single yet, and she hadn't even heard the song. I was excited for her to be let in on the plan, and I thought it might bring her some hope and give her something to focus on.

I was set up and ready to go before any of the others arrived, and as the band members started to filter in, I nervously watched out for Rosie. Then there she was, walking with Sally. I noticed that she was smiling and chatting with her friend, but as the two of them headed towards me, the smile disappeared. When I saw her bruised face, I felt a fresh surge of anger that made me want to storm from the building, find Alan, and kill him.

"We hear you've been busy, Nasher," Sally said with a crooked smile. Today her T-shirt said 'we are the granddaughters of the witches you couldn't burn'. "There's talk that you're going to try and use your big rock star connections to help us release a charity single."

"Yeah," I said distractedly, looking at Rosie and not her. She had cast her eyes to the ground and wouldn't look at me. "Are you alright?"

She glanced up briefly then looked away again. "Yeah, fine. I'm going to go and see Fred." She directed this to Sally. "I need a loaner instrument."

I caught a flicker of something in Sally's expression and she briefly rested a sympathetic hand on Rosie's back as she turned away from us.

"Anyway," Sally said brightly, making sure I didn't have a chance to ask any questions. "I can't wait to hear this song. Simon has been raving about it."

Once everyone had taken their seats, Fred addressed the room.

"Quiet everyone, and listen." The chattering stopped. "A lot of you were there the other night when this young man here suggested a new project. For those of you who weren't and haven't already heard, Nathan has written a song for us and, if all goes well, he'd like to help us record and release it to raise money for The Grange."

There were nods of murmurs of approval.

"You've all got some music on your stand—it's a bit rough and this isn't the final version, but we're going to try and give it a run through."

I glanced at Rosie, who was slotting a mouthpiece into a rather battered and tarnished old instrument. She gave the cornet a disapproving look. Once we were all ready, Fred counted us in and we began. The phrase 'car crash 'came to mind. Fred waved his hands frantically to silence us and shook his head before we had even finished the first chorus.

"What on earth was that?" he asked, sounding agitated. "Now I *know* you can do better than that."

Our second attempt wasn't much better. The players faltered, lost their place. The horns came in three bars two soon. The bass was playing at a different tempo to everyone else. The cornets clashed horribly with each other. The melody sounded like it was having a fight with the harmony. At least Fred let us make it to the end this time before declaring, "Abysmal. Absolutely bloody abysmal. Have you all forgotten how to count and keep in time?"

"Sorry," George piped up from the trombone section. "It's just a bit hard to hear yourself with that thing he's playing and all the shouting he's doing."

"Do you want to try it without the vocals? I can turn this down for now too if it's distracting."

"We gave it a try, Fred," said one of the back-row cornet players. "It didn't work. Can we just move on to something else?"

"Maybe this isn't for us after all..." Fred shuffled his papers nervously.

"Hey, wait a minute!" Simon stood up, glancing around the room in outrage. "I'd hardly call that giving it a try. Every time Fred gives us a new piece, it sounds like shit. You know that, but we always get there in the end with a bit of work."

"Yeah, but it's usually proper music we try to play. This is just...noise..." George said before swiftly adding:" Sorry, Nate."

I waved a dismissive hand. If they didn't want to do this, it was no skin off my nose.

"Come on, one more try," Simon pleaded.

"Alright then, after four."

It was marginally better, but not much.

"This is a joke," Brendan blurted out after we had finished. "It's just not us. We're a brass band, not a rock band. We've got a proud history, and this just pisses all over it."

"I wonder if Brendan might be right," Fred said with a disappointed glance my way. "It was a nice idea, and we do appreciate your help, Nathan, but it's not really working. We aren't some ska backup ensemble. You talk about having a reputation and an image to uphold, well, we do too, and I'm not convinced the two are compatible."

Simon now looked crestfallen. I took off my guitar and unplugged it, ready to abandon the whole idea, when a voice spoke up.

"Wait." It was Rosie, and she was now on her feet. "Will you all just humour me for a minute? Nate, that riff, the one that starts at bar thirty-four."

I looked at her blankly. I wasn't reading from a sheet of music. "Bar thirty-four?"

"She means the bridge," Simon said helpfully.

"Oh, the bit where you all come in?"

"Uh-huh, play that, just you. Everyone else; forget about the music Fred has given you and just listen."

Fred looked a bit put out, but he let her continue. I plugged the guitar back in and ran through the riff while Rosie continued to stand, listening hard.

"Yep, it's just what I thought," she confirmed, and the rest of us looked at her questioningly. "It's 'Slaidburn March'."

Brendan snorted and shook his head. "Don't be ridiculous."

"It's really not a million miles away," Rosie protested. "Listen. Play it again, Nate."

I started up again, and Rosie joined in with a phrase from 'Slaidburn' on her cornet. When I glanced at Fred, he was laughing and nodding. He waved his arms, and we fell quiet.

"She's absolutely right, you know!" he cried. "How did I miss that? What a fine ear you have, Rosie my girl!"

Rosie looked embarrassed, but at least she was smiling.

"Right, everyone, forget about those parts I spent hours writing for you; this changes everything. Nate, lad, I knew you had brass in your blood."

Rosie nodded, vindicated. Brendan, on the other hand, still looked disgruntled as he hugged his euphonium to his chest.

"We've been thinking about this all the wrong way," Fred said. "Brendan is absolutely right in that we have our own roots and our own traditions. If we're going to work together, not just as a back-up band, then we have to respect each other's styles. What I've tried to do is write something that fits with *you*. Really the brass side of things needs to still sound like *us*. With that in mind, what could be more appropriate than 'Slaidburn'?"

I stared at him, dumfounded. "You want to work 'Slaidburn' into 'Blood and Brass'? Into a punk song?"

"It fits, doesn't it?" Rosie pointed out.

"Exactly." Fred gave a triumphant nod.

"I'm sorry, I'm still not sure I'm hearing this right," I said in disbelief. "'Slaidburn'? That depressing dirge?"

"It's not a dirge, it's proud and triumphant," Brendan insisted.

"But you want to put it into a punk song?"

Sally beamed. Rosie looked hopeful. Brendan still looked unsure but the mention of a march seemed to have stirred a nostalgic chord in him.

"It's out of copyright too, of course, and every brass band in England knows it," Sally offered.

I opened my mouth and was about to protest again, but I sensed defeat marching my way.

I gave a resigned sigh. "Nothing gets the youth moving like a slow, minor key elegy…"

"I think it's perfect." Simon looked like he was about to burst.

"Fine. 'Slaidburn' it is then." I thought I might live to regret this. Dad, on the other hand, was probably bursting with pride, wherever he was.

Chapter Twenty-Two

Rosie

The rehearsal had ended on a high that night. I hadn't been sure I even wanted to go, given the circumstances, but Sally had talked me into it. When she had told me Nate had written a song for us, curiosity got the better of me. I had to borrow an old band cornet, and although it sounded okay, it just wasn't the same as my own, treasured instrument. Playing it was bittersweet, as music had always uplifted me, but that night I was reminded of my own instrument lying broken and battered in the fireplace. I wondered if it was still there, where I'd abandoned it after Alan's last blow.

Since I had walked out, my phone had not stopped ringing. Alan called relentlessly. He sent me text messages, left me voicemails, all saying how sorry he was. He told me he hated himself for what he had done. I ignored him.

I hadn't had the courage to go to my parents yet, and I felt like a refugee staying at Sally's. I didn't even have my own clothes—I just wasn't ready to go back to the house to pack up my things.

Sally had been running everything at the shop for the last couple of days. As we suspected, Alan had shown up there looking for me. Apparently, he had been full of remorse. He even brought flowers. Sally had given him a piece of her mind, and he had scuttled off again.

As I sat in the band room that night, I felt like they were all looking at me. I supposed they had all guessed that Alan was responsible for my bruised face.

As the tea break approached, I began to panic. Things had been going so well after I suggested we try and fit 'Slaidburn' into Nate's song, but as the prospect of having to talk to everyone approached, I started to feel sick. I contemplated sneaking out and going back to Sally's. I knew it would go one of two ways: either people would come right out and ask me about what happened, or they would awkwardly pretend they hadn't noticed and chat as normal. Should I make up an excuse? The old classic 'I walked into a door'? But why should I lie? *I* wasn't the one who should be ashamed.

As the tea was handed around, Simon was the first one to speak to me. He avoided the subject entirely as he started to chatter enthusiastically about the press coverage around the fundraiser. The rest of my bandmates acted in a similar way—they were going for the awkward avoidance tactic. They probably assumed I didn't want to talk about it. Despite my best efforts to stay out of his way, Nate eventually approached me.

"Thanks for ruining my song, Patches," he said with a face so straight I thought he was being serious at first. "Only kidding. It was a great idea; you seemed to have managed to unite everyone. Pretty impressive."

"Thanks," I said nervously, taking a sip of tea. I wondered how much he knew. Had Simon told him?

"So, walked into a door did you? Or do you have a more creative excuse? Maybe you hit yourself in the face with your cornet that is now also mysteriously missing."

"No, actually," I said, keeping the emotion out of my voice. "Alan hit me, then he stamped on the cornet, crushed it, completely wrecked it beyond repair."

I was amazed at how empowered I felt just by saying it out loud. No shame. No embarrassment. Just honesty. A few people around us who had overheard looked shocked, but Nate didn't seem surprised.

"Once a bully, always a bully," he observed.

"That's right," I raised my voice because everyone seemed to be looking at me now. "Let's just get it out in the open. My husband hit me."

I looked around at them. Fred was shaking his head, sadly. Brendan was looking at the ground and shuffling his feet. Some faces were shocked, some appalled and others looked uncomfortable. Sally gave me a nod of encouragement.

"I'm not looking for sympathy. I just can't bear you all looking at me and wondering," I continued. "I've left Alan, so it won't happen again. I don't especially want to talk about it. This here is my happy place—it's where I come to forget my troubles, not wallow in them."

I felt Sally put a reassuring hand on my shoulder. Nate was looking at me like he wanted to say something but was holding it in. There were nods and murmurs and reassurances that if I ever *did* want to talk, they would listen. If I needed help, all I had to do was ask, and they would do whatever they could. I felt a surge of love for all of them.

"Have you really left him?" Nate asked as he followed me and Sally out of the building after we had finished rehearsing.

I had told Sally I wanted to make a quick exit, but it seemed Nate was determined to catch me. I'd seen him brushing off Simon as he tried to talk to him, so he could hurry after us.

"Didn't you hear when she said she didn't want to talk about it?" Sally said sharply, and she took my arm, quickening her pace and steering me towards the gates.

"Yeah, but I'm worried about her, and I'm an old friend. "

I stopped walking, and Sally gave me a small tug. "Come on, you don't have to talk if you don't want to."

"It's okay," I told her, and turned back to Nate. "Can you give us a minute?"

"If you're sure." Sally looked doubtful. "I'll just be over by the gates."

"So we're friends now?"

"Well, yeah, aren't we?"

"I really don't know, Nate. You tell me. I haven't seen you for years, and then you show up again, and somehow my life starts unravelling."

"You can't possibly blame me for any of this?" He looked outraged.

"Oh, can I not? It's Alan's jealousy over you that's behind all this. You must know that."

"I don't see what he can possibly have to be jealous about. We were never a thing." Now he just looked pissed off. "And it's not like I chose to come back. I didn't come here to seek you out. I'm only here because I have to be."

"No, and you never tire of reminding us of that, do you?" I could feel myself growing angry. "You say you're a friend, but if you had it your way, you never would have come back at all. You've just said as much."

"Look, I just want to make sure you're okay, that's all. I care about you. I always have."

"Yeah, you cared so much that you pissed off to London without a word." I was starting to get worked up now. In my mind, I saw myself as a teenager writing his name in my journal, surrounded by hearts. Lying in bed at night, wishing he would ask me out. Wondering why he liked Hannah and not me. Crying in my room because he'd gone. And he said he'd always cared.

"How many times do I need to say I'm sorry for that?"

"You fucked everything up for me back then, even if you didn't mean to, and you've come back and done it again."

"I don't understand…"

I saw myself and how miserable I was. I was so heartbroken that when Alan started paying me attention, I jumped at the chance to be loved, to matter to someone.

"I loved you when we were kids, Nate, that's why Alan is so jealous. He's seen my diaries from when we were young. He knows what I felt for you. It doesn't matter to him that you never felt the same."

"What?" He faltered. "But you never said anything…"

"How could I, Nate? You were all over Hannah Ferguson with her cool clothes, perfect gothic makeup, and that amazing figure. I was just this…well…this patchwork mess."

I saw him take a deep breath. I was a teenager all over again; my hands were shaking, and I thought I was about to cry. He glanced over his shoulder at where Sally stood, pretending she wasn't watching us. When he looked back he looked conflicted, like he was fighting an internal battle. I was suddenly aware of how close he was standing. There was something in his dark eyes when he looked at me. Was it sadness? Regret?

It took me completely by surprise when he took my face in his hands and kissed me. It was completely reckless. I was in a vulnerable state, and I should have pushed him away. Yet I didn't, because inside my teenage self was giving me a high five. All those times I had dreamed of a moment just like this. Why did it have to come now? It only lasted seconds, but it was enough to send a wave of emotions cascading through me—guilt, giddy exhilaration, confusion.

When we pulled away from each other, I noticed Sally gawping at us from the gates.

"I'm sorry, I probably shouldn't have done that." He looked awkward now. "I might just leg it now like you did the other day." He gave a nervous laugh.

"I can't...I just..." I fumbled for the words. My stomach was in knots. "You're ten years too late, Nate. It would be a terrible idea for me to get involved with you right now..."

"I know, I completely understand." He ran his fingers through his hair and took a step back. "I'll let you get on. This didn't happen, okay? Last thing I want to do is make things more complicated for you. That was for our teenage selves, nothing more. Just friends, yeah?"

"Agreed," I nodded firmly. "I'll see you next practice then."

As I walked away to rejoin Sally, who was still gaping, I had butterflies in my stomach.

"Really?" Sally asked as we walked. "He shouldn't be taking advantage at a time like this."

"He's not taking advantage," I assured her. "Anyway, I did it first." I fought back a smile.

"What are you talking about?"

"I kissed him after the fundraiser."

Sally shot me a shocked glance. There was a chill in the air as we made our way through the village. Autumn was definitely on the way.

"It wasn't a proper kiss, but still."

"What did I say to you the other night? The absolute worst thing you can do right now is get involved with someone else."

She was right of course.

"Give yourself space to breathe and just be you for a bit, girl. Listen to your Aunt Sally; she knows what she's talking about."

"Don't worry." I swung the cornet case, the warm flutter in my belly fighting with the guilt I felt. "I'm not planning on getting involved with him. That was just for old times 'sake."

"Ok, but I'll be keeping an eye on the pair of you. If I see him try anything like that again, he'll have me to answer to."

"I'm lucky I have you looking out for me," I chuckled.

When we got back to Sally's house, Alan was waiting, and the warm sensation in my stomach was replaced by a heavy stone. My heart started to pound. He was sitting there in the dark on the front door step, his knees pulled up, and his head bowed low. He looked like a hunched gargoyle. I felt bile rise in the back of my throat, and I thought I might be sick. At the sound of the front gate opening, he had looked up, and I had frozen like a deer caught in headlights.

"Rosie." His voice was a miserable whine. The tension lessened ever so slightly—at least he didn't seem angry.

Alan got to his feet; his movements were slow and stiff. I wondered how long he had been sitting there in the cold. He was just wearing a T-shirt and no jacket, and he looked dreadful. He took a few steps towards us and stared at me with a haunted expression on his face.

"I just want to talk to you, Rosie, just for five minutes; that's all I ask."

"Alright, five minutes, Alan. After that I'm calling the police, no discussion," Sally threatened.

"Please," he begged, never taking his eyes off me. "Let's not throw away the last ten years. I can't lose you."

"I think it's a bit late for that," Sally scoffed.

Suddenly Alan lurched forward, and I jumped. Had I misread the situation? Was he angry after all? But he fell to his knees at my feet and grabbed both of my hands, clasping them tightly in his.

"I'm sorry, Rosie." There were tears in his eyes now. He looked so utterly bereft that I felt a painful pang in my heart for him. He wasn't all bad…" I'm going to get help, I really am. I've already phoned the doctor. My head's not right now. I don't know if it's depression or what, but I'm going to get it sorted. Counselling. Medication. Even Alcoholics Anonymous. Whatever you need me to do, I will do, Rosie, I swear."

Sally was still at my side, and she looked down at him with contempt. He squeezed my hands as a fresh burst of sobs wracked his body. I stiffened my resolve. I wasn't going to fall for this again.

"Just say something, Rosie," he pleaded. "Talk to me. I love you more than anything."

132

"I think it would be a start if you did all of those things, Alan," I said slowly. I found I was rubbing the back of his hand with my thumb in a soothing gesture. "It's a good first step."

"Really?" It hurt my heart to see the hope in his eyes as he looked up at me.

"Rosie, love…" There was a warning tone in Sally's voice as she put a hand on my shoulder.

"You're not well, and you need help." His grip on my hands tightened. "It's important that this isn't just empty words though. You actually have to do it."

Sally shook her head, her mouth opened and closed. She seemed lost for words.

"I will, I will!" He lowered his head and kissed the back of both of my hands. "I swear, Rosie, I'll do it for you. I'll be the best husband you could ever wish for."

"Alan, I think you should do these things for yourself, not for me." I pulled my hands away from his, and his arms flopped to his sides. "I hope you get the help you need and get well, but understand that you and I are done. It's over."

"No!" His cry was gut-wrenching, like that of a wounded animal, as he folded over again and pounded his fist on the path.

"You're lucky she's such a kind soul," Sally said, as she guided me around his slumped form towards the door. "I wouldn't have been quite so nice about things. Now get out of my garden, or I *will* call the police."

Chapter Twenty-Three

Nate

My emotions were all over the place by the time I got back to the house that evening. I felt completely exhausted as I walked home, the trombone feeling like a dead weight in my hand. Kissing her had been a stupid thing to do. I was the last thing she needed.

I dropped the trombone in the hallway with a heavy thud. The house felt damp and uncomfortable in the chilly autumn night. Outside, the wind was picking up and as I tried to light a fire it whistled down the chimney, blowing the match out before the fire lighter could even catch.

I really had no idea that she had liked me at school. I suspected that if I hadn't been so self-absorbed with my dreams of leaving Bramwick, I might have noticed. But would it have made any difference? I still would have wanted to leave, and she still would have wanted to stay.

"You'd have loved that, wouldn't you?" I looked up at the picture of my father as I struggled to get the fire to light. "If I'd stayed here and married Rosie Bell."

I struck another match, and this time a yellow flame leaped from the small square of paraffin. The kindling crackled.

I didn't kiss her because I thought I could fix everything, but because there was something about her that had always drawn me to her.

Another gust of wind blew pungent smoke back into the room, making my eyes water. The small flames quickly went out again and the flickering embers with their promise of warmth only made the cold feel sharper.

I had just made things a hundred times worse for her.

"Shit!" I threw the box of matches angrily on the ground.

The best thing to do now would be to keep my distance. I would be professional. I'd see her at rehearsals and I'd be civil, but I would stay out of her way.

In my pocket, my phone started to buzz, and I cursed. "Who the hell could that be?"

I retreated to the sofa and sat down while the wind continued to blow and the rain started to tap against the window. I answered the phone and was greeted by Maxwell's upbeat tone. As I looked around my cold, dank surroundings and the smouldering remains of my attempt at a fire, his voice might as well have been coming from another planet.

"Hey, if it isn't Mr Brass Punk himself. How's everything in the country? Have you bought a tweed jacket and a flat cap yet? No wait, you've got something better, haven't you? That blazer, man! Amazing! I'm absolutely digging the new look."

"If you've called just to take the piss, Maxwell, you can fuck off." I clenched my teeth.

"Woah, you *asked* me to call, remember? You sent me a message about some new material."

Of course. I'd forgotten about that.

"I must admit I was a bit intrigued," he went on. "A new song? Why, mate? The band's pretty much dead."

"Yeah, I know, but I need your help…"

I went on to explain about 'Blood and Brass', about the rehearsal and 'Slaidburn', and about The Grange and my intention to help by releasing the song.

"Are you having a laugh?" Maxwell asked when I was done talking. "This is a wind-up, right?"

"No, I'm serious."

"Mate, what the hell's happened to you? Have you lost the plot? You seem to have entered some kind of alternative dimension. Is there something in the water up there in Yorkshire?"

"I'm just asking for a bit of your time, that's all. I'm sure you haven't got that much else going on right now?"

"And I suppose you also want me to try and sell this madness to the others?"

"Preferably."

"Even Ritchie?" he asked suspiciously.

As much as it pained me to think of working with Ritchie again, I knew this project would be so much better with his vocal talents. Listed MIA wasn't Listed MIA without our frontman.

"Even Ritchie," I said at last. Outside, a real storm was kicking up. I'd left the doors on the burner open, and a fresh gust sent a small cloud of ash swirling out into the room.

"Bloody hell," Maxwell exclaimed. "Are we putting the band back together?"

"No, it's just for this one song."

"And what's in it for us? Are we meant to just drop everything because you called?"

"Come on, Maxwell, think of all the times I've bailed you out over the years. Quite literally once if you remember."

"You always have to bring that up. It was years ago," he grumbled.

"I suppose you've got so many other important things to do since the band split."

"Actually, I have," he snapped. "We haven't all just been pissing about doing nothing like you. I've got a gig as a session player with Giles Corrigan's new band. I'm due to leave on a two-week tour in a couple of weeks."

"Bloody Giles Corrigan? The guy is a total idiot, and his music's shit."

"That may well be the case, but he's a popular idiot, and the tour is sold out. Plus he pays well," Maxwell said defensively. "Anyway, you're one to talk, prancing around with those brass band losers."

I felt a surge of anger. The members of Bramwick Brass might have been the furthest thing from cool, but they were decent people, and I didn't like hearing him speak about them like that.

"Spare me just one day," I said, crushing down my annoyance. "Come up here and meet the band, have a jam, see what we're doing. You say you're going on tour in a couple of weeks? That gives me a month to get them in shape."

There was a silence on the other end of the phone, and I heard Maxwell sigh heavily.

"Why does this matter to you? I thought you hated that place and everyone in it."

It matters because it matters to Rosie, and Simon, and I owe them.

"It just does. A lot's changed, mate. I feel like I've lost everything— my dad, my band, my girlfriend. I've reconnected with a few people here, and I'd just like to help them out so I can feel like I've done something good before I bugger off again."

"It must be *really* important if you're willing to bury the hatchet with Ritchie. He and Freya have been seeing an awful lot of each other…" There was a slyness in his voice now. I walked over to the window and looked out at the front garden where the rusted barbecue was blowing across the tangled grass.

"Why would you bring that up now?" I had my suspicions, given the pictures that had been appearing on her Facebook, but having it confirmed hurt.

"Just thought you might like to know, in case them being a thing puts a different slant on things."

"Honestly, I don't care. They're welcome to each other."

"This is about a girl, isn't it?" Maxwell burst out triumphantly.

"What the hell are you on about?"

"Sure it is, it all makes sense now." He sounded smug and I wanted to reach down the line and throttle him. "Are you sure this isn't just some rebound thing? Digging up an old flame and all that?"

Maxwell was a little too sharp for his own good and I felt myself turning red.

"I know you, Nasher, there are only two things that would motivate you to do something so incredibly uncool and that's money, which there clearly isn't any, or love."

"For fuck's sake, Maxwell!"

"Just admit it, man, it's not a big deal. I totally get it. I'll help you win her over, don't worry. She's in the band, isn't she?"

It sounded like he had just put me on speaker phone and I wondered what he was doing.

"Just having a look at some of those pictures from the weekend now. Which one is she? They all look like dogs to me."

"That's totally uncalled for, you prat," I snapped.

"So there is someone! I fucking knew it." He was laughing down the phone at me now.

"Ok you got me. There's a girl I used to go to school with, but nothing is going on. She's married and it's a totally fucked up situation."

"This just gets better and better," he hooted.

"Look, will you come up here after the tour or not?"

"Yeah, man. It might even be worth it just to see you make a prat of yourself."

When we ended our conversation I went back to my attempts to start a fire, finally managing to get it to catch. Maxwell was right about one thing. I wasn't doing this for the band or out of some misplaced sense of duty. There was something about Rosie that I couldn't shake even after all these years. Maybe this song was about giving myself one last chance to put things right.

The storm outside was in full force now, whipping its turmoil across the village and all of us in it.

Chapter Twenty-Four

Rosie

In the days that followed, Alan continued to bombard me with messages. The more I ignored them, the nastier they got. What had started out as grovelling had, by the end of the week, turned into abusive rants full of cruel name-calling and insults.

Sally looked at my phone and read out loud to herself, with a growing look of revulsion.

"You really think you can just walk away from me? You've made a huge mistake. You know what happens when you push me too far. You'll live to regret this. I'll make sure no one ever wants you again. You think he'll put up with your bullshit? Newsflash: he won't. You're nothing without me Rosie, and I'll make sure you feel that. Every. Single. Day."

"Nice, huh?" I took my phone back from an appalled Sally.

"Men are such bastards," Sally spat viciously. "I had one once, before I realised I prefer women, who used to get jealous and send me messages like that. He lost it once because I went to a get a tattoo and he found out the artist was a bloke. Couldn't stand the thought of another man touching me."

"Wow."

"I know. You really should report him to the police though," she insisted. "It's harassment."

I had thought about it. Both Sally and Simon had urged me to press charges after he hit me, but something was stopping me. Dealing with the police just seemed like another burden that I didn't have the strength for.

I had wanted to tell my parents in my own time that we had separated and had hoped to spare them the grisly details, but Alan was spreading vicious and untrue rumours around the village, so I knew I would have to face them soon.

"Sandy was in the shop again today," Sally said with a sigh, as she hung her coat up. "Aw, you cooked dinner; you didn't have to do that, you know, love," she added when she saw that the oven was on.

"I wanted to," I said. "It makes me feel useful. Anyway, it's just pasta."

I had barely left the house all week and had mainly been wallowing around in my pyjamas, feeling horrible, avoiding both Nature's Bounty and The Grange. Sally hadn't even been able to talk me into going to rehearsals. The thought of seeing Nate made my stomach churn. Sally told me they were making good progress with 'Blood and Brass' and that Fred had evidently had a great time tinkering with 'Slaidburn' until it integrated perfectly with Nate's work.

"Honestly, the pair of them have a real chemistry going now that they've decided to put aside their differences and work together properly," Sally had told me. She also told me Nate had been asking after me, and my heart ached. I had been replaying the kiss over and over in my mind. It was a happy thought that temporarily cut through the gloom but also left me feeling guilty and confused. Just friends, he had said, and I had agreed. So why was I constantly suppressing the thought that just friends wasn't enough?

"You look a little better today," Sally observed as I drained the pasta in the colander.

"I haven't had quite as many messages from Alan," I said. "I think he's calming down a bit."

A shadow passed over Sally's face that suggested she knew otherwise.

"You said Sandy was in the shop today," I pressed, turning to mix the sauce in with the pasta. "Did she say something?"

"No, just the usual, you know what she's like." Sally sat down at the kitchen table and started leafing through a magazine.

"Tell me." I started ladling the food onto plates.

"You won't like it…"

"Honestly, I don't think anything could possibly make me feel worse than I already do, so you might as well tell me."

"Alan told her that you broke up because of Nate."

"Oh, brilliant, and now everyone's heard that, I suppose?"

"It's Sandy, of course they have," she winced as I put a plate down in front of her. "Sorry. I mean, I did set her straight and told her it was nonsense, that there was nothing going on between you and Nate, but she seems to have really taken a dislike to him. She wouldn't listen."

I was definitely going to have to go and talk to my parents. They didn't venture down the hill into the village all that often, but the last thing I wanted was for them to hear secondhand gossip. I told Sally I'd be moving to the farm, and when I called Mum to ask if I could stay, I got the impression she already knew what had happened. When I arrived, she was waiting at the front door with a big hug for me.

"Alan and I have split up," I said when she released me from her embrace. I immediately started to cry.

"I know," she said kindly. "Get yourself inside; your room's all made up. Dad had to go into Skipton today. He won't be back until later, so there's plenty of time if you want to chat, just the two of us."

I told Mum everything. I relayed how Alan and I had been having trouble for some time and how things had only got worse following his expulsion from the band and Nate's return.

"I think he suffers from depression," I confided. "I suggested so many times he get help but apparently that would make him look weak."

I told her about that first time he hurt me, and about how he had done it again. She listened with a devastated look on her face, her hands starting to shake. She had known things were not great, but I don't think she had any idea how bad things were.

"I know the physical abuse is bad enough," I said. "But that was only twice. It was the emotional abuse that was the worst. I lied to myself over and over about how cruel he actually was. I convinced myself it was normal."

I saw him sprawled on the couch, one of my teenage diaries in his hand as he read aloud from it in a mocking imitation of my own voice. It was a passage detailing how upset I was that Nate had got together with Hannah. He laughed and made fun of me and told me my teenage angst was pathetic. When I got upset, he became defensive and told me he was only having a laugh and I needed to lighten up. He was always using that excuse. He'd say something mean then tell me I was in the wrong for not having a sense of humour. He said it so often that I started to think maybe he was right. Before long, I had learned to laugh and act good-natured when he took the piss out of something I said or did.

"I know you must be wondering why I put up with it for so long," I sniffed.

"No love, nobody is judging you."

"I loved him, Mum." I blinked back the tears from my eyes. "How pathetic is that?"

Telling Mum about the cornet was the worst part, and I started bawling so hard I could barely speak. I sat there with my shoulders heaving and the air caught in the back of my throat. I choked on the sobs and I cried big, ugly tears that turned my face red and made my nose run. I had cried a lot over the last week but not quite as hard as I did that afternoon with Mum. It made me feel better.

Mum listened without judgement even when I told her what had happened with Nate and how confused the whole thing had left me. I wanted to do the sensible thing and not get involved. I knew I should just continue to keep my distance, but I couldn't stop thinking about him. My mind was full of 'what ifs?' and each one was like a tiny spark of hope amid the turmoil and the heartache.

"Well, you know this will always be your home," Mum said. "And we meant what we said about downsizing. The farm can still be yours if you want it. Whenever you're ready, though, there's absolutely no rush."

"Thanks, Mum." I blew my nose loudly and wiped at my eyes. The tears were finally coming to an end. "I don't see how I can now, though. I'll only get half of what our house is worth, and that won't be enough for you and Dad to get a new place."

"Don't worry about all that now, we'll work something out. You've a long road ahead of you. Separations take time. Will you promise me one thing, though?"

"What's that?"

"Don't go back to him. Someone who hits you will *always* do it again, no matter how much they say they've changed, or how much help they get."

"I promise, Mum."

I knew Mum and Dad had not been especially happy when I had got together with Alan. They couldn't understand it when they had seen me come home from school in tears so many times because of something he had said. Despite this, they had tried their best to support me and to make Alan feel welcome into our family. In the early days when we were dating, Alan had turned the same charm on them as he had used on me. Over time, he stopped making the effort with them. He made excuses not to join me when I visited them most of the time, and grumbled insistently when they were due to visit us. Alan's own parents had moved away from the village not long after we were married and now lived in Harrogate. Alan didn't really make an effort with them either. I didn't like his dad. He was old-fashioned, misogynist and bigoted. His mum was a sweet woman though— timid and quiet but very kind. She always struck me as being quite downtrodden, living a traditional, old-fashioned life as a housewife running after Alan and his dad. Now I wondered if she suffered from domestic violence too. It would not have surprised me to learn Alan had seen his mother on the receiving end of the odd slap from his dad. Maybe that was where he got it from.

I asked Mum if she would chat to Dad as I didn't really want to have the conversation again, and I knew he would be furious when he heard Alan had struck me.

"Don't let him do anything daft like going off and confronting Alan," I told her, "that won't help anyone, and tell him I don't really want to talk about it."

I went up to my room and sank down on the bed, where a tremendous sense of calm washed over me. I felt safe in my old space. It had been redecorated since I left. It was no longer full of posters of Steel Eye Span and Pentangle (yes, I was a weird child with weird taste in music), but it still felt familiar and comforting, and home will always smell like home.

I heard Dad come back around five o'clock, and I continued to linger upstairs. At one point, I thought I heard his voice raised in anger, and I had visions of him rushing off and hunting Alan down. When I thought I had given Mum enough time to talk to him, I ventured downstairs. They were in the kitchen, and I saw Mum give Dad a warning look when I entered.

"Hello, love," he said, and he too came and gave me a hug. "Your Mum says you don't want to talk about it, so I'll respect that, but I'm always here and ready to listen if you do want to talk."

"Thanks, Dad." I pulled away from him.

"I'm also ready to go and give Alan what's for; you just say the word."

"Vic!" Mum said sternly.

"Just so she knows that her old dad has her back."

After dinner, I took the cornet case out to the summer house. It was where I had always practised as a kid to avoid disturbing the peace in the house. Looking out through the window at the beautiful view of the fields, a view that was so familiar and comforting, I started to play.

Chapter Twenty-Five

Nate

Four weeks after my initial conversation with Maxwell, I took the battered old van to the nearest train station to collect my former bandmates. Now that the time was upon me, I felt sick at the prospect of my old life clashing with Bramwick. Maxwell had managed to talk Ritchie into coming, and I was apprehensive about seeing him. Mike, our drummer, was not available, so we would have to make do with Andrew, who had taken Alan's place.

The band had worked hard that month to get their part of the song in shape, and I was proud of their progress, but I was still concerned that Maxwell and Ritchie would be critical. I had sent them rough recordings, and though they agreed that the song itself was another of my special ones, Ritchie had been quite scathing about the inclusion of 'Slaidburn'. Neither of them seemed able to appreciate why I was doing this, no matter how hard I tried to explain in ways they might understand. I told them about Danny Henshaw, who was like a caricature of everything I knew they hated. I told them how slimy and odious he was and how if we helped save The Grange, it was a chance to stick it to the gentry. They continued to take the piss in every message, and I was sure they were only coming so they could laugh at us.

The train station was one of those twee old ones nestled in the rolling Dales. It had an old-fashioned waiting room and an ornate metal bridge connecting the platforms. I was sure I had once seen it in one of the period dramas Freya liked to watch. I half expected to see a steam train rolling up, perhaps with Maxwell and Ritchie leaning out of the windows in bowler hats. When the modern electric version arrived, it looked out of place; the illusion shattered.

As the train came to a halt, the tension that had been building in me all morning reached its peak, and my palms were starting to sweat. I waited anxiously as the doors slid open, and a few people disembarked. Then I saw Maxwell swing out of one of the carriages in his ripped jeans and battered old creepers, a bass guitar bag slung over his shoulder. I was glad to see him, and a smile crept across my face. Ritchie followed close behind, wearing his trademark sneer, and the smile slipped from my lips as I realised they weren't alone. I watched Freya step onto the platform and gave Maxwell a pointed stare. Ritchie turned to help her with her bag while Maxwell hurried over to me.

143

"Sorry, man," he said in a low voice, reading my expression. He leaned in and pulled me into an embrace. "I had no idea he was going to bring her."

I gritted my teeth and pulled away from him. "A text or something would have been nice. I'd have appreciated a bit of a warning."

"Yo, Nasher!" Ritchie called, waving his bottle of beer in the air.

"I think this was a mistake." All of the anger I had felt when I had found out about him and Freya had come surging back.

I turned away from the sight of the pair of them and started to walk.

"Hey, man, just chill. You asked him to come, and you know we need him. Part of the agreement with the label is that they'll only work with us on this if he's on board. "

My scowl deepened. "Did he have to bring Freya? You know he's only done that to piss me off."

"Look, we can always get back on the train," Maxwell threatened. "I have absolutely no desire to hang about and watch you two rip lumps off each other all weekend."

"You telling me to play nice, Maxwell?"

"If you want to help your new pals, I don't think you have a choice."

I forced myself to turn around and gave Ritchie the most sarcastic smile I could muster. "Ritchie, mate, it's great to see you."

I didn't acknowledge Freya, and she huffed moodily and looked off into the distance. Ritchie advanced, an obnoxious swagger in his stride, and extended his hand. "No hard feelings, eh, Nasher?"

When I didn't accept his handshake, he dropped it to his side and swigged the dregs from his bottle of beer, dropping the empty bottle into a planter full of pansies.

"There's a bin right there," I gestured, and he smirked. We started to walk towards the van.

"So, this is where you grew up," Freya observed. I ignored her.

Ritchie added, with a hint of revulsion in his low voice, "No wonder you thought it was better to top yourself than come back here…"

Freya shot a confused glance between the pair of us.

"What does he mean?"

"Nothing, Freya," I muttered as I yanked the side door of the van open. It crashed loudly at the end of its rusty rail. I'd never told her about that. It had been a long time ago, before we met.

"One of you will need to get in the back with the gear," I said.

"Maxwell likes riding in the back of vans, don't you?" Ritchie tipped him a wink. "Go on, son, get in; it'll give the three of us a chance to chat, clear the air if you know what I mean."

I exhaled slowly through my nose and watched Ritchie hold open the passenger door so Freya could climb in.

As I drove off, I tried to squeeze myself as close to the door as I could so I didn't have to touch Freya. Her presence had made me deeply uncomfortable. I gripped the steering wheel so tightly that my knuckles were turning white. I could have just about tolerated Ritchie, but not Freya. All the hurt and the fury I had felt at the time of our break-up was back. We hadn't spoken much following my discovery of her infidelity. We had shouted a lot, but we hadn't actually *talked*. Not really. And I had no desire to do so now. There was nothing to say as far as I was concerned. We weren't married, we didn't own property together, or have any kids, and I didn't especially care about any of our possessions. I had left with all I needed in the back of the van, and she was welcome to keep the rest.

"Christ, how can you stand it here?" Ritchie drawled, looking at the hills and the crisp autumn sky.

There was a time when I would have agreed with him, but things had changed these last couple of months. Bramwick wasn't the prison I used to think it was.

"It's not so bad," I said, keeping my eyes on the road.

"Pfft, you're kidding, right?"

"Remind me what picturesque part of the world you grew up in? Idyllic Bethnal Green wasn't it?"

"At least there were things to do there. You know, clubs, shops, transport links." Ritchie smirked.

"Yeah, and you probably ran the risk of getting stabbed every time you left the house." I gave him the side eye.

"At least when I was growing up, I didn't have to resort to playing in a brass band because there was nothing else to do."

"At least I didn't grow up being sent to the corner shop to steal cigarettes for my alcoholic mother."

"At least…"

"For fuck's sake," Freya shouted. We both looked at her in surprise. "Stop fucking bickering like a pair of kids. You always do this."

I glared back out of the windscreen. A black cloud drifted across the sun.

"You should have seen him when he first arrived in London," Ritchie sneered, nodding at me. "No street sense, no plan, just this country kid who had no clue. Bit of a baptism of fire wasn't it, Nasher?"

I ignored him. He was winding me up, and I took a bend too sharply, sending the van lurching to the side and making Freya exclaim loudly. Ritchie didn't miss a beat.

"He'd never have made it if it weren't for me. Reckon he was ready to pack it all in when we met."

Unfortunately, most of what he said was true. My early days in London had been a real shock. I didn't find the bohemian paradise I had gone in search of. Nobody cared that I could play guitar, or that I had dreams of making it as a musician. I didn't connect with like-minded artists as I had hoped. What I found was noise, crime, and a whole lot of people who were cold and indifferent. Instead of days spent making music and writing songs, I ended up with a depressing job in a dodgy bar. There were no artistic communities living together in squats, just rent so high that all I could afford was a single room in a damp flat which I had to share with an intimidating character from Birmingham and a man who I was sure was a drug dealer. I slept with a knife under my pillow. At times I cried like the kid I was and had to fight the urge to run back to Bramwick. When messages from home arrived, I ignored them lest I should have to admit what a disaster the whole thing had been.

I had been quite literally ready to top myself. It had seemed preferable to retiring home and admitting how much I'd fucked up. I had never told anyone, including Freya, the details of how Ritchie and I met, and I sat in the van, willing him not to elaborate.

We had met on the platform of the underground station at Camden Town. I had been preparing to throw myself in front of the next train. My mind was filled with images of Dad and his 'I told you so's'. The shame of having to go back with my tail between my legs. Having to return to working in the petrol station. As the train approached, I stepped over the painted yellow line. I saw the glare of its lights. It approached in slow motion. The driver saw me, and an expression of horror crossed his face. He couldn't possibly stop in time.

Ritchie had somehow picked up on what was about to happen, had grabbed my jacket, and pulled me back from the edge just in time. The train sped by, the warm, bitter air hitting our faces as we just stared at each other. Then, he took me for a pint to calm me down. I'd say we had been friends ever since, but I'm not sure friends is the right word to describe our relationship.

"I made him who he is today, you know? Moulded him with my own two hands. You might even say he owes me this life of his." Ritchie gave me a sly glance. "It hasn't taken long for all my good work to be undone."

"So why did you even agree to come?" I growled.

"We're here on a rescue mission, aren't we?" Freya said dramatically.

"And why would you even care?" I said, slamming on the brakes as we came up behind a tractor.

"I've seen the pictures, Nate," she said. "All the brass band stuff? It's not you."

"Yeah, well, what do you know?"

"That's exactly why we're here," Ritchie insisted. "To remind you that the real world still exists. I can't have my prodigy turning back into a country bumpkin."

I swerved around the tractor, and the van clanged and grumbled as we ratted past it. Having him here was going to be difficult.

I would have preferred to keep the three of them in Dad's house that night. I had got in a supply of beer, and I thought they'd be happy with that. But Ritchie insisted he wanted to go out and 'see the sights'. I told him there were no sights, just The Black Bull. I tried to make it sound as unappealing as possible. I told him how it was mainly farmers who drank there. I told him it was boring, quiet, and we'd have a much better time if we just stayed in where we could at least put on whatever music we wanted. The three of them ganged up on me, though, and so we found ourselves in The Black Bull. I gritted my teeth. Bramwick really wasn't ready for Listed MIA and our legendary drinking sessions.

"This isn't so bad," Ritchie said sarcastically as he cast his eyes around the place.

There were many raised eyebrows among the patrons as we approached the bar. By now, word had got around about the help I had offered the campaign to save The Grange, and Bramwick had started to warm to me again. That could all be about to change.

I trailed behind the group as Ritchie and Freya exclaimed loudly about how they felt like they'd stepped back in time. I gave the regulars apologetic glances and wished the ground would open up and swallow me.

"You said there would be no music!" Freya called. She had wandered off and found the jukebox. Great. "Give me a couple of quid, Nate."

"Right," I said tensely as I fished about in my pockets for some change.

Maxwell and Ritchie were at the bar now, ordering drinks. They were getting a lot of curious questions from the locals about the project we were working on. Ritchie could turn on the charm when he wanted to, and I was relieved to see he was being civilised.

"I still don't understand why you're here," I muttered to Freya as I stepped up beside her and dropped some coins into her outstretched hand.

She gave me a long look, green eyes peering out from below her perfect, glossy fringe.

147

"I just wanted to see you, that's all." I was struggling to read her expression.

"I can't imagine why."

A fragment of conversation drifted from the bar. Ritchie was telling one of his anecdotes to the young girl who was serving. She was laughing. He was flirting with her. I looked back at Freya, who didn't seem bothered by the advances Ritchie was making.

I turned away from Freya and went to take a seat next to the fire. 'Sex and Violence' by The Exploited suddenly erupted from the jukebox, and old Brian Mitchell, who was sitting at the end of the bar, jumped.

"Hey, you can get absolutely any song you want on here!" Freya's voice rose with delight as she made her way back to the bar.

"And you wanted us to stay at home like a bunch of boring old farts!" Ritchie put a pint in front of me, slopping the contents over the sides. "Just wanting to keep us away from all your new friends. Bless you, son, are you embarrassed by us?"

Ritchie patted my cheek, and I swatted him away.

"I wonder why you would think that."

I noticed Sandy Brown in the far corner with what I assumed was her husband. She gave me a scathing look and shook her head.

I leaned back in my chair, wanting to just disappear. I watched Ritchie resume his conversation with the barmaid. She seemed captivated by him. He had always had that ability. It didn't matter that he could be an obnoxious prat; people were just drawn to him. It was seriously annoying. I observed Freya closely. Just because she was happy to let Ritchie flirt with the barmaid didn't mean they weren't sleeping together...

I scowled and took a drink of my pint.

As the night wore on, Ritchie and Freya got more and more intoxicated. The tunes kept blaring out of the jukebox, and at one point, Freya actually managed to get Brian Mitchell up dancing to The Sex Pistols. The sight of the pair of them was almost enough to break through my bad mood.

All in all, it could have been a lot worse, I thought, as we walked back to the house. Freya staggered and grabbed onto my arm. I begrudgingly helped her stay upright. She'd probably just pass out when we got back, which was fine by me, as it meant I wouldn't have to talk to her.

Chapter Twenty-Six

Rosie

That Monday, the atmosphere in the band room was nervous and excited. Nate was bringing his bandmates to rehearsal. They had arrived the previous afternoon, and from what I had heard from Sandy Brown that morning, they had been in The Black Bull for most of the night. She had recanted with shock and horror the bad language they had used, how loud they were, and how they had taken over the jukebox while she and her husband had tried to enjoy a quiet drink.

"The state of them!" If she had been wearing pearls, I had no doubt she would have been clutching them. "Absolute vagrants. One of them was all over Georgia. Poor girl was only trying to get through her shift! And that girl! Wait until you see her! Bright green hair, covered, and I mean *covered,* in tattoos, and a skirt that might as well have been a belt."

I had been successfully tuning her out up to that point, nodding in all the right places, but I zoned back in when she mentioned the girl. I'd seen pictures of Nate's ex, Freya, on social media, and Sandy's description sounded an awful lot like her. I felt a tug of anxiety at the prospect of her being here.

Four weeks ago, Nate had kissed me, and I had let him. Four weeks ago, we had agreed that we wouldn't let it go anywhere. But in the time that had passed, my feelings towards him had only grown. Following that night, he had been avoiding me. He only spoke to me in rehearsals if he had to, but every now and then I'd catch him looking at me. He had said we were friends but now it didn't even feel like that. I had no idea where I stood and his ex being back on the scene complicated things further.

It was with great apprehension that I arrived at The Grange that night. Everyone had worked incredibly hard over the last few weeks, and we were ready. Fred had been full of praise for our commitment, and Nate had been suitably impressed, but the prospect of these professional, cool musicians in our rehearsal room remained a daunting one.

Fred had asked some of us to get there early to tidy the place up as he wanted to 'make a good impression'. He bustled around the place, completely ignoring Sally's jibes.

"They're a punk band," she reminded him as he straightened the chairs. "Not the royal family."

"He's even got the good biscuits in," I giggled. "Foxes creams, would you believe?"

"Will you lot leave off?" Fred pleaded. He was now lining up the music folders on the shelf so all the spines were all aligned. "This is important. We need to make sure we win them over, make them feel welcome."

"And you think Foxes creams and straight chairs will do that, do you?" Simon was at the other end of the room, dusting the drum kit.

"Well, what would you suggest?" Fred snapped irritably.

"This." Simon went into the Asda bag he had brought and lifted out a twelve-pack of beer.

Fred gave him a horrified look. "We can't have drinking during rehearsals!"

"You need to lighten up a bit. We need to offer them a bit more than tea."

Fred grumbled and shook his head. "No chance, we want clear heads. They did enough drinking last night by all accounts."

When Nate finally stepped into the room, I noticed how awkward he seemed. I caught his eye briefly, but he looked away as he dumped an amp on the ground. Behind him followed two men, both hauling equipment. They *would* have looked out of place in The Black Bull, but I thought Sandy's scathing description of them had been harsh. A girl with green hair trailed into the room, and I felt myself tense.

Freya.

It was definitely her. Even though she had dark circles under eyes and a tired look she was still pretty. Why had she come to the rehearsal? She wasn't part of the band. She hovered about as the members of Listed MIA deposited their instruments and amps on the floor, looking around with a bored expression on her face. She was quite striking with her perfect eyeliner, pale, flawless skin, and green hair. My mind flashed back to Hannah Ferguson. Nate certainly had a type. I was suddenly painfully aware of my messy hair and ill-fitting dungarees, and the earth under my nails from a morning spent weeding at the farm. I felt stupid standing there lamely holding the plate of biscuits. Simon was at my side, looking equally as uncool with his tray of mugs and a teapot. I glanced at him. He looked a bit star-struck.

Fred was shaking hands with the new arrivals and gushing about how great it was to meet them. Their expressions were indifferent as they nodded at him. Nate introduced them all to the room, still looking like he'd rather be anywhere else in the world. This wasn't the confident and passionate Nate that had pushed us through rehearsals these last few weeks. He seemed to have shrunk since the arrival of his bandmates. Or perhaps it was Freya who had him looking so on edge.

150

"Does anyone want a biscuit?" I said, after Nate had made his introductions. My voice came out in a strained squeak.

Freya turned to me and looked me up and down. I felt my insides shrivel.

"There's tea too," Simon chimed in. I stole a sideways look at him. He was staring at Freya with a big, stupid grin on his face.

Maxwell was the first to reach out and take a mug of tea and a biscuit. He gave me a warm smile and a thank you, and that eased my nerves a little. Ritchie was next, drawling something unintelligible but friendly-sounding. His sneer had twisted into a sarcastic sort of grin. Freya approached us and took a mug of tea, with an aloof expression on her face.

"I really like your hair!" Simon said enthusiastically. "It almost matches our blazers."

"Um, okay," Freya said dismissively. She looked hungover.

She stalked across the room to where Nate was busying himself setting up guitars and amps. She put a hand on his shoulder and leaned in to say something in his ear. He looked at her and shrugged. His expression was hard to read. Freya smiled and then retreated to the corner and pulled her phone out of her pocket, proceeding to type furiously on it.

The members of Bramwick Brass milled around, chattering and warming up their instruments. I drifted over to Nate, still holding the plate of Foxes creams.

"Biscuit?" I said, trying to sound cheery.

"What?" He looked at me distractedly. "No, you're alright."

He went back to fiddling with the dials on the amp.

"Can everyone take their seats, please?" Fred called. "We're going to have a bit of a warm-up while Nate and his friends finish setting up."

I was awful as we played through a hymn. My stomach was in knots, and I kept looking over at Nate and Freya for any sign that they were back together. She was now sitting on a chair against the back wall watching the room curiously.

"What's wrong with you?" Simon asked, turning his head to look at me over his shoulder.

"Just nerves," I said. "I'll settle down soon."

"I bloody hope so, you were blowing every note but the ones you're supposed to right in my ear."

"Sorry," I said through tight lips.

"Now then," Fred addressed the room. "We've been doing a pretty decent job with this, but things might feel a little different with our guests here, so let's just take it easy and get a feel for things."

151

He looked across at where the members of Listed MIA stood in their ripped jeans and studded jackets. He focused his gaze on Nate and raised an eyebrow the way he used to when we were kids. "Are you going to take your seat, Nathan?"

"I'm fine where I am actually," he said, indicating the guitar he was holding. Ritchie sniggered.

"This piece has a second trombone part."

"Yeah, it also needs two guitars," Nate countered.

"Nah, don't worry about that, *Nathan,* I've got it covered." Ritchie gave a loud strum on his guitar, and Nate glared at him.

"Thank you, Ritchie," Fred beamed.

"Come on, Nate, you're one of us now!" Simon encouraged.

"Go on," Freya piped up, "show them what a real musician can do, babe."

"Fine." But he didn't look fine. He looked irritated.

We waited for Nate to get himself organised with the trombone, and I looked at Freya again. I didn't like the idea of them back together.

"I can't *wait* to see this," Ritchie said, eyeing Nate with a cruel grin.

I caught Nate's eye again as he looked away from Ritchie, and some of the frustration disappeared from his face as he gave me a lopsided smile. I gave him a thumbs up, and his smile broadened. Freya eyed me with scorn and I shrank back in my chair.

"Are we ready then?" Fred asked. "Good, after four."

Everyone apart from me played well, and overall, it sounded great. Despite my initial dislike towards Ritchie, I had to concede that he was a good musician. His vocals and Maxwell's bass line added an extra dimension to what we had been practising. It might have been an exhilarating experience if I could have made my fingers do what I wanted them to, but I was still all over the place. As we ran through it again, I tried to stop thinking about Nate and Freya and just focus on the music. It sounded raw and powerful, Ritchie's vocals lending it a biting attitude of urgency that had been lacking before. I started to get a hold of myself, and when it was time for us to come in, I was able to play again. As we finished, I really started to believe that this could actually go somewhere. This song was the perfect way to stick it to Danny Henshaw and maybe, at the same time, make brass seem cool.

"Wow!" exclaimed Simon as the noise died down. "That was bloody amazing. I had no idea music could feel so good."

"That's punk rock." Even Ritchie had dropped his scowl and looked quite satisfied.

"I'm still not getting it." It was Brendan who had spoken up. He had a serious expression on his face.

152

"What's the problem?" Fred enquired.

"I dunno, I still don't feel entirely comfortable. It just seems wrong somehow."

"Wrong how?" Nate asked, looking annoyed.

"The words. I still can't get on board with a song that's so scathing about the past, like brass bands have something to be ashamed of."

"Oh come on Brendan, times change, you can't always stay stuck in the past," Simon said.

"Yeah and there won't be a band for much longer if we don't try *something*," Sally reminded him. "It's not just about The Grange either, it's bigger even than that. We could really reach the younger generation with this, inspire them, put brass on the map. Without new players coming through brass bands will just die out. It's already happening—bands are folding all the time because they don't have enough players."

"Maybe that's how it's meant to be," Brendan mused. "If there's no longer a place for us then perhaps we should just accept we've had our time."

"Look, if you don't want our help we'll just be on our way," Ritchie drawled, starting to take off his guitar. His movements were slow and lazy. He didn't care one way or another. "This whole thing is starting to bore me anyway."

"So you'd rather see brass bands die out than adapt," I snapped in Brendan's direction. "For nearly two hundred years this band has been there for Bramwick. And what about The Grange? We have a real shot at saving it. Though I suppose you'd be happy to see that die out too, yeah? Should we just open the gates to Danny Henshaw and his bulldozers and all lie down while he steamrolls over us?"

I had risen from my chair now and I realised I was shaking. Nate was grinning at me now.

"What's your name, love?" Ritchie addressed me and I looked at him in surprise.

"Rosie," I said, feeling the adrenaline subsiding.

"I like your attitude, Rosie. You've got the heart of a punk."

I saw Freya stiffen in her chair. She turned her gaze on Nate, a small frown furrowing her brow. Nate didn't notice—he was still smiling at me. I shifted, feeling heat creeping up the back of my neck. I brushed a strand of hair out of my eyes and looked away.

"Rosie's the reason we're doing this, really," Sally offered. "She's the driving force behind the campaign to save The Grange. I just wish everyone cared as much as she does." Sally gave Brendan a scathing look.

"Ah! You're the one, aren't you?" Ritchie said with an air of dawning recognition. "Of course, you are. It all makes sense now."

Nate stood abruptly, his chair scraping across the wooden floor boards. I noticed his clenched fists at his sides.

"Leave it, Ritchie," he said threateningly.

"What? I'm just saying, there's no need to be embarrassed, mate," Ritchie smirked.

Nate briefly turned his gaze to me, and behind the anger, I saw panic.

"She's quite pretty really," Ritchie continued. My cheeks were burning now.

Freya sat, arms folded and lips pursed. She gave me a disparaging look. "She's not really your type, is she, Nate? I would have thought it would have taken someone a little more interesting to rattle you."

"Nobody's rattled me, Freya," Nate snapped. "Least of all her."

I felt tears pricking the back of my eyes.

"Oh, get it over it." Freya stood up, never taking her eyes off me. "You were just a rebound thing, but I'm back now."

"Hey!" Sally shouted, getting to her feet and walking towards Freya. "How dare you come in here and start acting like that? Have a bit of respect."

"Wait a minute. We came here as a favour to you," Ritchie cut in.

Nate was now dismantling his trombone. He looked like he wanted to bolt for the door and never come back.

"*Protest like your future depends on it,*" Ritchie was now reading aloud from Sally's shirt. "Is this a midlife crisis T-shirt, love?"

"I've been an activist since you were a kid, *love.*" Sally looked like she might actually slap him.

"I think you should leave." Fred stepped up beside Sally. "We don't tolerate this kind of behaviour at Bramwick Brass."

"But the song…" My voice trailed off. Through my hurt and embarrassment I could see it all slipping away.

"I'm sorry, everyone," Nate said as he yanked the trombone apart and stuffed it into the case. "This was a stupid idea, this isn't going to work."

Ritchie was still leaning against the back wall, a smug look on his face. I felt deflated. This had been an absolute disaster.

Chapter Twenty-Seven

Nate

"You're out of order, do you know that?" I don't think I'd ever seen Simon angry. I tossed my guitar in the back of the van and looked back to see the others just coming out of the doors with the rest of the gear. "Did you see Rosie's face? She doesn't deserve this, not after everything."

"Yeah? Well, blame *him*." I spat the last word at Ritchie as he approached.

"Woah, it's not my fault you've got some stupid rebound crush on the hippy chick," he said with a roll of his eyes.

"And you," I rounded on Maxwell. "Why the fuck did you tell him? He didn't need to know."

Maxwell shrugged.

"And bringing *her* here," I pointed a finger at Freya. "You really did just come here to fuck with me, didn't you? You never wanted to help in the first place."

I was so angry I was shaking. I advanced on Ritchie. Nasher was back, and it looked like we were going to have one of our infamous brawls.

"Back off, Nate." Freya inserted herself between us, and I stood there, feeling the adrenaline pumping, furious at all of them.

"You have some nerve to even show your face," I growled at Freya. "All the bullshit you fed me about how it was a one-off, how it would never happen again."

"Ritchie and I aren't together, Nate," she said coldly. "Despite what you may have been led to believe. He's just a friend. He's been there for me because God knows I needed someone when you fucked off and refused to even talk about anything."

"Yeah, I really believe you."

I could see the door to the building over her shoulder. Some of the Bramwick Brass players were standing staring at us in disbelief. I briefly tried to search out Rosie, but she wasn't among them. I shouldn't have reacted the way I did. Simon was right; it was out of order. She'd probably never forgive me.

"It's true." Ritchie gave a nonchalant nod. "It was only that one time."

"But you said on the phone…" I turned to Maxwell.

"I just said they'd been seeing a lot of each other. I don't know what they get up to. Maybe he has just been supporting her…"

"You're all full of shit." I turned away, and slammed the van doors so hard the whole thing shuddered.

"To think *these* are the people you chose over us." Simon's voice was thick with contempt.

"What's that supposed to mean?" Ritchie started towards him, fists half-raised. "I saved his fucking life once."

Simon now looked worried and started to back up towards the small gathering of his bandmates. Ritchie stalked after him.

"Leave him alone, Ritchie." I dashed after him and pulled him back. Ritchie spun around to face me and before I knew what was happening I was seeing stars. He had landed a punch right in my face. I reeled back but regained myself and my fury spiked.

"Wanna hit me, Nasher?" Ritchie grinned at me. "Come on then."

I felt a trickle of blood run from my mouth. I raised my clenched fists.

"Both of you stop it!" shrieked Freya. "Why do you always have to do this?"

"Stay out of it, Freya," I warned. Ritchie's grin widened.

"What are you waiting for, Nate? Scared your sad little friends back there won't approve?"

I prepared to hit him. By the door, Fred was shaking his head sadly. Simon looked afraid. George was threatening to call the police, his phone held out in front of him. Then I saw Rosie behind them, still in the corridor behind the open door with Sally. I lowered my fists. This wasn't the answer.

"Knew this place had turned you soft," Ritchie said scathingly.

"You alright, man?" Maxwell put a hand on my shoulder and I wiped at the blood on my face with my sleeve.

"Course he's alright, he's had worse than that," Ritchie answered.

He was right. We'd had far worse fights over the years—and it was always me who came off worse, especially in the early days. Then it hit me. Just like Rosie, I'd been trapped in a toxic relationship for years. Only mine wasn't with a partner, but with my bandmate.

Ritchie had always had a hold over me, ever since that night on the platform when I was just a desperate, daft kid. He was ten years older and, back then, he'd seemed like the coolest person on the planet—confident, talented, effortlessly rebellious. He was everything I wanted to be and I idolised him.

I ignored the jibes and the constant needling, because he said it was just "banter." According to him, I needed to toughen up if I was going to survive in the city. He was always pushing my boundaries until I snapped—then he'd use it as an excuse to kick off. He loved provoking people; he always found a way to stir up trouble when we were at gigs or out drinking, winding up strangers until we got dragged into a fight. Then he'd just stand there watching, laughing, egging me on like it was some kind of dogfight. He claimed it was all part of being in the punk scene.

In the early days, he even discouraged me from keeping in touch with anyone back in Bramwick. He said they'd only ever held me back—and I believed him.

Now, thinking it all over, I realised the silent treatment I'd been getting since coming home was probably just another part of his game. I couldn't think of a single good thing to say about Ritchie. Asking him to come here had been a terrible mistake.

"I'm done with this," I said at last, feeling myself calm. "Maxwell, I've no issue with you, but you might want to think about the company you keep."

Maxwell looked sheepishly at his feet.

"Freya, I don't care why you came here, I don't care if it was just the once, I've had enough of you."

Freya looked outraged.

"Ritchie, I don't ever want to see you again."

"You're always so fucking dramatic, Nasher," Ritchie said cooly. "I know you'll be back; you need us."

"Not this time."

Ritchie smirked. I stepped away from them and approached the members of Bramwick Brass. They looked at me with expressions of shock and disbelief.

"I'm so sorry," I said to Fred. "This should never have happened."

Fred looked at me, the disappointment radiating off him. I shrank beneath his gaze. I looked down the corridor to see that Rosie was still with Sally, hovering in the background and looking upset.

"No, it shouldn't," Fred shook his head. "Brendan was right, our worlds don't mix. We don't need this type of thing."

"You're absolutely right," I agreed. "We don't need Ritchie, we can finish the project without him, don't worry. I'll find a way to convince the record company we can do it on our own, it'll be fine."

"No, lad," Fred gave me a sad smile. "We can't. We kicked one of our own out of the band for bad behaviour, what makes you think we can let you off?"

Brendan folded his arms and set his mouth in a smug, satisfied line.

"What? But the song…The Grange…" I floundered.

"I'd rather see Danny Henshaw's bulldozers flatten the lot than have anything more to do with you, Nathan." Rosie had come forward now. Her face was tear-stained but now she looked resolute.

There was a ghost of a smile on Freya's lips as she looked at Rosie.

"Rosie," I felt my heart breaking. "I didn't mean what I said, it's just him, he winds me up."

"Sorry, Nate, it's over," Sally said as she stepped up beside Rosie.

"But I love you, Rosie," I pleaded.

"For fuck's sake," Freya rolled her eyes and folded her arms.

"This is precious!" Ritchie guffawed from behind us.

"But I do." I started to walk towards her but Simon put himself in my path.

"Leave it mate, you've done enough damage."

I looked at Rosie.

"Like I told you, you're ten years too late," she said. Freya gave her a conceited look. She turned and went back inside.

"Come on, Nate." Freya approached me and put a hand on my shoulder. "You don't need these people, it's time to come home."

Chapter Twenty-Eight

Rosie

By the next day, the whole village had heard *some* version of what had gone down at the rehearsal with Nate and Listed MIA. Rumours spread like wildfire, and soon enough, I was back in the middle of it all. Of course, Alan heard every last word.

In the weeks after Sally had chased him from her doorstep, he hadn't given up—bombarding me with texts, pleading for forgiveness. Then one evening, a new cornet turned up at the band room, a bow tied to the case and a tag with my name on it. For a moment, I thought maybe the band had clubbed together to get me a new instrument. But Fred quickly set me straight—it wasn't from them. When I read the card, I found out it was from Alan.

I couldn't accept it. The cornet sat untouched in its case, pristine and silent, while I kept playing the battered old loaner and wrestled with what to do with it.

Eventually, things began to calm down. Alan's messages grew less frequent. But after the Listed MIA rehearsal—when Nate blurted out that he loved me in front of everyone—the tide turned again. This time, Alan's messages were venomous. It gave weight to the narrative he'd been spinning: that Nate was the reason we split. And just like that, I was recast as the cheating wife who'd run off with a rock star.

As if that wasn't enough, Nate started messaging too. He wanted to meet up, talk, clear the air. I ignored him, and eventually, he gave up.

The whispers behind my back, Nate's messages, and Alan's increasingly vile texts all started to wear me down. Morale in the band dropped, too. We were back to playing marches and hymns, and soon, the Christmas carols began and Bramwick saw its first snowfall of the season. The village's excitement over our big plan to save The Grange fizzled out when people realised the charity single wasn't happening. The whole thing was beginning to feel hopeless.

In November, I got a call from Greenhill Leisure. After a formal interview, they offered me a part-time admin job—afternoons behind a desk, sorting contractors, chasing invoices, preparing for the centre's spring opening. Ironic, really. I wasn't with Alan anymore, but I still took the job.

By December, with the crisp air settling in, fairy lights twinkling in windows, and the first trees going up, I was miserable. I blamed Nate.

Once again, he'd vanished, leaving me hurt and rejected. I took a walk past his dad's old house one day, but there was no sign of the rusty van. I assumed he had left the village again. Running away, as he always did.

"You need to pull yourself out of this slump," Sally said one evening as we sat in The Black Bull.

I hadn't wanted to go out—she'd practically dragged me—but here I was, slouched by the fire with her and Simon, while Mrs Thornton sang along loudly (and off-key) to the pub's Christmas playlist.

"I agree," Simon added. "I hate seeing you like this."

The pub was buzzing, the whole of Bramwick apparently in the festive spirit. Everyone except me.

"I heard you skipped the last meeting about The Grange," Simon said carefully.

"I think I've just about given up on The Grange," I muttered, swirling the wine in my glass. Across the room, Nigel Dunnock was drunkenly pulling tinsel off the taxidermy fox and wrapping it around his neck like a scarf.

"This isn't you, Rosie," Sally said softly.

"This *is* me now," I said, barely above a whisper. "The me who finally stopped living in a dream world."

Simon and Sally exchanged a glance. There was a spark in Simon's eye.

"Let's tell her," he said.

"You think? Shouldn't we run it by Fred first?"

"Nah," Simon grinned.

"What are you two on about?" I asked, not really expecting to care about the answer.

"Let me grab another round," Sally said, already getting up. "Then we'll tell you everything."

Ten minutes later, I stared at the pair of them, one eyebrow raised.

"Let me get this straight," I said slowly. "You want *us* to release the single. On our own?"

"Yep," Simon said proudly, practically bouncing in his seat.

"Even though the only person with any contacts, any clue how to actually *do* this, has buggered off?"

"Exactly."

"It's a terrible idea," I said, folding my arms.

"We thought you'd be excited," said Sally, her face falling. "There was a time you'd have jumped at something like this."

"Yeah, maybe back when I had the energy to care."

"It's not as mad as it sounds," Simon insisted.

"Have you actually thought this through, or did you just wake up one morning and think, 'Let's release a single!'?"

"Of course we've thought about it!" Sally said indignantly, taking a drink of her gin.

I straightened up, the heat from the pub fire making my head throb. Mrs Thornton's off-key warbling didn't help either. I peeled off my cardigan, trying to stay focused.

"Okay," I said. "Tell me how this is supposed to work, and I'll decide whether you've totally lost the plot."

"Sleigh bells ring, are you listening…" Mrs Thornton's voice rose in a painful crescendo.

"I think *she's* the one who's lost the plot," Simon muttered. "Wish she'd shut up."

"Right," Sally slapped her palms down on the sticky table like she meant business. "You don't need a label anymore to release a single, right?"

"You don't?" I blinked. I was surprised.

"No," Simon chimed in. "Anyone can put stuff on Spotify. Where've you been for the last decade?"

"Sorry I'm not up to date on the inner workings of the music industry," I shot back. "Even if that's true, how are we meant to record it? Nate was supposed to handle all that."

"We don't need him," Sally said. "Lancaster College has a studio. I've already spoken to someone there. The students will help—for a modest fee."

I felt the first flicker of something like excitement.

"You're serious about this?"

"Dead serious," she nodded.

"Alright, next problem." My interest was growing. "Say we do record a song. How do we get anyone to *notice* it? Listed MIA had the contacts. We don't."

"We make it go viral," Simon said, like it was no big deal.

"Oh, sure. Easy," I snorted.

"We can try," Sally said. "Social media, press releases, a few well-timed stunts—"

"No gluing yourself to anything," Simon warned.

"So?" Sally raised an eyebrow. "What's the verdict? Have we lost the plot?"

I chewed my lip, Mrs Thornton now launching into a mangled 'Jingle Bells'.

"It's not the worst idea I've heard," I admitted. "But you're both ignoring the biggest challenge."

161

"Which is?"

"No one in the band can write a song like Nate."

Sally sighed. "Yeah. That song was brilliant. Imagine if we let Fred write something."

"We'd get another depressing march," Simon muttered. They looked as gloomy as I had felt half an hour ago. But my own spirits were lifting.

"We could always use a classic, something out of copyright," Sally offered.

"Nah," Simon shook his head. "That won't make headlines. The whole point was that it was brass-punk fusion—something *new*."

Sally sighed again. "Unless one of us has a secret songwriting talent..."

I leaned in like I was planning a heist. "We could use the original song."

Sally frowned. "'Blood and Brass'? Are you serious? Now *you've* lost the plot."

"Why not? Nate's not going to use it—not for his band. It'd be weird for them to sing about brass band traditions. Besides, he feels guilty. I've had so many messages."

"Same," Simon nodded. "Apologies, all very heartfelt. I ignored them."

"Me too," I said.

"Good," Simon grinned. "I'm pretty sure he's back in London now."

"I thought as much," I said.

"This feels very dodgy," Sally said. "You're talking about stealing his song."

"He wrote it for *us*. We were meant to perform it. It's basically ours."

"Yeah," Simon agreed. "Like we commissioned it."

"But we didn't," Sally reminded us.

I sighed.

"I could always ask him. See if he'll let us use it." The words tasted sour. The last thing I wanted was to reach out to Nate.

"He'd say yes if *you* asked," Simon said, grinning again.

"Why would you think that?"

"Because he said he loves you, obviously."

I gave him a look. "He doesn't love me."

"He might even come back to help if you asked," Sally said.

"No." I shook my head firmly. "Even if he did, we'd still have to convince Fred. If we're doing this, we're doing it without him."

Chapter Twenty-Nine

Nate

"For fuck's sake, Nasher, are you even with us today?" Ritchie glared at me.

It had been a rough couple of months. Ever since my last rehearsal with Bramwick Brass, I hadn't known what to do with myself. I meant what I said to Rosie—I did love her—but I'd fucked it up, and now there was no way back. It could have been perfect, like something out of a movie. I should have told her how I felt the second Ritchie started mocking her, but instead, I acted like a complete idiot. No amount of apologies could fix it. My messages went unanswered. Eventually, I took the hint, left Bramwick, and had been sleeping on Maxwell's sofa ever since.

"Sorry," I muttered, stuffing my phone into my jeans pocket. "What were you saying?"

"If I see that phone out again, I swear I'll stamp on it." Ritchie's eyes narrowed. "It's A, G, C for the chorus. Got it?"

"Yeah, yeah."

Listed MIA were back together. The money we'd been offered for a new album was too good to turn down. That meant working with Ritchie again. I told myself I could keep it professional—so long as I didn't have to socialise with him outside the studio, I'd get through it.

"Let's start from verse two. See if you can get it right this time."

I had received a message from Rosie just as I arrived at the studio. She was the last person I expected to hear from. I'd just about managed to put her out of my mind, but the second I saw her name on the screen, my heart flipped. She wanted to talk.

It had been months.

I quickly replied, telling her I was in rehearsals and asking what she wanted. Her response was simple: *Call me when you get a minute.*

I hadn't been able to concentrate since.

"Stop, stop, stop!" Ritchie threw up his arms. "Are you stupid or something? It's the easiest riff in the world, and you keep fucking it up."

I wasn't going to play a damn thing properly until I spoke to her.

"Sorry, guys," I said, taking off my guitar. "Give me five minutes—I need to deal with something."

"It better be a fucking emergency, Nasher." Ritchie's voice was a low growl. "Just hurry up. We've got a lot to get through."

I bit my tongue and stepped into the corridor, my hands already scrolling through my contacts for Rosie's number.

She picked up on the second ring.

"Nate," she said briskly. "Hi."

A smile tugged at my lips. It was good to hear her voice. "Hey. Did you have a nice Christmas?"

"Oh, you know. It was okay. Passed by in a bit of a blur—endless carol concerts, you know what it's like."

Christmas had always been Bramwick Brass's busiest time of year. I pictured them playing at the lights switch-on, the church service, and the legendary Christmas Eve gig at The Black Bull. Dad used to take me every year once I was old enough. The band would cram into the pub, tinsel wrapped around their instruments, and play carols while the villagers got drunk. The music went on until midnight, when Mrs Thornton would buy a round for the entire pub to toast Christmas.

"It's good to hear from you," I said. "I really am sorry about everything that happened."

"I know." Her voice was tense. "You told me a hundred times. That's not why I called."

I frowned. "Okay... so why *did* you call?"

"The band wants to release 'Blood and Brass'."

"Really? That's great!" This was my chance to win her over. "I've got some stuff going on here, but I can definitely help."

"I'm not asking for your help," she said sharply.

My stomach dropped. "Then I'm confused. What do you want?"

"We want to record the song ourselves."

For a moment I was speechless. That was not what I had been expecting. "Wait—what?"

"You let us down, Nate. I know you don't give a damn, but we're struggling up here and we have to do *something*."

"So you want me to just *give* you 'Blood and Brass'?"

"Yes, please."

It was like a fresh kick to the gut. She still hadn't forgiven me.

"That song is gold, Rosie. What makes you think I'd just hand it over?"

"You wrote it for us. What use do *you* have for a song about brass bands?"

"I could rework it for Listed MIA. Change the lyrics—they're the least important part."

"We're fighting a losing battle with The Grange, Nate." Her voice sharpened. "You *owe* us. After the way you behaved, it's the least you can do."

"You don't know the first thing about recording music," I shot back. "You don't have the contacts or the equipment."

"That's not your problem."

I sighed. "Just let me help. You know I can make this a success for you."

"I really didn't want to get into this, but clearly, you still have no idea how much you hurt me." Her voice wavered. "You humiliated me in front of everyone. Then you had the *audacity* to say you loved me—*with all those people listening.* Do you have any idea how much trouble that caused me?"

"I heard the gossip too," I snapped. "I couldn't leave the house because half of Bramwick hated me."

"Oh, well, what a *shame* for you," she said mockingly. "At least *you* could leave. I had to *stay* and rebuild my life. You don't have a clue how the real world works, do you?"

"I said I was sorry. I *know* what I did was awful. I'd take it back if I could." My voice softened. "Don't cut off your nose to spite your face. Let me make it up to you."

"You really are that arrogant." She let out a bitter laugh. "You think *you're* the only person who can make this work?"

"That's not what I meant."

"Don't you think we're *capable*? Don't you believe *I'm* capable?"

I hesitated. "You know it would be a hell of a lot easier if you had me on board…"

"I know." She sighed, and for a moment, I thought she was softening. "But maybe it's not meant to be easy. And maybe—just maybe—I can make this work."

I swallowed hard. "I think you can do anything you put your mind to, Rosie. You're the strongest, most determined person I know."

There was a beat of silence.

I heard her take a deep breath, steadying herself. "So… you'll sign the rights over to us?"

"Yeah." My voice came out quieter than I intended. "Go on, then."

"Thank you, Nate."

"If you change your mind about me helping—"

"You had your chance," she cut in, her tone turning cold. "I'll be in touch. Take care."

The line went dead.

Chapter Thirty

Rosie

It seemed like the whole village had crammed into The Black Bull that night. Even Alan was there, a can of coke in his hand, looking a lot better than he had in a long time. It had been a gruelling two months. There had been arguments, financial challenges, dozens of bus trips to Lancaster and back— but we had done it. The determination and commitment of everyone in the band, the unbelievable support from the community, and the kindness of the students at the college who gave up their time to help us out had all led to this moment. Simon had been amazing with his campaigns on social media, and it seemed our story had captured the hearts of the residents of Yorkshire and beyond. Everyone had been talking about the brass band that was soon to release a punk fusion single. We had even been approached by a ska punk band based in Blackpool who had offered to take the place of Listed MIA. They had done a brilliant job— we hadn't needed Nate after all. They had even extended an invite to us to join them at Rebellion festival in the summer, but I suspected that might be a bit much for some of the others, especially Fred and Brendan. They had been sympathetic when I told them how badly let down we had been by Listed MIA. They had seen the articles about Nate being involved in the fundraiser, and they were determined to show they could do just as good a job.

We had made so many new friends, and the whole thing had been a great adventure. Now we were about to unleash our masterpiece on the world.

"Every town has that one building. You know the one, the place where the community gathers, full of memories and music and maybe the odd dodgy rifle prize over the years." The presenter smiled into the camera.

We had been delighted when *Tonight's Take* got wind of our story and wanted to do a feature. This was proper prime-time national television. We had decided that it would be the perfect platform from which to launch the single. The episode was airing that night, and Mrs Thornton had borrowed a projector from one of the pub regulars so we could all gather to watch it.

"Well, in a small village in the heart of the Yorkshire Dales, there is such a place that is especially important to its residents," the presenter continued as the pub watched in awed silence. "The Grange, with its community centre and gardens, was gifted to the people of Bramwick nearly two hundred years ago, but now it is under threat, with plans to redevelop the site putting its future at risk."

"Yeah, fuck you, Danny Henshaw!" Someone who'd had one too many yelled out from the back. Mrs Thornton made a loud shushing sound.

"So what's a community to do? Well— in true Bramwick style— this group of local residents are turning up the volume."

Sally was standing behind me, and she gave my shoulder a squeeze. I looked back at her, and she was grinning excitedly. On the screen, the camera cut to footage of the band practising, of The Grange, of the villagers waving their placards as they marched to the pub. When I saw Nate among them, my heart skipped a beat. We had exchanged the odd message here and there— and he was always the first to comment with words of encouragement on the band's Facebook posts about our progress— but he hadn't been back to Bramwick, and I still wasn't sure I had forgiven him.

"The local brass band has decided to record a charity single, hoping to raise both money and awareness, and it's already striking a chord, not just in Bramwick, but far beyond."

"God, look at my hair," said Sally as she appeared on the screen with the rest of the band in some footage of a rehearsal.

"Liam has been to meet the people behind a very local campaign with a very catchy tune."

The Grange appeared on the screen as the show ran a montage of footage of the building, the grounds, the volunteers working, and the various clubs and groups meeting.

"It may not be glamorous, or modern," a man's voice began to speak over the footage. "But to the people of Bramwick, this glorious old hall and its grounds are the beating heart of the village."

The scene cut to us practising again, and the sound of our music drifted behind the presenter's commentary.

"You're out of tune there, George," Fred observed, and a few people laughed while George looked indignant.

"For decades, this hall has been the home to Bramwick Brass Band, who have been a part of the community for over a hundred years."

"It's more than just a building." A cheer erupted in the bar as I appeared on screen, and I blushed. Simon nudged me with his elbow, and Sally tightened her grip on my shoulder. "It's where I learned to play, where we hold weddings, grow food, and come together to celebrate."

Now the screen was showing archived footage— old photographs of parties, jumble sales, and the May Day festivities.

167

"But now, The Grange faces closure. There are plans for it to be redeveloped into luxury houses, and the community has been left fighting to save this space that holds generations of memories."

"Where are the kids supposed to go?" Now one of our older residents was on screen. Gladys was in her kitchen with a cup of tea in front of her. "Where will the pensioners go to dance? If they take The Grange away, they erase the soul of this place."

Now the screen was showing footage of us in the recording studio at the college. Fred was wearing headphones and waving his baton while some skinny youths in ripped jeans played guitars and sang.

"To raise awareness— and some much-needed cash— Bramwick Brass Band have formed an unlikely partnership with punk band The Splinters."

"We knew we needed something different." I was back on the screen now, the rest of the band behind me in the studio while someone fiddled with buttons and dials on the mixing desk. "And that's when we had the idea for this brass-punk fusion. We wanted to honour Yorkshire's traditional brass bands but at the same time create something memorable and unusual."

"And the campaign has brought the community together in more ways than one." They were now showing footage of a bake sale the WI had hosted. "From bake sales to bucket collections, Bramwick is pulling out all stops to keep its community and its heritage alive."

It was Simon's turn to appear on camera now. "We just hope people hear the song, see the campaign and realise that these types of things are worth fighting for." There was another cheer and Simon grinned.

"It's not just a song." Liam was now standing outside The Grange with all of us behind him. "It's a stand. And for the people of Bramwick, The Grange is worth every note."

Back in the studio the presenter smiled into the camera. "Well, if that doesn't warm your heart... 'Blood and Brass' is out now on all available streaming platforms, with all proceeds going to the Save The Grange campaign. And we're told there's even talk of a national tour..." The presenter chuckled, as did my band mates. "Best of luck to them."

The pub broke out in cheers and applause. There was much back slapping and hand shaking and clinking of glasses. I couldn't stop smiling. It had been a beautiful feature, the perfect launch for our song. All the hard work was paying off and we had done it all without Nate. I wondered if he had been watching tonight. Was he proud of what we had done or was he bitter and resentful that we hadn't needed him? I instinctively checked my phone to see if he had been in touch, and was a little disappointed to see he hadn't. I shook myself. Why did I care?

168

"Well, that was all very touching." I hadn't even noticed Danny Henshaw, but there he was, lurking at the door. He was leaning on the frame with his arms folded and looking very relaxed. He had the air of someone who was completely confident he was going to win. "I mean it. It was lovely."

"Why are you here, Danny?" I asked, my joy evaporating.

"Just stopped in for a drink, that's all."

"Well, you aren't welcome." It was Alan who had challenged him, and I looked at him in surprise.

"He's right, get out," Mrs Thornton demanded. "You're barred."

Danny gave her a smug look. "That's fine, I've been thrown out of much better places than this, believe me."

He turned and left. I was so angry I had started to shake.

"You okay?" asked Sally.

"Yeah, he just winds me up. He's so sure that he's going to get his way."

"Well, he's wrong," Simon assured me. "Forget him, this is our night, come on, I'll get you another drink."

The bar was filled with excited chatter, and the mood was jubilant. I decided I wouldn't let Danny Henshaw spoil it.

"You've done a good job." Alan approached me, looking sheepish. "I can't believe you pulled it off."

"Thanks," I said, eyeing him warily.

"So how are you?"

"I'm okay. Rushed off my feet really. You?"

"I'm good." He gave an affirming nod. He looked good. "Haven't had a drink in two months, been seeing a counsellor, sorting myself out, you know."

"Is everything alright here?" Simon said suspiciously as he came back with my drink. He looked at Alan reproachfully.

"It's okay, Simon," I said, touching his arm and taking my glass from him.

"Right, I'll just be over there," he said as he retreated to the bar and continued to glance at us.

"It's nice how much they look out for you," Alan commented, and he sounded genuine.

"They've been a huge support," I said.

"I miss them."

"Well, you've only got yourself to blame for that."

"I miss you too."

"Alan, let's not do this," I groaned, feeling my defences going up. "I'm happy that you're looking so well and that you're getting help, but we won't be getting back together, ever."

"I know that," he said. "I didn't mean to imply we might. I know it doesn't mean anything, and I know I've said it a million times, but I really am sorry. For everything."

And I believed he was. It would have been so easy to fall back into my life with him. To return to our house, to keep working at the spa, to have the children I had always wanted. But I wouldn't.

"I know, Alan," I said softly. "You take care of yourself."

I left him standing there and went to join Simon at the bar.

"What a night, eh?" he said happily. "You're amazing, Rosie, do you know that? None of this would have happened if it weren't for you."

"Hmm…" I gazed thoughtfully at my glass of wine, starting to feel a little down for some reason.

"What is it?" Simon asked, frowning. "Is it Alan? What did he say?"

"No, no." I shook my head. "I was just thinking about Nate."

"What about him?"

"I just feel a bit guilty, that's all. This is as much to do with him as me."

"Hardly," Simon snorted.

At that moment, I felt my phone buzz.

"Speak of the devil," I said, opening the message.

"Is that him?"

"Yeah." I read the message, then showed Simon.

Hi Patches. Just saw you on the tele, and I've listened to the song. I am unbelievably proud of you. I knew you would pull it off, but I didn't think it would be that good. You were right. You didn't need me after all. I hope you make a million pounds. Thanks for doing my song justice.

"Pff." Simon looked irritated.

"Should I write back?"

"Have you been talking?"

"Not really, just the odd message here and there when I've needed to talk to him about something to do with the song."

"I'd ignore him," Simon insisted. "You just got rid of one arsehole man. You don't need another."

"You're probably right," I sighed, putting my phone away.

Around me, the excited buzz continued, and I started to smile. Everyone had been telling me how proud they were all night, but now I had heard it from the one whose opinion mattered most to me.

Chapter Thirty-One

Nate

"What are you grinning at?" Ritchie said with disdain when I arrived at the studio that morning.

Listed MIA were nearing the end of recording our new album. Normally, I enjoyed studio work— writing and recording songs— but not this time. The band had lost its shine for me, and working with Ritchie just felt like a chore.

"Bramwick Brass released their single yesterday," I said. "They were on *Tonight's Take* last night. I'm just looking at some of the feedback— it's pretty positive."

I felt more connected to this than anything I was doing in the studio with Listed MIA. I had messaged Rosie to tell her how proud I was, but I was yet to get a reply.

"Let's have a look." Ritchie snatched my phone from my hand. I had been reading an article about the song on *The Metro* website.

"For fuck's sake, they've made a video and everything."

The video Ritchie was talking about had warmed my heart. It was cheesy, not exactly what you'd call "cool"— the old me probably would have mocked it with Ritchie— but there was something charming and fun about it. It looked like they were all having an absolute blast. I wondered how they had talked Fred into allowing them to customise the blazers. They were now adorned with safety pins and slogans scrawled in Sharpie. I had a feeling Sally was behind this. To his credit, Fred was right there at the front, conducting proudly with 'Corporate Greed Destroys Communities' written across his back. When I saw Simon had scribbled 'Band Sucks' on his sleeve, I got unexpectedly emotional. Perhaps he didn't hate me after all.

From my phone, 'Blood and Brass' started to play, and I watched Ritchie's lip curl into a sneer.

"What a bunch of losers," he drawled. "Look at the state of them; they think sticking a few safety pins in their coats makes them punk. They've murdered your song, Nasher. I can't believe you let them have it."

When I had signed over 'Blood and Brass' to them, a selfish part of me had wanted them to struggle and come back begging for my help, but now that they had nailed it, I felt nothing but admiration. I would have gladly gone back if they had asked me, though. I had even kept playing the trombone in hope that it might happen. But they had proved they didn't need me. They had done it on their own.

My return to London hadn't been the great thing I had hoped it would be. I had once been desperate to get away from Bramwick, but I hadn't found my old life waiting for me when I returned to the city. Everything was different, and I felt hollow and unfulfilled. My friendships were shallow and revolved mainly around childish banter and getting drunk. Freya and I had agreed to give things another go, though I hadn't moved back in yet— I was still sleeping on Maxwell's sofa. I didn't feel the connection anymore. My mind wandered back to Rosie frequently. In all honesty, I was pretty miserable.

"I think you're being a bit harsh, Ritchie," Maxwell said, peering over his shoulder at my phone.

"Ha ha ha look!" Ritchie blurted. "There's that bird you fancied. What the hell is she wearing?"

I made a grab for my phone, but Ritchie stepped back, and I overbalanced and went crashing to the floor. He laughed harshly and continued with the insults.

"You dodged a bullet there, Nasher," he cackled, finally tossing my phone back to me as I got to my feet. "You should be thankful I rescued you, *again,* or that could be you making a tit of yourself."

I felt angry. He was pushing me again, hoping for a reaction, and as much as I wanted to resort to my old ways and punch him, I stopped myself. I had had enough. I wasn't going to fall into that old pattern. Ritchie enjoyed physical violence, and nothing would please him more than if I started a fight. I took a deep breath and put my phone in my pocket.

"Have I offended you?" he said with mock surprise. "Should we show this to Freya? Let her size up the competition? Not that it's much of one."

"You know something, Ritchie," I said calmly. "You're an arsehole."

"So what?"

"So I'm done with you. And I mean it this time."

Rosie had found the courage to leave Alan. If she could do that, I could walk away from Ritchie.

I crossed the room and started to pack away my guitar.

"Oh look, lads, I've hurt Nasher's feelings. He's going to run away again."

"I'm not running away," I said, zipping the bag shut. "I've just had enough of this. I should never have agreed to come back."

Had Rosie stayed away? Or had she gone back to her marriage?

"Oh, so dramatic! You've made your point. I won't mention her again."

Maxwell glanced between us, visibly uneasy. I slung my bag over my shoulder.

"We've got an album to finish, Nate…" Maxwell reminded me.

"It's nearly done," I said. "Get a session player to fill in the rest of my parts, pay them out of my cut."

Maxwell looked helplessly at Ritchie, whose expression was now thunderous.

"You can't just walk out on us!"

"Watch me."

As I headed for the door, Ritchie shoved me. Not hard, but just enough. Words had failed—so now he wanted a fight. It would've felt good to land a punch. But I didn't.

"You need us, Nasher!" Ritchie yelled.

"Maybe I did once," I said, a hand on the door. "but not anymore."

"Fine, fuck off then! I'm still screwing Freya, you know? I've got your band and your girl now."

It didn't surprise me, nor did I feel hurt. It just confirmed what I already knew: nothing about being back in London felt right.

"Maxwell, Mike," I said, nodding at the other two and ignoring Ritchie. "Give me a bell if you ever fancy getting together for a jam without this tosser."

And with that, I left.

As I stepped out into the street, I had didn't know what came next. But for the first time in a long while, I knew I was heading in the right direction.

Chapter Thirty-Two

Rosie

Everything was moving at a million miles an hour. I'd hoped our song might get a bit of attention, but it had gone far beyond anything we'd imagined. Simon's relentless efforts—his press releases, the countless social media posts—had really paid off. Our story was out there. People knew who we were. And with that raised awareness came a surge in donations to our GoFundMe page.

Support from other brass bands across the country began pouring in too. We could hardly keep up with the messages, emails, and offers to help. It was exciting—thrilling, even—but the excitement was laced with a creeping anxiety I couldn't shake.

The developer was pressing the council to finalise the sale of The Grange. Our community group had fought hard and managed to buy us a little time, but that grace period was slipping away fast. The donations were coming in, but not quickly enough—and donations were all we had to rely on.

It didn't matter how many people were listening to the song—no one buys music anymore. They streamed it on Spotify, shared it on social media. There was no money in that. We had to appeal to people's generosity, their empathy. And the longer this dragged on, the more I feared it wouldn't be enough.

"We need to do more," I said, trying to keep the panic from my voice as I glanced over the figures during a meeting with the group. "We've made huge strides, but we're running out of time."

"I can ask for another review," Sandy Brown offered. "Try to buy us a bit more breathing space."

"On what grounds?" Alex asked, clearly just as frustrated as I was. "We already made up that thing about the endangered newts in the pond. It worked for a while, but what else can we possibly say now?"

"Bats?" Helen suggested. "Aren't bats protected? I heard if they're nesting in your loft you're not allowed to move them."

"Do bats even nest?" Christine asked, chewing the end of her pen.

"No, they don't nest," I snapped, more sharply than I intended. "And anyway, we can't go down that road again. They already did a full wildlife survey after the newt incident. According to their report, there's nothing there worth saving—not to them, anyway. Just the rabbits, the mice, the butterflies, the birds... all the small lives they're about to destroy."

"So what then?" Sandy asked, exasperated.

"I honestly don't know," I sighed. "If it comes to it, maybe we follow Sally's lead and chain ourselves to the railings when the diggers arrive."

"Can the band do anything else? More appearances?"

"Honestly, they're at their limit. Everyone's exhausted. We've dragged them all over the place for weeks now."

"It's not going to work, is it?" Gerald said quietly, staring down at the calculator in his hands. "There's just not enough time. We're still short about fifty grand."

That evening at rehearsal, I looked around the room and saw it on every face: weariness. The high from the single's success had kept us going, but now it was wearing off, and reality was setting back in.

"We've had another request for a radio appearance," I told them, trying to sound upbeat. "BBC Radio 4 this time. It's for a programme about women and their success stories—they want to interview me, but they'd also love it if some of you could come and perform a live piece."

Silence. A shuffling of feet. Eyes on the floor. Biting lips. No one rushed to volunteer.

"Rosie, love," Fred said gently. "We're all tired. We tried our best. But we've got jobs, families... I think we've done all we can."

"But if we could just push a little harder, maybe we'd—"

"Fred's right," Simon cut in softly. "This has been incredible. The best time of my life, honestly. But we're out of time. What is it—four weeks until the council votes? And from what I've heard, we're still way behind what we'd need to buy the Grange."

"But..." I faltered, my voice trailing off. My shoulders sagged. The crash after all the excitement was brutal.

Sally stood and came over, wrapping an arm around me.

"You did your best," she said quietly. "Whatever happens, you've achieved something incredible. You should be proud."

"*We* did," I corrected her.

"Yeah, but none of it would have happened without you," Brendan added kindly.

I started to cry, and Sally hugged me tighter. Then Simon stepped forward and wrapped his arms around us both.

"You're absolutely exhausted," Fred said. "You need to rest before you burn yourself out. It's not over yet. It only takes one generous donor. There are people out there with the means to make a real difference."

I wiped my tears away with my sleeve and nodded, managing a small smile.

"You're right," I said. "What we've done is amazing."

"Even if it doesn't save The Grange," Simon added encouragingly, "you've started something, Rosie Fenn. You've sparked something real. There are kids all over TikTok playing brass instruments now. It's a thing."

"What?" I stared at him, surprised. I'd been so focused on saving The Grange that I hadn't even considered the wider impact.

"It's true," Simon grinned.

"Absolutely," Fred confirmed. "I've got kids at the school coming to *me* wanting to learn for a change. Looks like we'll be restarting the youth band."

"Whatever happens next," I said, looking around at them, "we've started something special."

Driving back to Mum and Dad's that night, I took a detour without really thinking about it—and found myself passing Nate's dad's old place. I told myself I was just curious. That I just wanted to see if it was still standing, if the ivy had finally choked the gutters. But when I turned the corner and saw his van parked out front, my stomach flipped.

A 'Sold' sign was staked in the front garden like some kind of declaration. He was back. And I hadn't been ready for that.

I pulled up at the kerb and cut the engine, my hands still gripping the wheel. For a while, I just sat there—chewing at my bottom lip, fingers drumming out an anxious rhythm on the wheel. Every part of me felt torn. Part of me wanted to march up to the door and demand answers, to force a conversation we never finished. The other part wanted to put the car in gear and pretend I'd never come this way at all.

Eventually, I chose the easier path. I started the engine and drove off. I wasn't ready to open that old wound—not yet. Maybe not ever.

Chapter Thirty-Three

Nate

And so I found myself back in Bramwick.

When I let myself into the house, the air inside greeted me with a stale, musty smell. It felt emptier than it had on my first return—stripped down to its bare bones. Only the last of the furniture remained, waiting to be cleared before the place would be ready for its new owners.

I dropped my bag and the trombone case in the hallway and let out a heavy sigh. In truth, I had no idea why I'd even brought the instrument. I had no plans to contact Bramwick Brass. After the way I'd treated them, I knew I wouldn't be welcome.

My intention was to keep a low profile for the duration of my stay. No pub visits, no idle wandering around the village. Just finish what needed doing—clear out the house, load the furniture into the van, take it to the big charity shop in Skipton. Job done. Then I'd be gone.

Still, there was one thing I wanted to do while I was back, which meant braving a short walk through the village. I put it off for as long as I could, but on the fourth and last day, I decided it was time.

I had to walk past The Grange to get there. On its rusted gates, someone had hung a placard scrawled with the words: *RIP to The Grange*. The letters looked angry, hastily painted. A wave of sadness washed over me. I'd been following the social media updates, rooting for them, hoping against hope that the single's success would be enough to save it. But clearly, it hadn't been. The Grange was lost.

My feet carried me through the gates anyway, giving me an excuse to delay my original errand. On the door, a poster invited everyone to the final May Day celebration—a last chance for the village to say goodbye and to share fond memories.

I drifted onwards, letting myself be drawn to Lady Henshaw's oak. This was where Rosie always used to come when she needed to think. I used to tease her for talking to the tree when we were kids, but now, standing beneath its ancient boughs, it didn't seem quite so silly.

I looked up at the few tattered ribbons still clinging to the branches from last year. It was a beautiful spring day: the apple trees in the orchard were heavy with blossom, and the air thrummed with birdsong and insects. Everything felt alive—everything except me.

"Rosie always used to ask you for guidance," I said quietly, placing a hand on the gnarled bark. "So what about me? Got any wisdom for me now? Where do I go next?"

A breeze stirred the leaves above my head, setting the ribbons dancing.

"No message for me?" I whispered. "Didn't think so."

I turned to walk away—but then I stopped. I knew, suddenly and with absolute clarity, what I had to do.

I had been avoiding Rosie. I wasn't even sure she knew I was back. But I owed her more than silence—I owed her a proper apology. So I made my way to Nature's Bounty, hoping she was still on the morning shift.

The bell above the door jingled cheerfully as I stepped inside, and the smell of incense hit me—comforting and familiar. It reminded me of her. And there she was, behind the counter: hair in a messy bun, chewing on a pen, eyes fixed on her laptop. She looked tired.

When she heard the door, she looked up. For a moment, her face was blank with non-recognition. Then her eyes widened.

"Nate," she said, pulling the pen from her mouth and straightening up.

"Hi Rosie," I said. I glanced around the shop—so full of colour and life. Red tomatoes, green peppers, yellow squash. Shelves of beeswax candles and Indian wall hangings. It was as vibrant and warm as she was.

"How've you been?" she asked. I tried to read her tone. No hostility, just a distant politeness.

"You know. Just back to sort through the last of Dad's things. The house finally sold."

"I saw the sign," she said. "You must be pleased."

I gave a half-shrug. "I suppose. At one point, I'd have been over the moon. Now... I'm not sure how I feel."

She nodded slowly. I hesitated, then added, "I know I've sent a million messages, but... well done. What you did with the song—that was incredible."

"Yeah, but it wasn't enough, was it?" Her tone cooled.

"I know. I saw the posts. There's going to be one last May Day, right?"

"Are you sticking around for it?"

"I don't think I'd be welcome."

"Probably not."

There was a moment of quiet and she looked back at her laptop.

"I feel awful about everything. About how we left things."

"Don't," she said quickly. "I've had worse to deal with since."

178

"I just wanted to apologise in person. I hurt you. I was an idiot. And I'm sorry."

"Okay," she said, looking back at her screen. She started clicking the mouse. It didn't feel like forgiveness.

"How much are you short?" I asked.

"Why do you care?"

"Just tell me. Or is it a big secret?"

"About twenty-five grand now. We've got no chance."

"You remember how you used to go to Lady Henshaw's oak when you needed guidance?"

"I remember you and Simon laughing at me for it."

"Well, I was there today." I swallowed hard. I hadn't planned to say any more, but I found myself going on. "Something came to me while I stood there. I want to give you the money."

She blinked. "I can't accept that. That money's from your dad's house—it's your fresh start."

"There's still enough for that," I said. "I'll be okay."

"You can't buy me back."

"I'm not trying to," I said, meaning it. "I just want to help. It's not about us—it's about making something right."

"This feels wrong. I'm sorry. It's generous, but…"

"You'd rather let The Grange be torn down than swallow your pride and accept help?" I said. "This place feels like unfinished business to me. Let me do one good thing. Let me move on."

She gave me a long, sad look. I could see how hard this was for her.

"You don't get to turn it down," I added gently. "This isn't just about you and me. Say no, and I'll donate it anonymously."

"Maybe you should've done that in the first place," she said, her voice clipped. "If it's only The Grange you care about."

"Alright, you got me. It's not just about The Grange. I still care about you. I know you'll never feel the same way. That's fine. I just wanted you to know there's still something good in me."

The door jingled again as a young woman walked in. Rosie gave me a look.

"I'm sure people will appreciate your generosity," she said, her tone brisk. "But this doesn't change anything between us. I hope you're clear on that."

"Crystal," I said, trying to match her detachment while my heart cracked in two.

I left the shop and headed back to Dad's.

When the last of the furniture had been taken away, I sat on the living room floor, drinking, into the early hours. Outside, the sky was dark, and the first spring storm had rolled in. Rain tapped the windows. Thunder grumbled across the valley.

The trombone lay beside me on the carpet. On the mantelpiece, my parents 'wedding photo still stood, next to an envelope addressed to the Bramwick Community Group.

"Well, Mum, Dad," I said, looking up at their smiling faces. "I'm sorry. I was a terrible son. I ran off to London. I stopped calling. I didn't appreciate the life you gave me."

Lightning flashed. Thunder followed.

"I used to hate this place. I couldn't wait to leave. I never saw what was good about it—about the people. I judged them, mocked them. I wish I'd realised sooner. I wish I could've figured this all out before you died, Dad."

I stared down at my clasped hands, feeling the burn of shame.

"The house is sold now. A young couple's buying it—planning to start a family here. I thought I'd feel free. Like I was getting a fresh start. But I don't. I feel lost. I don't belong anywhere. Not here, not in London…"

I choked on a breath and felt tears threaten.

"I've really fucked things up. With the band. With Rosie. With you."

I looked out at the quiet street. A cat crept along the front wall, soaked, its fur clinging to its sides.

"Anyway," I whispered, picking up the trombone. "I thought maybe you'd like to hear this one last time."

I raised the instrument to my lips. Thunder rolled like a count-in. I began to play 'Memory' from *Cats*. It wasn't perfect, but it was raw, and it was real. As the notes filled the room, the rain softened, accompanying me with a gentle rhythm.

When it was over, I laid the trombone in front of the old wood burner. Beside it, I placed a second envelope, addressed to Bramwick Brass.

I crossed the room and paused at the door, glancing back at my parents 'photo.

"I'll see you around," I said, then stepped into the night.

The rain had eased to a fine drizzle, but by the time I reached the oak tree, I was soaked to the skin. I didn't care.

Twice in my life, I'd wanted to end it all. The first time had been dramatic—a cry for help, really. I just wanted someone to notice.

The second time was serious.

I had planned everything as those hours in the old house wiled away. Written a letter requesting the proceeds from the house sale go towards saving The Grange. I'd even thought about the method. At first, I considered the banister in the house. But then I thought of that young

180

couple, so excited to build a life there, and I couldn't do it. I couldn't stain that space with death.

Lady Henshaw's oak felt more fitting.

Male suicide figures are higher than that of women. The biggest cause is loneliness.

It was getting light now. A sliver of orange had begun to stretch across the horizon. A blackbird sang into the gloom, its song hauntingly beautiful.

I had climbed that tree countless times when I was a kid and as I did so for the last time, its branches welcomed me like an old friend.

Chapter Thirty-Four

Rosie

I took an early morning walk through The Grange that morning. I had been doing that a lot recently. I liked to go before the village woke up so I could soak up the peace. The dawn chorus and the dew on the hems of my dungarees, the slightly damp, earthy smell of early spring, and the mist hanging over the Dales were like a calming balm for my soul.

The previous day, Nate had offered to donate the remaining money to save The Grange. I had tried to turn him down, but he was right; it wasn't up to me to refuse. I had tried to act aloof and cold because I still felt his betrayal, but his offer had been a lovely gesture. It was the answer to our prayers, really. So why did I feel so conflicted about the whole thing?

I took a deep breath in, inhaling the beautiful spring morning. At least I could tell Philomena Henshaw that it looked like The Grange was saved after all. It seemed like all I had brought her of late were problems and sadness. It felt like a chapter was finally closing, and I wasn't sure how to feel.

Nate was the last person I expected to see that morning. But there he was, under the oak, bending over and picking something up out of the long grass. I felt a stab of resentment. Morning walks were my time, a time to clear my head, and I wanted to speak with the tree alone. What was he doing anyway?

As I drew nearer, he noticed me and straightened up abruptly, a sheepish look on his face. I narrowed my eyes and looked at him suspiciously as I approached. He was dishevelled and appeared unwell— a bit like how Alan used to look after a heavy night of drinking. Is that what he had been doing? Sitting here all night drinking in the park like a teenager? I was ready to point out to him that drinking wasn't permitted in the park outside of organised events. Was that why he was scrabbling about in the grass? Was he picking up empty cans?

"Nate?" I addressed him coldly, coming to a stop and folding my arms. "What are you doing?"

He picked up the small backpack that was at his feet. Whatever he had removed from the grass was obviously now inside.

"Umm, not much, just saying a last goodbye before I leave," he mumbled, starting to walk away. My intuition told me something wasn't right.

"Nate, hold on a minute," I called, my tone softening. "What are you really up to? You look very shifty."

"Nothing," he said defensively.

"A likely story." I caught up with him, and we fell into step.

"Listen, I might have been a bit harsh yesterday," I said. He didn't look at me, just kept staring straight ahead, his jaw set firmly. "It was a kind gesture, and if you're really set on helping, then we'd all appreciate it."

"I meant it when I said I wasn't trying to buy my way back. I'm leaving today, and I'll never bother any of you again. I'll sort everything so that the money gets to you as soon as possible."

"Do you have to go today? I think the others might like to thank you when they find out."

"It's better this way, trust me." He looked sad. "A clean break."

"Okay," I said gently, feeling my heart grow heavy.

"You did an amazing job with it all, you know." There was a hint of a smile on his face as he glanced at me before quickly looking away. "I always knew you could do anything you put your mind to."

"Fred says it's given the band a new lease of life," I told him. The early morning air was chilly, and I wrapped my cardigan more tightly around myself. "He has new people wanting to join for the first time in ages."

"See, you're changing the world." This time he gave me a proper smile, and it warmed my soul. Then the expression turned serious. "Why did we never tell each other how we felt when we were kids?"

"Because we were immature and awkward. You were so cool, I didn't think you'd ever want to be with the compost queen. You saw me more as an annoying sister."

"I never thought that."

"No? But you were so into Hannah Ferguson, she was more suited to you than I could ever be."

"I'd have preferred to be with you, Patches."

"Then why didn't *you* say something?"

"I dunno, I kind of always thought you'd end up with Simon." He shrugged.

"Things would have been a lot easier if I had..."

"We really made a mess of things, didn't we?" he mused, shifting the weight of the backpack.

"We were kids, that's what you do when you're that age. You make mistakes and you learn from them."

"Only you learned, and I didn't." He stopped walking. We had reached the building now with its posters about the goodbye celebrations.

We could take those down now, thanks to Nate. "I'm sorry, Rosie, for everything."

"It's okay, I think I can just about forgive you now."

"Friends?" He raised an eyebrow.

"Yeah," I nodded, giving him a smile.

The tension had lifted from the air now, and I looked around at the beautiful surroundings— the wildflower meadows, the apple trees in the orchard, the beautiful old building that meant so much to us all.

"I can't believe we're going to get to keep it." A happy glow was growing in my belly.

"You deserve it. You all do, everyone in Bramwick."

For a moment I just smiled at him; then something caught my attention.

"Oh my God, Nate!" I exclaimed, and my blood turned to ice as my stomach plummeted.

I hadn't noticed because he had the collar of his jacket upturned. I thought he was just cold, but now I saw he had been hiding something. There were angry red marks around his neck that were starting to bruise and turn purple. The broken tree branch lying in the grass under the oak had not registered at first, but now it did.

"What's in the bag, Nate?"

"Nothing." He started to hurry towards the gates, but I dashed after him.

I made a grab for the bag. He tried to wrestle it back, but he didn't seem to have any strength. I yanked the zip open and looked inside. Among some bundled-up clothes, his wallet, and some paperwork, was hiding a length of rope.

"Jesus Christ, Nate," I said in a low voice. "You absolute idiot."

He looked away, shame written across his face. I stared at him, not sure what to do.

"Do you need me to take you to a hospital?"

"No," he said without looking at me. "I'm alright. The branch broke. I guess Lady Henshaw is still looking out for brass players, eh?"

I took a deep breath in and exhaled a long sigh. "Don't be daft, it's not Lady Henshaw— the tree is sick and rotting. If you'd come to me, I could have pointed you in the direction of a nice, strong one."

There was a pause before he started to laugh, and I soon joined in. When the awkward laughter died, I went to him and pulled him into a hug. He laid his head on my shoulder and started to cry. He smelled of morning dew.

Chapter Thirty-Five

Nate

None of the Bramwick Brass members mentioned my suicide attempt. Still, I could tell they all knew. The marks around my neck looked worse than they had on the day it happened—no longer just red, but a mottled mess of deep purple and sickly yellow. I caught Fred trying to hide a wince when he looked at me. George didn't even bother—he just avoided my gaze altogether. It stung. It hurt to talk, to swallow, even to move my head. But none of that mattered. For the first time in a very long time, I felt genuinely happy.

Simon and Sally were the only ones who brought it up. Simon couldn't really avoid it—I was staying in his spare room. He asked if I was alright, awkwardly, like he felt he had to say something but didn't know how. I told him I was fine. After a couple of tense days, tiptoeing around each other, we slipped back into our old rhythm—messing about, sharing stupid jokes, and reminiscing about the good times.

After Rosie found me that morning, she'd taken me back to the shop and made me some tea. It was from her range of herbal blends—it tasted flowery, with a bitter aftertaste. She said it would make me feel better. It didn't, but being there with her did. We talked and talked, and by the time the bell above the door announced Sally's arrival, we were both in a much better place.

When she saw us sitting there, she looked stern at first, like she was about to reprimand me. Her T-shirt that day featured a semicolon with the words 'Stop! Wait! Your fight is not over! You got this'. It couldn't have been more fitting. But then her face turned chalk white and she looked at me with a frozen expression of horror. Rosie stood up and went over to her.

"He's had a bit of a rough morning, don't be too hard on him."

But Sally was anything but.

"You poor thing," she said, tears in her eyes. She came over and gave me a big hug and had been a huge source of support ever since. She'd been over to Simon's three days in a row to check on me. Rosie had been a little more distant, but I understood—I'd given her a lot to process. She still messaged me every day.

She'd told the community group about what I'd planned to do, and at the end of the week, she asked if I felt like going to band rehearsals.

"You should come," Simon said as I read him her text. He was lounging on the couch, glancing up from the video game he was playing. "Everyone's been asking after you."

"They all know?"

Simon looked at me like I was stupid and started to speak, but I beat him to it. "This is Bramwick—everybody knows."

"Well, yeah…" he turned his gaze back to the screen and resumed punching buttons on the controller.

"I'd love to see everyone," I said. "But can you do me a favour? Tell them I don't want a fuss. I want things to be normal."

"Yeah, I can do that—ah, crap!" Simon tossed the controller aside. He'd just lost.

"Thanks, mate."

"Don't expect Fred to accept an attempted suicide as an excuse not to have been practising, mind you," Simon warned with a chuckle.

"I think he might actually be pleasantly surprised."

"How do you mean?"

"I didn't stop playing when I went back to London."

"You didn't?"

"Reckon I'm back to my best now."

Simon grinned and offered me the second controller.

"Want a game?"

It felt awkward when I first arrived at rehearsal that night, but once the initial looks of shock and pity were out of the way, things soon settled. It felt like I'd never been away. They were practising for that year's May Day concert. The event was now to be a celebration of the village's victory. A selection of music was put in front of me—show pieces, classical numbers, marches, and hymns. As we started the first piece, I caught Rosie's eye across the room, and she smiled. I managed to play along with only a few mistakes, which of course earned me sharp reprimands from Fred. When we stopped for a break, though, George turned and told me he was impressed with how much my playing had improved. I was struggling a bit toward the end of the last piece—blowing the instrument made my bruised neck hurt.

I looked for Rosie as mugs of tea were handed around, but she'd disappeared. As everyone took their seats for the second half, she still hadn't returned.

"Alright, everyone, we've got a bit of a surprise for you tonight," Fred said, a glimmer in his eyes. "Especially for you, Nate."

"What?" I blinked at him.

"Rosie, come back in, love!" he shouted toward the door.

She entered the room, followed by two guys I recognised from the music video. One was carrying a guitar and an amp, the other a mic with its own speaker. I started to smile.

"We can't have our celebration without playing the song that made it all happen, can we?" Fred beamed.

"There's one more thing," Rosie said, practically bouncing with excitement. She turned toward the door and beckoned.

"Maxwell!" I exclaimed, jumping out of my seat.

"Hey, mate." I dashed across the room and hugged him.

"It's good to see you, big idiot," he said, setting his instrument bags down. "Here you are."

He handed me a very familiar bag, and I unzipped it. I looked at Fred questioningly as I pulled out my guitar.

"I think George will be alright on his own for this one," Fred said, then added sternly, "but don't get too comfortable over there—we still need you on the trombone for the rest of the set."

I pulled the strap over my shoulder and watched as the other musicians carried in more amps and cables. Rosie introduced me to Kevin and Greg, from The Splinters, and I briefly told them what a fantastic job they'd done on the single. Once we were all set up and ready to go, Fred counted us in, and we launched into 'Blood and Brass'.

Chapter Thirty-Six

Rosie

It was the best-attended May Day celebration The Grange had ever seen. Everyone in the village had thrown themselves into the preparations that year, eager to play their part in what felt like a real turning point for Bramwick. The place was alive with a party atmosphere—bright bunting strung between the trees, gazebos overflowing with homemade crafts, the smell of the barbecue drifting lazily on the breeze. There were games to keep the kids entertained, and beneath the great oak tree, a makeshift stage where local musicians had been playing all afternoon, filling the air with music and laughter.

The weather had been kind to us—one of those perfect spring days when the sun shone warm and golden, a gentle breeze stirred the leaves, and only a few soft, cotton-wool clouds drifted across the blue sky.

Because of the attention our single had received, there were local press dotted about, and *Tonight's Take* had even sent a crew to film an update for their show. They'd followed me around the gardens and the orchard while I talked about my volunteer work maintaining them, their cameras catching the blossom in the trees and the careful planting we'd done over the past few years. They'd interviewed Fred about the band and captured our rousing performance of 'Blood and Brass'—complete with Maxwell on drums and our two new friends from The Splinters lending their unmistakable energy.

They'd even spoken to Nate.

He hadn't wanted it made public that he'd been the one to donate the money we needed to save The Grange—typical, really—but word had got around. It was Bramwick, after all. Secrets didn't stay secret for long around here. Still, he wasn't embarrassed about his involvement like he'd been at the fundraiser. I watched with something like pride as the interviewer asked him about his motivations. He handled it beautifully, steering the conversation away from himself and back to the music, back to the community he'd once tried so hard to distance himself from.

"It's important we give new players a reason to pick up an instrument," he said, standing there in his green blazer—albeit customised now with a few punk touches: badges, safety pins, a patch on the sleeve. "This is really just the start for Bramwick Brass. We might have saved The Grange, but there's still so much work to do if we're going to preserve our banding heritage for the next generation. Music matters. It brings people together. And I think we've proved that today."

"You really are a proper bandsman now, aren't you?" I teased as we watched the last of the film crew pack up their gear.

The day was starting to wind down. We'd played our set. The oak tree had been toasted with cider and song. The craft stalls were being dismantled. The kids had been taken home, sticky with sugar and flushed from excitement. All that remained now were a few hardy souls lingering in the warm dusk, finishing off the last of this year's cider beneath the lantern-lit trees.

"Yeah, and?" Nate grinned. The bruises on his neck were fading now, their angry colours softening.

"Are you sure you won't stay?"

He looked out across the hills, a distant, thoughtful expression on his face. The air shimmered with the late evening haze. Bees hummed lazily around the apple blossom, and a white butterfly bobbed past us on a drifting current of warm air. Earlier that day, when I'd tied my ribbon to the tree, I'd wished—foolishly, perhaps—that he wouldn't leave. I knew I couldn't hold him here forever. But these past couple of weeks had flown by too fast. They hadn't felt like enough.

"I don't think I can," he said softly, shaking his head with a small, regretful smile.

"No," I sighed. "The outside world will always be calling you, won't it?"

"That—and I think I might have outstayed my welcome at Simon's," he added, with a wry glance. "You could always come with me…"

But I was already shaking my head. "I belong here. Just as much as you belong out there."

"I know." He let out a long, steadying breath.

In the last couple of weeks, he'd convinced me to leave the spa job behind for good. The house I'd shared with Alan was on the market now, and I was planning to invest my half of the proceeds into the farm—to finally create the wedding venue I'd always dreamed of. It felt unbearably cruel that Nate and I should be destined for such different paths.

"I've loved these past two weeks," I said quietly, feeling the threat of tears but determined to hold them back. "It was like old times. You, me, and Simon."

"Yeah…" he agreed, his voice sounding rough. Somewhere in the trees, a robin sang a wistful little melody.

"Can you not wait until tomorrow?" I asked. "Come by for one last rehearsal? Let everyone say a proper goodbye? They'd love that."

189

"I can't," he said, shifting awkwardly. "I'm not good with things like that. The van's all packed. I've said my goodbyes to everyone in my own way."

"Okay." A tear finally escaped.

"Come here." He opened his arms and I stepped into them, letting him hold me as the tears came quietly.

"It won't be like last time," he promised, his voice close to my ear. "I'll stay in touch. I'll visit every chance I get. It'll be like I never left."

"Do you promise?"

"I promise."

He drew back, hands warm and steady on my shoulders, and kissed me—a kiss full of memory and sadness and something I didn't quite have words for.

"I'll always love you, Patches," he said. "Remember that."

And then he turned and walked away, his shadow long in the low sun. I stood there watching him go, thinking of the tree and the pink ribbon I'd tied to it.

Not all wishes come true.

But some loves—the best ones—never really leave you.

Epilogue

The old oak tree that stood in the grounds of The Grange had been sick for some time. The villagers still gathered every May Day to pour cider on its roots, tie ribbons to its branches, and toast its health—but still, the tree ailed. Then one morning, after a winter storm, the people of Bramwick woke to find the tree had fallen.

It lay like a wounded giant in the snow, defeated. Its great tangle of roots—which had grounded the village for generations—were ripped from the earth. Its gnarled old branches, still clutching some of the wishes tied to them, stretched across the cold landscape as the low winter sun rose over the hills.

But that was not the end for the tree.

Rosie had always been an early riser, but that May morning she was up with the sunrise. It was a special day, and there was plenty to do. By the time Simon came downstairs, she'd already made good progress with the morning's tasks.

"Morning," Simon mumbled, shuffling into the kitchen in his pyjamas, rubbing his eyes. "How long have you been up?"

"Couple of hours," Rosie replied. "I've mucked out the alpacas, fed the chickens, and hung the clean tablecloths on the line."

"You should've woken me. I'd have helped."

"I thought you could use a lie-in."

She poured coffee from the cafetière as Simon came up behind her, wrapping his arms around her waist and resting his chin on her shoulder. Together, they looked out at the sunny morning.

"I'll make a start on clearing the rest of the stuff up in the barn after breakfast," Simon said, taking a mug.

"Oh, don't worry about that today," Rosie told him. "We've no wedding for another two weeks—there's plenty of time. Is Daisy not up yet?"

"No sign of her," Simon grinned. "She was up late last night. I peeked in on her about ten o'clock and she was sat up with her torch, studying her music."

"Bless her," Rosie smiled, cupping her mug in her hands. "Oh, I meant to tell you, I got a letter from Mum and Dad yesterday."

"Only your parents would still send letters when there are about a hundred easier ways to stay in touch," Simon chuckled.

"I think it's sweet," Rosie replied. "You know they won't go near social media. They don't even have camera phones. But they sent that."

She nodded towards the mantelpiece, where a photograph was propped among the knick-knacks—her parents, grinning at the camera, the Taj Mahal rising behind them.

"They look like they're having a great trip," Simon said.

"I'm starting to wonder if they'll even come back this time."

There was the sound of hurried footsteps in the hall, and a small girl with a shock of red hair burst into the room.

"Mum! Dad! Can I go out and practise?" Daisy brandished her trombone at them.

"Steady on, love," Simon laughed as she bounced impatiently on the spot. "Breakfast first."

"But Dad—"

"He won't be up yet," Rosie told her gently. She took the trombone from her daughter and set it down. "Come on—sit down. I'm making eggs."

As Simon washed up after breakfast, he spotted a figure emerging from the field where the glamping pods stood, heading towards the house. Daisy, standing on a stool to help with the drying up, caught sight of him too—and her face lit up.

"Uncle Nate's up!"

She jumped down and ran for the door, darting across the grass. Nate crouched to catch her as she flung herself at him.

"Hey, Daisy-Moo!" he laughed, lifting her off the ground and spinning her around.

She giggled as he set her down. Rosie came towards them from the doorway.

"There's coffee and eggs in the kitchen if you're hungry," she said.

"Brilliant, thanks." He gave her a lopsided smile. "Big day today. I'd better check my blazer's ironed."

"Oh, don't worry too much," Rosie said as they headed back inside, Daisy skipping ahead. "The new conductor's not anywhere near as strict as Fred."

"I was up all night studying the music," Daisy told him proudly.

"Which means you'll be shattered," Rosie said.

"Nah, she'll be fine— won't you?" Nate gave her a wink.

Where once stood the old oak tree, there now stood a new bandstand. Upon it, a group of people in green blazers clutched shiny instruments. Coloured ribbons were tied to the wooden frame, streaming in the breeze.

Fred Black stood before the gathered villagers, the marquees, and the apple trees.

"It is with great pleasure that I stand before you all today," he began. "I may be handing over my baton, but the Bramwick Band still means the world to me. It has been the greatest pride of my life to watch its growth over these past years. There was a time when the future of this band—and this place—looked doomed. But Bramwick folk won't be kept down. With your resilience and support, this band has gone from strength to strength. Nothing makes me happier than to see all these young faces joining us today."

Fred turned to look at the band—its numbers no longer struggling, its ranks full of new young players, including Daisy Hunter, seated beside Nate.

"And I am delighted today to hand the band over to the next generation. Please give a big round of applause for our new conductor—Sally."

As the crowd clapped and cheered, Sally stepped forward, a delighted grin spreading across her face. Nate noticed that under her blazer she wore a t-shirt that read: 'My body is an instrument, not an ornament'. She caught his eye and grinned cheekily.

"Well, this is a real privilege," she said, taking the baton from Fred. "I don't know how I'll ever fill Mr Black's shoes."

A ripple of laughter spread through the crowd.

"There was a time when this would've been unheard of—a woman leading the band? And a blow-in, no less. But here I am: Bramwick's first female conductor. And that's what this band does—we lead the way, we shake things up, we do music differently. And with me, we'll keep pushing boundaries—because music should be for everyone."

A cheer went up. Across the stage, Rosie caught Nate's eye, and they shared a look.

"Anyway, enough about me," Sally smiled. "Let's get down to why we're really here. Last winter, we lost a beloved resident of the village— a two-hundred-year-old oak tree, planted by the late Lord Henshaw. But she's not really gone. The wood we could save has gone into making the beautiful bandstand you see here today. We hope it will serve the band for many generations to come."

Nate picked up his trombone and looked at Daisy.

"You ready, kid?"

She gave a resolute nod.

"We're going to finish today with the song that set us on the path to where we are now," Sally announced proudly. "You all know it—so please, sing along. This is 'Blood and Brass'."

www.ingramcontent.com/pod-product-compliance
Ingram Content Group UK Ltd.
Pitfield, Milton Keynes, MK11 3LW, UK
UKHW041823270625
460106UK00012B/83

9 781915 975171